"Power's work, already cover-to-cover forceful, keeps getting better. Boston has never had a better P. I."

—John Lutz
Edgar & Shamus award-winning
author of *Single White Female*
past president of Mystery Writers of America
& Private Eye Writers of America

Praise for Jed Power

"The ghosts of hard-boiled legends such as John D. MacDonald ...and—yes—Dan J. Marlowe himself haunt these pages. Pure pulp pleasure."   —Wallace Stroby
Author of *Shoot the Woman First*
and *Kings of Midnight*

"Author Jed Power has the...touch...it doesn't get much better..."
—Charlie Stella
Author of *Rough Riders*
and *Shakedown*

"...Jed Power channels the tough-as-nails prose of Gold Medal greats Peter Rabe and Dan Marlowe."

—Shamus & Derringer
award-winning author
Dave Zeltserman

"Fans of Dennis Lehane will revel in the settings and atmosphere ...an absorbing read...a hard-charging plot...Boston nitty-gritty."
—Charles Kelly
Author of *Gunshots In Another Room*
a biography of crime writer Dan Marlowe

Jed Power

THE
COMBAT
ZONE

Dark Jetty Publishing

Published by
Dark Jetty Publishing
4 Essex Center Drive #3906
Peabody, MA 01961

Cover Artist:
Brandon Swann

ISBN 978-0-9858617-8-0

10 9 8 7 6 5 4 3 2 1

ACKNOWLEDGEMENTS

Thank you to my editor, Louisa Swann, for her exceptional help in launching this new series.

Also, a huge thanks to my writing buddies, Amy Ray and Bonnar Spring, for reading the first draft and offering helpful suggestions.

CHAPTER 1

STONEY SUNDOWN had his brown Frye boots propped up on my desk, a burning joint in his right hand. I didn't appreciate either, but refrained from saying anything. After all, I had invited him up to my office for a chat. I got up from the chair behind my battle-scarred wooden desk, went into the small bathroom, returned with a towel, and shoved it along the floor crack of the room's front door. I didn't need the landlord smelling what was going on in here. I already had enough trouble with him regarding my habitually late rent payments. When I stood, I could see the inscription in reverse on the outside of my office door's glass panel—Michael Malloy, Private Investigator.

When I sat down again, Stoney offered me the joint. I waved it away. Sure, I'd tried the stuff once or twice before, couldn't help it. This was Harvard Square and hippies were king, after all. But I didn't like pot. It made me nervous and I could do that all on my own.

"So what's happening, Mikey?" Stoney blew smoke rings with the last of the weed, stubbed it out in my ashtray. I made a mental note to flush the joint as soon as he left.

"I had a visitor yesterday." I rummaged through the mass of papers on my desk. You'd think by the looks of it I had a lot of work; I didn't. I was just a lousy housekeeper. "Figured I could use a *little* help on this one and you might need a *little* money." I emphasized the words little, even though I didn't think money was the real reason Stoney had helped me out in the past. I thought it was more that he enjoyed playing amateur detective. But whatever his reasons were, there was no doubt he could go places in the Square and make discreet inquiries where my presence would cause the same reaction as if a narc had just strolled through the door.

"I can always use bread." Stoney took his feet off the desk. His bell bottom jeans were more flared than a sailor's. He held them up with a thick brown belt wrapped around his thin waist. A huge brass buckle and a paisley shirt finished off his wardrobe.

I finally found the paper I was looking for. It contained notes I'd taken during my client's interview. I sat up straight, tried to look professional. "A father was in to see me, Stoney. He's looking for his daughter. Pretty broken up, too. She's sixteen."

"Runaway?"

"That's how it started. But the old man thinks it's a lot more than that now."

"How so?" Stoney flipped his head, moving his shoulder-length, reddish-blonde hair away from his blue eyes, and stroked his short, scraggly beard like he was impersonating a head shrinker.

"Well, the father's been coming down from Maine for about six months now. Weekends. I guess a friend of his daughter's tipped him off that she'd mentioned the Square."

"No surprise there, Mikey. Half the runaways in New England end up here. And why not? It's a happening place— music, crash pads, plenty of dope, not too much heat. Christ, I'd probably come here myself if I wasn't already here." He let out a little chuckle.

"Yeah, good one. But this is serious." I rubbed my face hard, up and down. "Anyhow, Cambridge PD gave him no help. They're swamped with runaways."

"Has he had *any* luck?"

"A little and it wasn't good. That's what brought him to me." I put my arms on the desk. There was a coffee stain on the sleeve of my white shirt. "He almost caught up to her a couple of times, but just missed her. He didn't miss a couple of people who'd seen her, though. The old man knew enough to put out some green, and it bought him the same story from both of them—that she was living with some speed freaks somewhere around here. He wasn't happy with that. In fact, he panicked. Probably read all about the stuff in *Time Magazine* and imagined his little girl coming home with no teeth and a pockmarked face. I guess someone told him I was in the Square. He showed up and hired me to find her. Maybe help get her out of here before it's too late."

Stoney made a face like he'd just gotten a mouthful of sour milk. "Speed kills. It's nasty shit, man." He reached into his jeans pocket, pulled out a small glass vial with a black screw top that had a tiny spoon hanging from it.

"What the hell are you doing? Put that stuff away."

He waved at me like he was waving goodbye. "Take it easy, man. It's just blow. The exact opposite of that crank crap. Nice mellow high. Not addictive. Sigmund Freud used it in the old days. Indians down in South America use it for energy to hike around the mountains. Comes from a natural plant. Not much different than pot. But better. Taste?"

Cocaine. I'd heard about it, of course. It was getting as much press as the president recently. The articles I'd read said about what Stoney was pitching—that it wasn't a hard drug and not addictive. Many users said it helped with their thinking, made it more clear. Popes and presidents had indulged. Even one of my heroes, Sherlock Holmes, had used the stuff to help solve cases. I don't know if it was because of what I'd heard, or because the time was just right. Maybe even the four bottles of Schlitz I'd already consumed had something to do with it. Roaming the Square like I did, I'd been offered the chance to try coke a couple of times previously. I never had; it scared me too much. Until today, that is. I shrugged.

Stoney smiled. He was in his early twenties; I was in my late twenties. Not a huge age difference, but looking at us you'd think we were from different planets. I'd missed being a member of the Age of Aquarius. On the other hand, Stoney looked, sounded, and acted like he'd invented it.

While I watched, he unscrewed the vial's cap and used the attached spoon to dig out an overflowing heap of the white powder. "I'll demonstrate for you." He set the vial down and used the forefinger of one hand to block off a nostril. He then brought the spoon up to the other nostril, and noisily inhaled the cocaine. He shook like he got a shiver up his spine. He repeated the process with the other nostril. "Now you," he said.

I stared as he dug the tiny spoon back into the vial and pulled it out with a full load of the drug. As he brought it close to my nose, I noticed his eyes were sparkling. I tried to imitate what I'd seen him do, and I guess I did all right. I got it all up my nose anyway. When he made a move to do my other nostril, I waved him off.

I sat there for a moment, waiting to see what was going to happen. Except for a medicinal taste in my throat and a slight burning sensation in my nose, nothing did. "That it?" I finally asked.

"You don't feel *anything*?"

"Nothing."

"Hmm. Happens sometimes at first."

I got up, walked to the small fridge, pulled out a bottle of Schlitz, and looked at Stoney. He shook his head. I returned to my desk, popped the beer, killed half in one swig, and set it down.

"Well, what's her name?" Stoney asked.

"Who?"

Stoney looked impatient. "The girl. The runaway. How am I going to help you find her if I don't know her name?"

"Oh." I picked the paper back up. "Susan Worthman. But the father said people in the Square told him she goes by the handle Susie Sparkle now." I had no idea why everybody in this counterculture thing had a nickname. I just accepted it. I'd never even asked Stoney what his real name was.

"Well," Stoney said, his eyes still shining. "She shouldn't be hard to find. The Square isn't that big."

I put the paper back down, adding to the mess. "Yeah, it should be an easy one. I got a couple ideas I'm going to look into. And maybe you know some places these kids hang out that I don't. You can check those. You find her, don't bother her. Just let me know. Of course I'll throw you a little something."

Stoney shrugged. "I'm not worried. You always treat me fair."

He was right about that—I had. In this area called Harvard Square, I needed the services of someone like Stoney occasionally. He was the modern day equivalent of an Indian guide. "So let me know if you have any luck."

Stoney hopped up from his chair. He was taller than me and I'm six two. But he was a real beanpole. And the beanpole had a big grin on his face. "You got it, Mikey." He headed out the office door, but before he closed it, he turned, flashed me a V with his fingers and said, "Peace, man."

"Yeah, so long," I said to Stoney. To myself, I said, "Peace, shit." Kids like Stoney didn't seem to have a care in the world. I must have inherited their share along with my own somehow, because I had plenty of worries. I finished my beer and pondered how it must be nice to be a member of the Now Generation, without a trouble on your mind. I couldn't even imagine what that would feel like. I'd never felt that way. And today my worries centered around dough and how I was going to keep up with the bills and not get tossed out of my office onto a Harvard Square side street. I had to come up with something. It certainly wouldn't be the little case I'd just discussed with Stoney. That'd probably be wrapped up in a day or two. Not enough of a fee to keep me in beer. Well, something would turn up. I hoped.

CHAPTER 2

AN HOUR LATER I found myself seated in an office of the Cambridge Police Department on Western Avenue, sucking Wint-O-Green Life Savers one after the other. The office was a notch above mine, but not by much. And it wasn't really an office, just a cubicle inside an office with lots of other cubicles. This cubicle had the same framed photo of Nixon on the wall that I did, though. Of course, I figured he was well-liked in this building. Me? I just had the slug's photo up on my wall to help convince possible clients I was a rock-solid professional. I needed every edge I could get.

I was seated facing a metal desk in a chair that was so uncomfortable it could have been used to break suspects. Seated behind the desk, elbows on it, hands under his chin, was my cousin, Billy Skinner. Thin with receding brown hair and a skinny dog face, he was at least six inches shorter than me and looked like he weighed about 140 pounds. A Barney Fife twin. Mentally, though, he was a lot smarter than Barney and temperamentally, a lot more arrogant. A Napoleon complex for sure. I'd come close to smacking him a couple of times in the recent past. Matter of fact, when we were kids,

I had done just that more than once. And I knew he remembered it, too.

See, our branches of the family had never been close and he and I had never really liked each other much. So it was no surprise that Billy was none too happy when I took up my new profession almost a year ago, swallowed my pride, and began approaching him for a little help with my cases.

"So what is it you need this time, Mike? You didn't come here to take me to lunch, did ya?" He didn't try to hide the sarcasm.

I didn't like being here anymore than he liked having me, but Billy was a detective, a half-dozen years my senior, and double that time a Cambridge cop. He had access to a lot of info and other things that could be useful to me in my investigations. So I humbled myself and did the best I could with it. It wasn't easy though. I didn't like crawling. Billy did like it. Me crawling, that is. But I figured it was something I had to put up with. So I did.

Billy was a straight arrow as far as his job went and was always hesitant to do anything against PD rules. But a man like him, with our history, couldn't resist the sight of me squirming and practically begging. I knew that and took advantage of it, playing the role. To make it go down easier for him when he did help, I'd usually toss in something he could use to fool himself into believing he was assisting me for an honorable reason. Sometimes I'd try a different approach—the family card. And today, that's how I started.

"How's Aunt Gertrude, Billy?" I asked.

He was even more feisty than usual. "Cut the bullshit, Mike. You know my mother's a pain in the ass just like she's always been. And don't call me Billy, either. It's Bill. Now what the hell do you want? Can't you see how busy it is around here?" He waved one hand over his head.

No, I couldn't *see* how busy it was, but I could sure hear it. Outside the little space there was a cacophony of noises—shouts, doors slamming, police radios, typewriters clacking away. The place was a regular madhouse. And a lot of the people I passed getting to my cousin's little cubicle had looked like that was where they belonged—in a madhouse. And I don't mean just the criminals either.

Before I started my spiel, I mentioned one more name—his daughter's. This time I was genuinely interested *and* concerned. "Dottie?" I asked.

I didn't mean it to, but that little question took the wind out of his sails. He slumped. "The same. I don't want to talk about it, Mike. You know the story anyway."

I did. The drug part anyway. So I changed the subject to the one I had really come to talk about—Susan Worthman and her father.

While I talked, he tugged at his loosened tie. I watched his prominent Adam's apple bob up and down. I could read his mind, and it was telling me to hurry the hell up. So I did.

When I was finished, Billy turned his palms up. "You're talking about a freakin' runaway. Don't you know what year it is and where the hell we are? You ain't that dumb, are you?"

I'm not dumb at all. But I do have a red-hot temper, and it took every ounce of restraint I could muster not to go over the desk and break his pencil-thin neck. I tried to control my voice. "All I need from you is any info the department might have picked up after the father filed the runaway report. If they found out anything, it would've been added to her file, right?"

"Of course it would have," he said, sounding like he was talking to a child. "But the odds of that are next to zero. Runaways around here are loooow priority."

I gritted my teeth and said, "I could use the favor if you would just check. See if there is anything in there at all."

"A favor, huh," he said, a big smirk on his homely face. He let me sit there and squirm for a minute before he finally continued. "All right, seein' you're a relative." He made a motion like he was a king dismissing a subject. "You can go now. I'll give you a buzz if I find out anything."

I got up from my chair and felt like I should hide my face as I left the building. I knew it was flushed and I was steaming.

I banged a right when I left the cop station and headed for my car, a rundown green Volkswagen Karmann Ghia. I was just one corner away from it when I came to an Army Recruiting Station. Marching in a tight circle near the front door were a dozen or so protesters holding the customary signs—"End the War," "Army out of Cambridge"—stuff like that. I really had no beef with the protestors or their signs, but ahead of me other pedestrians were forced out onto the street to get past them. I'd already been humiliated once today; that was enough.

When I reached the demonstrators, I just bulled my way through the first side of the circle and they parted like snow before a plow. I trudged through the center of the circle and started to exit that side of the marchers. Just as I was almost free, I felt a hand grab my arm.

"Hey, man, we're protesting here. Can't you show some respect and walk around?"

I turned to see who had grabbed my arm and called me "man." I was pleased with what I saw. The guy was as tall as me, although he could have used some fat in his food. He looked more like a beatnik than a hippie, what with the black beret and Van Dyke beard. I glanced at the hand still latched onto my arm.

He must have been a little crazy or burnt out because he said, "I'm talking to you, man."

That's when I lost it. And even though I did, I had enough sense not to use my right. That could've gotten me in a lot of trouble. I pulled my arm free, used it to give his chest a little push. He stumbled back—just far enough. My left fist shot out straight and hard, and I caught him dead center on his beak. I could feel it collapse under my fist. Blood gushed and he let out a wail. His picket sign flew into the air and his hands covered what was left of his nose. Blood streamed out between his fingers, down his denim shirt, and onto the pavement. Girl protestors started screaming and a couple of guys ran to help him with his busted schnoz. No one came near me. Most, in fact, backpedaled away. I made a fast walk down the street, turned the corner, hopped into my little car, and got the hell out of there.

I didn't feel any better thinking about it later. In fact, it took quite a few more beers to wash the guilt away. Instead of pulverizing the face I'd wanted to—my cousin's—I'd clobbered some poor protesting slob. I knew I'd probably done some permanent damage too. After stewing on it for a while, I finally rationalized that at least I hadn't hurt him too bad. His nose might never look the same, but at least it could be fixed. Somewhat.

I finally fell asleep with one thought in mind—too bad the face I'd popped hadn't been my cousin's. My damn freakin' cousin's.

CHAPTER 3

THE NEXT DAY I woke up with the usual hangover, in the usual place—my apartment, a second floor walk-up just a few blocks from my office. It had one bedroom with a bed that only a fairly young guy like me could sleep comfortably on. The bed had been here when I took over the apartment. In fact, everything had. The small main room had a tattered couch, a television with rabbit ears that often had trouble with the Boston stations, an easy chair that threw up the last tenant's farts when I sat on it, a battered coffee table, a couple of lamps that would cause a twenty-year old reading difficulties, and a tray table for dinner that I left permanently open and within arm's reach of the easy chair. Jammed in one corner of the room was my only addition to the decor—an old teacher's desk and chair that I'd picked up at a secondhand store on Mass. Ave. I used the desk to do paperwork at night when I had a case, which wasn't often. A black telephone sat heavily on one edge.

I had some toast, coffee. Then shit, showered, and shaved. I dressed, then slipped into a sport coat. It was far from new but the elbow patches had come with it. When I left I had with me a photo of Susan Worthman—aka Susie Sparkle—that her father had given me. I figured the next thing to do was hit the Square and show the picture around. Between that and Stoney covering the more hidden areas of the Square, I hoped I'd get a lead. I know it's nothing original, but I'm fairly new at this racket and it was about all I could think of for a start.

It was a beautiful spring day. The long winter was over and the heat of summer was still weeks away. The sounds of a rock band rolled into the Square from Cambridge Common. Coats were a thing of the past. No bras on the women and shirts opened wide for the men was more the fashion now. And the Square was bustling with every kind of character imaginable. There were professors and students from Harvard and MIT. Street panhandlers with holes in their jeans. A soapbox Lenin haranguing a crowd with political fire and brimstone. Hippie kids from the suburbs looking to score. Sidewalk musicians with guitar cases open, hoping to catch a quarter from time to time. And everywhere there was hair. Lots of hair. In fact, determining someone's sex from behind was often impossible. Only the bald didn't have long hair. At least not on the top of their heads.

I made a beeline for the Out-of-Town News Agency that was located dead center in Harvard Square. I knew a lot of street kids hung around there, and if Susan was in the area, someone should have seen her.

The front of the building was covered with displays of magazines and newspapers from around the world. I'd spent many a lazy day there perusing the periodicals, even occasionally buying a provocative one to take home with me if the need arose.

I walked up to the closest group of kids lounging at one side of the building. Males and females. Ages hard to tell, anywhere from fourteen to twenty. The girls all had on those long dresses—peasant dresses I think they call them. The guys—jeans, boots, paisley shirts. Some of both sexes wore bandanas. They all had long hair. I got a whiff of marijuana as I approached and saw one kid flip something over his shoulder.

"Can I talk to you?" I said to no one in particular. I didn't get an answer. And no wonder. I don't think you would have seen a more nervous bunch of hippies if I'd pulled up in a police cruiser and jumped out with a German shepherd and a foot-long skull cracker. A couple of the kids even looked like they might make a run for it.

Finally, a kid with long, greasy blonde hair spoke up. "You a cop?" he asked. If he was trying to hide his nervousness, he wasn't successful.

I spoke as reassuringly as I could. "No, I'm not. I'm just trying to locate someone. I thought one of you might be able to help me." Then I added quickly, "She's not in any trouble. Her family's just worried about her."

I studied their faces and I could see that they might not help me even if they could. They looked as tight mouthed and loyal to each other as a band of gypsies. I pulled the photo out of my jacket pocket. Held it up for them to inspect. "Anyone seen her?"

I saw a couple of flickers of recognition. They were just kids after all and they couldn't hide it. So I repeated myself. "She's not in any trouble. Her parents just want to make sure she's okay." My gypsy analogy had been right. If they knew her, no one was talking. "If anyone changes their mind, give me a call." I passed out a few of my business cards. As an afterthought, and I figured it a good one, I added, "There'll be some money for whoever gives me some helpful information." I didn't mention that it wouldn't be much. I didn't have George Worthman's okay for that, so the dough would be coming out of my fee.

And that's how the rest of the day progressed—flashing the photo of Susie Sparkle and handing out my cards to street people and to store workers in any establishment I thought she might have patronized. Before I knew it, it was almost supper time. I'd grabbed a couple of hotdogs from a street vendor for lunch, and now I was hungry. But to be honest, I was more thirsty. So I headed over to O'Toole's Tavern, my favorite Square watering hole, for cocktail hour.

When I arrived, I walked the length of the mahogany bar and plunked myself down on my customary stool. The lone TV was located up high on this end of the bar's wall and I had a good view of the newscast that was just starting. The lead story, of course, was about an anti-war rally to be held on Boston Common tomorrow. It seemed something like that led the news almost every day. I was glad now that I'd hit the streets today. I knew most of the Cambridge long hairs wouldn't be around tomorrow. They'd be on the other side of the Charles River, in Boston, at the demonstration.

I looked away from the TV. The bartender approached. He also happened to be the owner.

"What's up, Shamus?" Jake asked, setting a frosted glass of draft Schlitz on a cocktail napkin in front of me. When he'd first learned of my occupation and had referred to me as Shamus, I had to look the name up at the Cambridge library, make sure it wasn't an insult. It wasn't—just dated. Jake and I were of two different generations. He looked it too. He also looked like he'd come out of central casting ready to play an old-time bartender. He had a round, rosy Irish face; blue eyes that sparkled; and wispy white hair. His belly was ample and he wore his white apron high.

"Going to the demonstration, Jake?" I asked, pointing at the TV.

He let out a fake laugh like he'd been asked the question before. "Not likely. Although I'm not really as sure as I used to be about this damn war. They got us mixed up in something that . . ." His voice trailed off. He must've remembered the first rule of tending bar—never talk politics or religion with the customers. I knew that because I'd worked on the business side of the bar when I was younger.

It took him only a few seconds to change the subject. "Working on anything new, Mike? It's pretty boring around here. I wouldn't mind hearing about some juicy case you're working on."

Jake knew the few cases I had were anything but exciting, so he was being kind that way. On the other hand, he had helped me a little in the past with tips and scuttlebutt about various Harvard Square characters and goings on. I was about to respond when he got a shout from the other end of the bar for his services. He spun around and was gone.

I was fast, too. I had the beer up to my lips and more than half the liquid down my throat before he made it to the other customer. It tasted awful good, like the first one always does. I set the glass down and at the same time let out a sigh. I relaxed a bit and surveyed my surroundings.

The decor of O'Toole's probably hadn't changed much since opening day right after Prohibition. Behind the bar was a mirror that ran almost the entire length of the wall. Set up along it in three ascending levels were the same types of liquor bottles you'd find in any good neighborhood bar, nothing too fancy either, thank God. There were already enough places that specialized in the pretty colored drinks starting to pop up in Boston. I hoped they'd stay on that side of the Charles River. Plunked about midway down the bar were six draft beer spigots, one of which held my brand. That was another reason I loved this place. Although with Schlitz being so popular, most joints probably carried it anyway. I hadn't bothered doing a survey though; I was happy here.

Scattered along the bar's length, seated on backless stools, were an assortment of Square characters. Most were regulars, although a newcomer never felt unwelcome at O'Toole's. On any given day the ancient stools could be supporting a Harvard professor, an MIT student, a few nearby store workers, a hippie or two who still liked the old way of getting high, some locals who'd been coming since they were kids, or a private dick (that'd be me). It was a very friendly crowd. Rarely was there a problem, especially in the daytime. And just in case any tough guys from out of the area started trouble with a customer who had his hair halfway down to his waist, I knew there was a baseball bat, a genuine Georgia toothpick, kept under the bar. It wasn't there to hit a baseball with either. I was sure Jake and the other bartenders wouldn't hesitate to use it if they had to. Not that they ever did. The display of the bat, if necessary, was usually enough to encourage any troublemakers to do their drinking elsewhere.

Behind me, running from the front door to the end of the bar, were more than a half dozen booths. All but one were already occupied. Each had a small contraption that looked like a miniature jukebox where you could drop in coins and make a record selection from the real thing against the back wall. The tunes were as eclectic as the clientele—anything could be spinning, from Sinatra to Patsy Cline to Janis Joplin. I didn't have any preference myself. I was good with them all, depending on my mood.

The facilities, men's and women's, were located down a corridor in the rear of the place. The patrons were mostly male with a few more women present at night. There was a pay phone stuck to the wall back there, too, and near the end of the corridor was Jake's small office. Beyond that, just a door that led out the rear of the building.

The small kitchen was at the far end of the bar behind a wall. A square wooden door, just large enough to pass meals through from the kitchen, would bang open every so often and a bar customer's order would slide out.

I was just pulling my empty beer from my lips when Jake returned and plunked down another. He set me up with a place mat, napkin, silverware, ketchup, salt and pepper, rolls. Then he leaned his butt against the back bar, folded his arms. He had on a white shirt with sleeves folded up to his elbow, exposing the white hair on his arms. He scanned the length of the bar, surveying his customers, waiting for me to christen the beer he'd just brought. I did. Then he spoke.

"So what are you working on?"

I guess he had a bartender's sixth sense or I was an awful easy read because he didn't say that every day. I pulled out the photo, handed it across the bar to him.

Jake took glasses from his shirt pocket, perched them on the tip of his nose, studied the photo. "Pretty and young. A runaway?"

"Yeah. Her father's hired me to find her. Afraid she might be mixed up with hard drugs." I told him the story while he stared at the photo.

Jake shook his head. "Possible. It's not all Flower Power and pot around here anymore. That's for sure."

As straight and as old as Jake was, he still knew if someone farted the wrong way around Harvard Square. He'd been here a long time and was plugged in with the Cambridge cops, many of whom were longtime customers of O'Toole's. On the other side of the fence, it was rumored that Jake had some underworld connections in his hometown of South Boston, where he still lived. I knew, like everyone, that he made book out of the bar.

"Anything?" I asked.

"Nothing." He handed the photo back to me. "I'll keep what you told me in mind though. You never know. Bartenders hear things."

Just then the little hand-through door slid open a few feet from us. I didn't have to look to know it was my meal being passed in from the kitchen. I could smell O'Toole's famous baked haddock instantly. Jake grabbed it, along with the vegetables—peas and carrots today—and a side of french fries and put it all in front of me. He added a third draft before he left to attend to other customers.

I dug in. The meal was usually the only healthy food I had every day. I know—french fries—but you can't be a saint. And these were damn good fries, too. The moment I put a forkful of haddock in my mouth, I tasted the unique flavor, which I believed had something to do with some kind of cheese, although Jake would never give up any of his recipes. I was hungry and it didn't take long for me to polish it all off.

When I was done, I did a couple of hours of beer drinking until I noticed it was dark outside and the place was filling with a noisy crowd. I wasn't up to that tonight. I had a case to work on tomorrow after all. I paid my bill, left a hefty tip. I nodded to Jake, slid off my stool, and headed for the front door and home. Little did I know that this walk, the walk I could probably make blindfolded, would be a bit more difficult than usual tonight. And it wouldn't be because of the beer.

CHAPTER 4

I'D BARELY TURNED the corner and was walking along the sidewalk when I fell for the oldest trick in the book— "Hey, Buddy, you got a light?"

I would've been a lot better off if I hadn't had one, but I did. The man who'd spoken the words stood at the head of a dark alley. When I struck the match to light his cigarette, the face I saw told me I was in trouble. Too late. He grabbed my wrist, gave a pull, caught me off balance. I stumbled a few steps deeper into the darkness. That's when I felt a sharp blow to my kidney and it hadn't come from the guy with the smoke. The pain doubled me over and I went to my knees. The smoker let go of my wrist and a forearm the size of a fireplace log wrapped around my throat from behind. I didn't have to see him to know he was powerful. The guy was having no trouble cutting off the air to my lungs. And he was toying with me, too—one moment letting me get air, the next cutting it off.

The one who'd done the possible kidney damage stepped in front of me. In spite of the dark, he was close enough that I could make out his *Devil's Demons Motorcycle Club* insignia on his denim jacket. He stood beside the biker who had asked for the light, turned, faced me. The gorilla behind me eased up on his choke hold enough that I could breathe, barely. That wasn't all good though—his body odor was overpowering.

My eyes were adjusting to the dark and I could get a better look at them now. The one who'd asked for the light was shorter than me, but built solid as a safe. His hair was short, beard scruffy. His face read like an advertisement for the Massachusetts penal system. On his denim vest was a sergeant at arms patch. I knew enough about biker gangs to know what that meant—he was the club enforcer. I'd have to play this just right. I'd already been kidney punched by one member of the club and I didn't want to find out what the enforcer could do for a follow-up. The one who'd clobbered me was just a standard dirtbag outlaw biker. They both stared at me, smirking, for a short minute.

Then the sergeant spoke. He had a voice that fit his looks. "For a big guy you went down easy. But I'll give ya credit. Jojo is an expert at them kinda punches and you didn't pass out."

Jojo let out a laugh like you'd hear in an insane asylum.

I had to say it; I couldn't help myself. "Yeah, he's an expert when someone's not looking."

Jojo's face shape-shifted crazier looking than it already had been and he started to take a step toward me before the sergeant threw out his arm to block him. The gesture stopped Jojo cold, but he continued to glare at me. I was glad the sergeant was there.

"You're not too bright, Malloy," the sergeant continued. "Jojo could hurt you bad if I let him." I wasn't surprised he knew me. Bikers like this didn't go in for common street muggings. "I hope you're a bit smarter with what I'm gonna tell ya now. And listen good, too." He nodded. The gorilla behind me tightened the squeeze on my neck, choked off my air. He waited for a sign from the sergeant and when it finally came, he eased up. I gasped, hauling in air.

The sergeant took something out of his vest pocket, flipped it toward me baseball-card style; it bounced off my chest. One of my business cards lay on the ground right in front of my knees.

"You've been passin' these out like candy," the sergeant said. "And ya can keep passin' them out. Just not in regards to the chick. Whatever you been paid, it ain't gonna be worth it to you." He glanced at a grinning Jojo, then looked back at me. "You get what I'm saying, shithead?"

I nodded. The kidney blow and the on again/off again loss of oxygen had taken any disagreeability out of me. At least for now.

"Good. If this is the end of it, you got out lucky."

Jojo spoke. "I owe him one." The grin was gone, replaced by something more fitting for someone called a Devil's Demon.

"Forget it, you had your fun," the sergeant said.

Jojo got indignant. "He insulted a full patch member."

I must've made a major violation because the sergeant looked troubled for a moment, then said, "One. That's it."

The maniacal grin came back on Jojo's face. He reached into a pocket of his greasy jeans, pulled out something metal I didn't like the look of. When he began to fit the device over the fingers of his right hand, I liked it less.

The sergeant grabbed his arm. "Put that the fuck away." Jojo did, although he didn't seem happy about it. "Do it once and don't put too much into it. There's no point in killin' him. He's already gonna stay away from the girl." The sergeant looked at the gorilla behind me, nodded and said, "Go ahead."

The gorilla was strong. I was almost a dead weight, still he got me to my feet, brought me over to the alley wall. He propped me against it so my back rested on the red bricks. If someone had taken that wall away, I would've gone down on my ass hard. The gorilla backed away slowly, gently releasing his hold, making sure I didn't collapse. I didn't, but I should have.

JoJo's motorcycle boots scrapped on the concrete as he came closer. Sick animal sounds came out of his mouth. When he reached me, he put his mouth close to my ear. I could tell by his breath he didn't believe in dentists. "No one fuckin' disrespects me, dipshit. Next time you won't get out so easy."

The sergeant spoke. "Don't forget to pull that punch, Jojo."

Jojo grunted, cocked his right arm, and if he did go easy, it sure didn't feel like it. The blow was as hard and heavy as the last one, but this time I got it square in the gut. I couldn't judge which punch had been worse, because the second it landed all thought left my head. My knees buckled, and I was giving up my baked haddock and beer before I hit the ground. I lay there in a fetal position, puking and feeling like someone had hacked away at my stomach with a bayonet.

I think I heard the three of them leaving, I'm not sure. And I don't know how long I lay there, even though I don't think I passed out. After a while, I knew I was coming back to Earth because I started wondering if I had any permanent damage. I dragged myself up with the aid of the alley's wall, and stumbled, like Quasimodo, out onto the sidewalk and into the street. The first two cars I tried to flag down both accelerated. The third car I waved to was a taxi cab. It pulled over. I fell into the back.

"Hospital," I said in a voice that sounded like I had pebbles in my throat.

The black driver turned, stared at me. "What the hell happened to you?"

"Fell off a roof."

"Jesus Christ."

He faced forward, slammed the shift into drive, and peeled out.

CHAPTER 5

THE FOLLOWING DAY I crawled out of bed with a body that hurt so bad I almost crawled right back in. I guess Jojo must have held his punches because at the hospital they'd run some tests and found no lasting damage, although they did say to watch for any blood in my piss for the next few days. They'd given me a shot of morphine and sent me out the door with a scrip for Percodan. I'd had that filled at an all-night pharmacy on the way home. Between the hypo, the pills, and the beer I had when I returned to my apartment, I slept, if that's what you can call it, despite the pain.

I had just struggled out of the shower—where I'd been debating how to tell my client I was going to extricate myself from the case—when the phone rang. I recognized the pipsqueak's voice.

"How ya feeling, Mike?" Cousin Billy said.

I knew he knew—he'd never asked about my health before. "I'm all right, Billy," I answered, emphasizing his name. The kidney and stomach pain tended to make me forget that I'd been choked over and over, until I actually had to open my mouth and say something. My voice sounded like a frog's and it hurt to talk. "That was fast."

"You sound good." The skinny turd actually let out a snicker. "The hospital let us know about the beating you took and someone here recognized your name, let me know. I thought you were supposed to help victims, not *be* the victim."

I wanted to slam down the phone and then slam down his head, but like I said, I wanted to succeed in my chosen profession and a pipeline into my local police headquarters was a big plus. So I ground my teeth down another fraction of an inch and then spoke. "You got any information for me, Billy?"

"I asked ya to call me Bill."

He sure had thin skin for a guy who liked to dish it out. "Hmm. Right, Bill. Now what about the info?"

"Nothing. I checked and the girl's report is just listed as your average dime-a-dozen runaway. Nothing in there you wouldn't already know."

"Great. You looked at everything?"

"Of course. And as far as your hospital visit goes, you want me to handle the paperwork for you?"

I knew where he was going, but I asked anyway. I wasn't going to give him any help. "What paperwork?"

"Assault and Battery, kid. Whattaya think? The hospital said you mentioned that a biker club did the dance with you because of a girl. I figured it was the Worthman chick. Which gang was it?"

That'd been a mistake—spilling that bikers had assaulted me over a girl. I didn't recall saying it. But between the pain and getting jabbed with the spike, I could've said anything. "Not sure," I lied.

"You didn't see any colors?" He didn't try to hide his skepticism.

"No." There were a few reasons I didn't tell him it was the Devil's Demons I'd had the run-in with. Number one—time was money in my profession, and if I got tied up in the court system, I'd lose a lot of both. Number two—I'll admit it—I didn't want to antagonize the Demons. I knew their reputation and I was just one solitary private eye. Number three—I was a big boy and could take care of myself, at least one on one, that was for sure. Matter of fact, I even liked it sometimes. And maybe someday I'd get a chance to "like it" with those three dirtbag Demons.

"You're not afraid of them, are you, Sherlock?"

"I'm not afraid of anyone." And I meant it—any *one*. I was just trying to be smart in this situation.

It didn't surprise me when Barney Fife didn't let it go. "Sure, Mike. That's what you try to make people think. I figure you'll be bowing out of the Worthman case sometime before dinner. Am I right?"

"I'm not bowing out of anything, Billy," I said.

"If you say so. And you're not pressing charges either?"

"No. I wouldn't know who to press them against." I'd had enough of my cousin. Besides, the more I talked to him, the greater the chance I'd say something I'd regret. "Do me a favor and let me know if anything comes in about the Worthman girl."

"Sure, sure. Be glad to. *If* you're still working on it by then."

I actually heard him snicker again as I slammed down the phone.

CHAPTER 6

IT WAS AFTER noon before I finally headed for the office. It was only three blocks, but with the pain still more than moderate, even with a couple of Percodan in me, it was a long three blocks. The walk did give me time to think and that's what I did.

It was clear that the Devil's Demons had an interest in keeping me away from Susan Worthman. The obvious reason, and the only one I could come up with, was that she'd become the old lady of a club member. That presented a problem—I'd already found that out the hard way. And if I was right, it would be very difficult to get the girl alone to talk to her, let alone get her away from the Demons. As far as her father went, that was a tough problem, too. If I told him about his daughter, there was a chance he'd head for the Demons' local hangout or clubhouse, and I'd have his blood on my conscience. Any way you looked at it, it wasn't good.

I knew the smart thing to do would be to back gracefully out of the case. I could give George Worthman back his retainer. Maybe I could even come up with something to tell him so he didn't stumble across the Demons' connection on his own and get himself hurt or worse.

That's what I should have done—stepped away from the case before someone, most likely me, got hurt. That would've been the smart way to go, but there were a couple of things gnawing at my brain. First off—that little snipe of a cousin of mine who'd been so cocksure I'd dump the Worthman case like a hot potato. That really got me. Second—I didn't like the idea of leaving a job because there was the possibility of danger involved. I was determined to make it in this racket, not run every time things got a little difficult. I'd already done that enough in my short life, burned a lot of bridges, both personal and professional. I knew this was my last chance. I'd promised myself that I would stick with it, no matter what.

But who am I trying to bullshit? It was the third reason—the real reason that I couldn't turn my back on Susan Worthman and her father—that kept my hand in the game. It was the nightmare that had haunted me every day since I'd returned from Vietnam. The memory that wouldn't let me get a night's sleep without booze. And even that sleep was filled with the visions. Visions of what I'd done. Done to a family—mother, father, and of course, daughter—who now in my mind might as well have been the Worthman family. And even though I was scared and told myself I was a sap if I didn't get out of this, I just couldn't allow myself to do it again. Jesus, I couldn't kill her again . . .

THERE WERE ONLY seven of us on patrol that day. It was supposed to be routine, like patrols usually were. We were winding our way through chest-high grasslands, taking it slow because it was as hot and humid as it gets on this damn earth. Made Florida in July seem like Alaska. We were out quite a ways from base camp. It was me; my best buddy, Johnny Dawson; Lieutenant Strickman, a West Point grad who talked with an Ivy League accent; two good old Southern boys; and two black kids, both from Chicago. Surprisingly, except for the lieutenant, we all got along pretty well.

We'd been out for a few hours. Johnny was out on point. Nothing unusual, something we usually took turns with. I could see him ahead of us and when he turned to signal us forward, the shot that rang out and caught him might as well have hit me, I was so stunned. He dropped hard; we all dropped hard.

"Johnny!" I shouted. "Johnny!"

"Keep your heads down," the lieutenant yelled.

Except for our breathing and the sound of my own heart it was deathly quiet. The rest of the patrol was spread out on their bellies in a row. Watching, waiting, sweating, hoping. Hoping that they got the hell out of there in one piece.

I was hoping Johnny was still alive. "Johnny," I shouted again.

"Malloy, shut the fuck up." The lieutenant had a tremor in his voice I didn't like. "You'll get us all killed."

It was right then that they opened up with their AK-47s. We couldn't tell how many gooks were out there, but we could hear their bullets flying over our heads. It only lasted a few seconds.

When they stopped, that's when the lieutenant said, "We're moving back out of here. Get up but stay low." His voice was even shakier now.

I raised myself on one elbow. "What about Johnny?"

The lieutenant said, "He's gone; we're getting out."

"He might just be wounded."

Grif, one of the big Southern boys, said, "Could be right, sir. One of us could go out there. See how bad he is."

"No one's going anywhere except back the way we came." The lieutenant tried in vain to get some authority in his voice. "Now get moving."

As we stood up in a crouched position, I saw the grass move where Johnny had gone down. I saw it plain as day. "He's alive. I see him moving out there. Lieutenant, he's alive."

Loop, one of the black privates, backed me up. "I seen it too. Johnny moved. The man *is* alive."

The lieutenant's face flushed and his voice came out in a rush. "You're seeing things. Nothing moved out there."

Just then the AKs opened up. The shots were high but they sounded closer this time.

"Come on," the lieutenant said, sounding panicked. "We're moving out. Go. Go."

I took a look back to where I'd seen Johnny fall. That damn grass was moving again! And I could tell just as well as if it'd been me out there, that Johnny was crawling on his belly in our direction. My friend was alive and he was trying to reach us. I didn't have to tell the others. I could see by their expressions that they saw it, too.

"Come on, Johnny!" I yelled as loud as I could. "You can make it!" I raised my M-16 with both hands and gave an arcing burst over and behind him toward the area where I thought the enemy fire had come from.

"Move, move, move!" the lieutenant yelled.

"But Johnny's headed this way," I said.

"Bullshit. You're seeing things. Get fuckin' movin' now." The lieutenant's face was red, sweaty, his eyes darting. I'd seen that look plenty on grunts like me, never on an officer before.

A few of the men started to move back, a couple held with me.

The lieutenant was screaming now, almost hysterical. "I told you to fuckin' move! That's an order!" The others finally did start to pull back; I didn't. When the lieutenant saw I wasn't planning on leaving Johnny behind, a crazy look came over his face.

He leveled his weapon at me and said, "You're disobeying an order during combat, Malloy. Move or I'll shoot you, you stupid bastard."

I didn't have to wonder whether he meant it or not. I could tell by his eyes he'd lost it and that there was no doubt he'd kill me. The man was yellow and he wanted out of there. Now. He kept his rifle pointed at me as I began, slowly, to follow the others. As I did, I glanced over my shoulder. Nothing. I wondered for a moment if I'd been seeing things. No. I knew what I'd seen.

It took us about ten minutes to reach a small hill where we could overlook our old position. My stomach collapsed when I saw that Johnny had reached where we had been. I could see his hand, above the grass, waving in our direction. I didn't know if he could see us or not, but he was definitely trying to let us know where he was. I turned to the lieutenant. He could see Johnny's frantic signal too, but he wasn't saying anything. By the look on his face, I didn't think he was going to. When I turned back, that's when I saw it—the grass moving behind Johnny—someone heading towards him. By the size of the swath, I figured it was at least two or three VC moving low through the grass toward Johnny.

Bodies around me stiffened. Everyone else had seen it too.

"We gotta get to him before they do," I yelled. "Come on."

"We're pulling back, Malloy," the lieutenant said. "Get moving."

Something in his voice told me he wasn't sure we would this time. He was right. I didn't care if he was General Westmoreland. I was going back for Johnny. And Grif and Loop must have felt the same. They were right behind me. We moved down fast from the hill. I don't think the gooks could see us, but as our elevation lowered and we reached the tall grass we couldn't see exactly where they were, either. That's when we heard automatic weapons fire ahead of us. We picked up our pace as much as we could, still trying to suppress any sounds of our approach. Within minutes we broke through to a little area where the grass was trampled down. Two gooks were busy going through Johnny's pockets. The little bastards didn't see us in time to use their weapons. We just about cut the two of them in half.

There wasn't much left of Johnny. They'd shot him up bad. There wouldn't be an open casket, that was for sure. After the shock wore off a bit, replaced by rage, we riddled the VC some more and then checked out the area. There were no more VC. It had only been the two of them. We took what was left of Johnny back with us to camp. On the march, no one spoke. We all knew we could have saved Johnny except for the lieutenant's orders and his yellow streak. I think he knew it, too. He wouldn't look any of us in the eye on the way back.

I knew it was a bad idea to drink that night with the feelings I had in me, but drink I did. We all did. And I drank a lot, even for me. I don't remember much of that night. I do remember that Grif, Loop, and the others tried to talk me out of what I was raving about doing. I don't know how hard they tried though—they were drunk and steaming, too. I do remember the bad part, the part that's haunted me every night since then. I remember somehow making it to the lieutenant's tent, a fragmentation grenade in my hand, me pulling the pin, throwing the grenade through the front opening of the tent, and stumbling away. And just as I tripped and hit the ground, I remember the sound of the explosion tearing at my ears.

When I turned and looked behind me, even with my drunken double vision I could see smoke pouring from the tattered tent. Then to my horror, someone who wasn't the lieutenant came running from the tent, and when they passed by my nostrils filled with the stench of burning flesh. It was a young Vietnamese girl—what was left of her. Most of her clothes were either blown off or shredded. But what was worse, what sobered me up real fast, was that her left arm was missing from the shoulder and her side was split open with something hanging out. I'd never, and still haven't except in my dreams, heard screams like what came from that young girl. The screams stopped before she did. She'd been running dead.

Somehow I got out of there without being seen. At least no one ever said they saw me.

I learned the next day that the lieutenant hadn't been inside when I lobbed the grenade, just some fifteen-year-old girl he'd picked up in the local village for the night. Worse still was when her father and mother came to pick up her remains. Their wails were the stuff night sweats are made from. I'll never forget those horrible sounds, either. I brought them home with me to the States, like they were dog tags I couldn't take off.

No one ever talked. I don't know why. Maybe they weren't sure it had actually been me. That I'd followed through on my drunken threats. Or they'd had pity on me and knew I'd pay for it the rest of my life anyway. And the brass didn't investigate too hard. I guess because the only one hurt was a Vietnamese girl. *And* an underage one. *And* in an officer's tent.

Since then I've often wondered if my guilt would have been less and if the visions of those three faces—mother, father, daughter— and the screams and wails never far from my mind would have eventually given me some peace if I'd been caught and had paid a price. But I hadn't been punished and I had no peace. Somehow I had to live with that.

CHAPTER 7

BY THE TIME I'd reached the office building, I'd resolved to stay on the Worthman case for a bit longer. I'd just reached my office door on the second floor when I heard the voice of my landlord on the stairs behind me.

"Malloy, I wanna talk to you."

I glanced back at the man. He resembled a weasel who'd decided to dress for the day. His face was thin and conical, ending at the sharp point of his nose. Black hair that could use a shampoo was slicked straight back. His suit not only came off the rack but off the rack of somewhere very cheap. He tried to act tough but his lack of size meant he couldn't intimidate a church mouse. All and all, he and his building went together like peanut butter and jelly.

"I got work to do," I said. I hurried with the key, tried to unlock the door. I wasn't fast enough. He got right up close to me; his pores were huge.

"I got work to do too and I can't waste my time chasing people for my rent. You're two months behind. Where's my money?"

I tried to appease him. It was either that or throw him over the bannister. "I'm working on a case now. I should get a good fee soon and I'll square with you then. I'll throw a month's advance in, too. How's that?" I knew how it was and so did he.

"Bullshit. We've done this tango before. You could say you're gonna give me a year in advance. Zero still equals zero. I got bills to pay."

"So do I and you'll be the first."

There wasn't much he could do, physically at least, and he looked about as frustrated as a man could look. "This is it, Malloy," he spit out. "Your last chance. If I don't get paid and soon, I'll evict you. Put that in your pipe and smoke it." He turned on his heels and went down the stairs as fast as he'd come up.

I didn't know if the pipe reference was just a cliche or he'd been reading an old detective novel and was throwing a dig at me. I didn't give it any extra thought. I went in the office, banged my leg against the damn Naugahyde couch as I passed it, and plunked myself down in the chair behind my desk. I was just about to get a beer when there was a knock on the office door. I hoped it wasn't the landlord back for another go around.

"Come in," I said. Through the door came two block-heads I was vaguely familiar with—Cummings and Dalton from the Cambridge PD. Plainclothes. I didn't know a lot about either, except that they'd been working the Square for quite a while. A lot longer than I had. They didn't wait to be asked, just sat in the chairs in front of my desk.

"Can I help you gentlemen?"

"You know who we are, Malloy?" Cummings asked. He was the bigger of the two, refrigerator size. Iron gray hair, standard buzz cut. His partner was thin, younger, with curly black hair and shifty eyes. One of them gave off an odor of cheap cologne so strong I almost gagged. I was pretty sure it was the younger guy. Both wore dark slacks, white shirts, and cheap sport coats. I wondered if the few people in Harvard Square who wore sport coats—including these two cops, my landlord, and even myself—patronized the same store.

"The police," I answered, pointing at the gun exposed on the big man's hip.

"I'm Sergeant Cummings," he said. "He's Inspector Dalton." He jerked a thumb toward his partner. "We'd like to discuss something with you."

"I figured that." I was feeling a bit uncomfortable now. I didn't like the look of these two generally, and I hadn't had an office visit from the law since I'd opened shop. I sensed this couldn't be good.

"Don't be a smart-ass," Dalton said. He pulled out a pack of Lucky Strikes, fired one up. I slid an ashtray stenciled with the words *Greetings From Harvard Square* towards him.

"We want to talk to you about a case you're apparently working on," Cummings said.

"I'm listening." And I was happy to. It gave me a break from talking. My throat was still sore from the previous night's neck massage I'd received courtesy of the Devil's Demons.

Cummings started to speak, stopped when I held up my finger. I felt I'd need a beer for what was coming and I didn't try to suppress the urge. Maybe it was the pills. I got up, went to the fridge, grabbed a Schlitz, sat back down, opened it. "I'd offer you fellows one, but I know you're on duty." They both eyed the beer bottle in my hand.

I took a large swig and let out a sigh. That broke their spell.

"Never mind that," Cummings said. "We heard you're working a runaway case. Worthman? Susan Worthman?"

I took a smaller sip of beer. It was nice and cold and tasted good, like the first brew of the day always does. "That's right."

Cummings put his hands on the desk, leaned in a bit toward me. They were very big hands. He spoke like he was talking to a child. "We were hoping you'd back off the case."

"Why?"

Again in a reasonable tone, Cummings said, "Well, Malloy, the department is working an investigation and the Worthman girl is . . . I guess you'd say . . . involved on the sidelines. Without getting into a lot of confidential police intelligence, it's enough to say that you poking around might foul up a lot of hard work." He looked at me intently. His partner just smirked.

"What kind of investigation?"

Cummings' voice got a bit less reasonable. "Doesn't matter. We couldn't go into it anyway. You'd be doing the department a favor. Isn't that enough? Especially the line of work you're in. You know, licensed and all."

Dalton snickered. Cummings gave him a disapproving glance.

I raised the beer bottle to my lips and took a long, slow sip. I was trying to stall for time. They were both staring at me, or maybe the beer, I couldn't be sure which. When I finally finished making love to the bottle and set it down, I said, "Well, I have a client who's very concerned about the safety of his child. Also, I've taken a retainer. So I'm obliged to finish the job."

Dalton fired first. "Look, asshole. You're gonna forget about the Worthman chick if you know what's good for you."

"Shut up," Cummings growled. Dalton looked at me like I'd said it.

Cummings leaned in even closer. I moved back. It wasn't because of his breath, which wasn't sterling, but I didn't want to be within sucker punch range in case it came to that. He'd given up the nice guy routine and changed tack. "You could be charged with interfering with police work, Malloy. Your ticket could be pulled in a heartbeat."

I already had antagonized the Demons, and before I made any new dangerous enemies, like these two cops seated in front of me, I had to figure out if there was a way around this or if I was playing with a losing hand. So again, I had to stall. "All right. Let me talk to my client. See if he'll let me excuse myself from the case. That's the professional way to do it."

Cummings studied me. I could tell he was trying to decide if I was bullshitting him or not. Before long, he pushed himself away from the desk and stood up.

"And of course you're a professional, Malloy," he said, then shrugged. "All right. We'll give you a little time to talk to your client. But not long. I'd suspend your inquiries about the Worthman kid 'til then if I were you. I'd also do everything I could to make sure the old man releases you from the case. It'd be in your best interest." He looked at Dalton. "Come on, Vinny. I think Mr. Malloy is going to do the right thing."

Dalton scrapped his chair loudly on the floor as he got up. He put on what must have been his idea of a hard guy face. It wasn't convincing. But behind it all I could see a touch of genuine evil. That's why I didn't totally ignore it when he said, "You better if you know what's fuckin' good for you, Dick Tracy."

Cummings grabbed his partner's arm, spun him around. "Put a sock in it, will ya."

Just before they reached the door, Cummings stopped, looked at my framed PI license on the wall, and said, "That's a real beauty, Malloy. Hard to get, too." He looked back at me over his shoulder. "And harder to keep sometimes."

Dalton let out another snicker.

When they were gone, I quickly grabbed another beer and tried to figure out what the hell was going on. My first thought was that Cambridge PD had some investigation going on concerning the Demons. That made sense. The Demons were known to be into a lot of shady things and were probably the subject of various law enforcement probes. And if Susan Worthman was somehow involved with them, maybe it was possible my inquiries would spook the Demons into temporarily tightening up their act. That could throw a monkey wrench into any police scrutiny of the biker gang. The cops wouldn't like that.

Probably why they had threatened my PI license if I didn't back off. I wasn't sure they could do that, but I certainly wouldn't have bet against it. And I needed that ticket. It was the road I'd chosen—the only road I had open to me.

So the obvious thing to do was tell George Worthman I hadn't been able to find out anything and back off the case. Yeah, that was the obvious thing. But there was something getting in the way of me making that decision. As I sat at my desk, hands cupped behind my head, my eyes closed, I kept seeing a face. And it wasn't Susan Worthman's. It was the face of a young Vietnamese girl, running from a shredded tent, a bloody stump where her arm should have been. I couldn't get it out of my mind. And if I walked away from this case, I knew I never would.

CHAPTER 8

THE PHONE RANG just in time to save my thoughts from turning even darker. "Michael Malloy."

It was Stoney on the other end. He asked if I could use a late lunch. "No, but I could use a beer." We agreed to meet in a half hour at O'Toole's. I played around with my collection of papers on the desk for a bit, then got up and left. It had been a short shift even for me.

When I arrived at O'Toole's the lunch crowd had already left. A handful of patrons were at the bar and all but one booth was empty. There was no sign of Stoney. I nodded to a couple of the regulars as I sidled up to my usual stool at the end of the bar. I glanced up at the overhead TV. It was a game show I had no interest in.

Jake was working the bar and he quickly had a frosted glass of Schlitz draft in front of me.

"Stoney been in, Jake?"

He furrowed his white brows, gave me a disapproving look. "Not today. And he better not bring any dope in here with him either if he does show up. For Chrissake, the last time he was here he smelled like a damn head shop."

I tried to look concerned. "You know how the kids are today. They don't think anything of grass."

Jake flicked the dishrag in his hand at the edge of the bar. "He better think something of it when he's in my place. And he better not be selling the stuff around here. I'm trying to run a legitimate business. I don't want any problems with the cops. I got my liquor license to think of and my . . ." His Irish face got a little redder.

Bookie action to worry about, I finished for him in my head. I figured he was afraid if Stoney was caught selling pot in the bar, it might attract heat to Jake's side business. "I don't think he sells the stuff," I lied. "Even if he did, he'd never do it here."

Jake put his hands on his hips and shook his head. "I hope you're right. But still, you better talk to him. Otherwise, I'm gonna ban him." He stalked off to the other end of the bar.

I made a mental note to speak to Stoney about it. The last thing I needed was friction between Stoney and Jake. I considered the two of them friends and they had both provided valuable assistance with my cases at times. Also O'Toole's was one of the three places I hung my hat, my office and my apartment being the other two. I didn't want Stoney tossed out the door. It would put a damper on the enjoyment of my one place of escape.

While mulling this over, I'd finished my beer. I waited an inordinate amount of time before ordering a refill, hoping to give Jake time to cool down. Finally I couldn't wait any longer. "Jake, another beer, please."

He glanced toward me, went to the draft spigot, delivered what I wanted. It had a perfect white foamy head, as usual. "Thanks." He nodded and left.

My side was bothering me, so when I was sure Jake wasn't looking, I pulled a vial from my jacket pocket and with my hands below the bar, shook out two Percodan, washed them down with the new beer. I reminded myself to check my piss for blood when I went to the head. I hadn't seen any yet.

I took another pull on the brew and looked up at the clock, a wooden replica of the Budweiser Clydesdales. Stoney was almost a half hour late. Unusual for him. He was a business-man and always prompt. I nursed the beer. When the half hour grew to forty-five minutes, I pushed myself off the stool and headed for the pay phone in the back corridor. Tossed in coins and dialed his number. It rang six times before I hung up. I decided my best bet was to head over there.

When I slid back onto my stool, I glanced toward Jake. He was kibitzing with someone who if he wasn't a college professor, then I wasn't a private eye. Normally, I would have asked Jake to let Stoney know what my game plan was if he came in. I thought better of it today. I drained my beer, dropped some dough on the bar, gave Jake a nod that he re-turned, and went out into the Harvard Square sunlight.

The Square was crowded with both pedestrian and car traffic. I wound my way along the sidewalk, on automatic pilot. I waited for the light and crossed the street over by the Out-of-Town News Agency kiosk. None of the kids I'd seen there the previous day were around. Matter of fact, I didn't see any kids there. The area almost always had a contingent of young hippies hanging around. Then I remembered the demonstration on Boston Common. That's where they probably were—where the action was.

I headed down Mass. Ave. toward Central Square in the direction of Stoney's apartment. I weaved my way around other people coming and going on the narrow sidewalk. I paid little attention to the storefronts on my right or the cars backed up on the street heading for Harvard Square. I'd gone a couple of blocks and had broken free of a lot of the foot traffic. Still no Stoney. And he would have to come this way. I wondered what could have delayed him. The possibilities ran the gamut from him passing out to being busted. It was just then that I spotted some furtive movement in a doorway ahead. I couldn't see who it was, but there was definitely someone there, concealing himself deep in the doorway.

Even though this was a safe area and it was broad daylight and people were around, I was still jumpy from what had happened the night before. I suddenly wished I hadn't left my .38 in the desk drawer back at the office. I slowed my pace, balled my fists at my side. No way was I going to let my kidney be used as a punching bag again. It couldn't have taken it. By the time I reached the doorway, my heart was beating as if I'd never had the beer or the percs. I kept my eyes on the doorway as I passed. I could see the shadow deep inside. It didn't move. It did whisper, "Grass, acid, hash?" as I passed by.

I kept on moving, shook my head. My heart stepped on the brakes, my hands opened like they were released from springs, and a smile spread across my face. Just another area entrepreneur. The smile lasted all the way to Stoney's apartment building.

Stoney's building was on a side street off Mass. Ave. It was a regal late nineteenth century three-story wooden structure with two apartments to each floor, just like the surrounding buildings. They all had been single family homes at one time, but converted to apartment buildings decades ago as the demographics and economics of the area had evolved. Stoney's apartment was on the top. I walked into the vestibule. Five of the apartments had a last name listed beside a buzzer. One buzzer had no name beside it. That was Stoney's. I pressed it, waiting to be buzzed through the next door. Nothing. I tried a couple more times with the same results. I gave the other five buzzers a tickle. One responded and I was in.

The inside was clean and well kept, especially considering that many apartments in the area were rented to students. The hardwood stairs and wooden bannister were polished. On my walk up to the third floor, I noticed the distinct odor of marijuana. It could have been coming from any of the apartments or even all of them. That didn't surprise me. Pot had been a more prominent smell than farts, breath, or body odor for years now in Cambridge. I was used to it.

When I reached Stoney's door I gave a hesitant rap on the heavy wood. When I received no answer I gave the door a better beating. Nothing. I tried the knob. It turned; the door opened. I didn't like that. Stoney never left his door unlocked, whether home or not.

I stepped inside. I was in the main room. I'd been here before, a few times. Psychedelic posters plastered the walls. Jimi Hendrix, Timothy Leary, and one from the Beatle's *Yellow Submarine* movie. I was familiar with them; everyone was. Some of the others—the political ones—not so much. There was an array of various colored bean bag chairs surrounding a beautiful hand-carved table with what looked like Hindu symbols adorning it. A round plate-like object sat in the middle of the table. There was pot spread out on it. The odor that filled the room wasn't from the pot, though; it was a heavy incense smell. Some type of oddly shaped lamp over in the corner was on. It threw off a soft red-tinged light.

I stood just inside the door, listening. There wasn't a sound. For the second time today, I wished I had my gun. Across the room were two adjoining doors. I knew one was the head, the other, Stoney's bedroom. "Stoney?" I hesitated a moment, then called again, louder, "Stoney?" No response.

I wondered if Stoney had gotten a little too high the night before and was sleeping it off. Then remembered he'd called me less than two hours ago and had sounded fine. Maybe he had left the door unlocked. Maybe we'd missed each other in passing. Maybe he was at O'Toole's now waiting for me. Maybe . . . maybe. These maybes were getting me nowhere. I headed for his bedroom, knocked on the door forcefully. Again, nothing. Gave it one more shot, then opened the door, looked in. The shades were up and sun illuminated the entire room. A king-size water bed plunked down in the middle took up most of the space. The bed was empty except for an array of brightly colored pillows.

Only one more door to check. I turned, took a few steps, and opened the bathroom door. That's when I found Stoney. He was on the floor on his knees, his head in the toilet bowl, jammed under the seat. "Stoney!" I threw the toilet seat up. His long reddish-blonde hair covered his face and hung in the water. I pulled his hair aside. Fortunately his face wasn't submerged. I grabbed him from behind—under his arms—and dragged him to the bedroom. I maneuvered him around so that he was on his back on the bed. The water-filled contraption rolled with the weight of his body.

He was wearing jeans, as usual, a denim shirt, and the same brown boots he always wore. I could also see that he'd taken a beating and that he was semi-conscious, groggy, moaning. There were a few bruises on his face and some dried blood, but it didn't look like serious damage.

I went back to the bathroom, got a wet facecloth, came back, and used it gingerly on Stoney's face. He slowly came around.

His blue eyes began to focus on me. "Mikey, Jesus Christ, I'm glad to see you."

I stood looking down at him. "Are you all right?"

He struggled up onto his elbows, shook his head. His hair was matted and drops of water flew off. One hit me in the face. "Yeah, I think so." He turned his head from side to side, checking himself out, maybe trying to confirm the truth in his statement.

"What happened?" I asked.

Stoney let out a deep sigh. "Fuck, man. I was just ready to go meet you when there was a freakin' knock at the door. Stupid shit, I opened it right up and they barreled in." Stoney reached up, gently touched his jaw. "Fuck."

I pulled out the vial of percs, shook out two. "Here take these. I'll get you some water."

He waved at me, then grabbed the two pills. "Don't bother. Whataya got these for?"

"I'll tell you about it later."

He swallowed them dry, gagged a bit, then continued talking. "Told me to sit down, they wanted to chat. One had a piece, so that was enough for me." Stoney ran a hand through his wet hair, moved his neck like he had a kink in it. "Let me sit up here." I grabbed his arms and he struggled up, throwing his legs over the edge of the bed so he was in a sitting position. He put his face in his hands for a minute, then looked up at me.

"What did they want?" I asked even though I already had a good idea.

"At first I thought it might be dope and money. You know, a rip-off. They looked the type and there's been more of that going on around here lately. But right away they asked about Susan Worthman and what I was doing asking questions about her around the Square. That's what they came about, Mikey—Susie Sparkle."

I wasn't surprised, my idea had been right. "Did you tell them?"

Stoney nodded, winced, and grabbed his head. After a minute, he continued. "I told them her father was looking for her. Figured that couldn't hurt anybody. But when they asked who else was looking for her, I said nobody, just me. That's when they started with a few slaps and punches. Said they didn't believe me. I swore it was just me. I thought I had them finally convinced—until the bigger of the two suggested having some fun with me in the bathroom. The freakin' ass-holes kept shoving my head in the toilet, Mikey. They were asking for names. I thought I was going to drown." Stoney adjusted his shoulders. "But I gave them nothing."

I believed him. Sure, Stoney was a drug dealer, if you can call a marijuana seller that, but he was a hippie dealer. I knew he lived by a code—never, ever rat. He believed in that more than a Mafia member.

"Did you notice if one of them had a sergeant at arms patch?"

"Sergeant at arms patch?" Stoney gave me a quizzical look. "These guys weren't in the army."

"They were bikers, right? Devil's Demons?"

Stoney shook his head very slowly. "No, no, no. Yeah, they were demons, but not Devil's Demons. They were Italian, man. They were from the *dem*, *dese*, and *dose* crowd. And if they weren't mob guys, I'll volunteer for Vietnam."

That caught me off guard. I thought for sure that Stoney had been visited by the Devil's Demons, just as I had. That he'd been worked over to keep him away from asking questions about Susan Worthman. I was right about half of that obviously. Wrong about the Demons part. It looked like someone else, someone besides the Demons, didn't want questions asked around the Square about Susan Worthman. And if Stoney was right, it sounded like they might be connected to the North End mob in Boston. I couldn't even speculate on what the hell the Mafia's connection to Susan Worthman might be. Whatever it all meant, I knew it couldn't be good.

"Did they mention the Demons?" I asked.

"No."

"They say anything else?"

Stoney rubbed his scraggly red beard. "The last thing I remember was my head in the toilet, the jerk flushing it over and over, him laughing like the sick fuck he was, and the other one telling me to keep my mouth shut about Susan Worthman. Forget all about her or they'd be back to see me, and the next time they'd flush me down the hopper in little pieces. Then a thump on my head and lights out." Stoney gently touched the back of his head. "Jeez, I got an egg there."

"I must've just missed them coming in," I said. "You couldn't have been in there long." I hesitated, then added, "I'm sorry I got you into this, Stoney." I felt as lame saying it as it sounded. "I didn't know until yesterday that this could be a little more than a missing person's case. I was going to tell you today at O'Toole's. It was my fault."

"*Mikey.*" Stoney forced a smile on his face even though I could see he was in pain. "No way. I took the job. I should've been more careful. It was my own stupidity opening the door. Not your fault."

"Thanks, Stoney," I said, even though what he'd said hadn't made me feel any better.

He sniffled. "So what were you going to tell me at O'Toole's?" Before I could answer, he spoke again. "Did you notice if there was any weed on the table out there?" He nodded in the direction of the main room.

"Yeah, it's there."

His face brightened. "Good. At least they didn't take that. Let me fire up and then tell me."

I helped him off the waterbed and into the other room. He sat, rolled a joint, lit it. I made myself uncomfortable in a red beanbag across from him. He offered me the joint; I refused. I could get nervous enough without it. As he handled the stick of weed like it was a valuable jewel, I told him what I knew.

When I was done, Stoney shook his head, stubbed out the joint in an ashtray. "What the hell do you think it means, Mikey?"

"I don't have a clue." And I honestly didn't.

"Well, maybe this'll help us figure it out." Stoney reached into his jeans pocket and pulled out a small clear plastic baggie. I could see the cocaine inside. I felt my heart speed up.

"At least this didn't get wet." He dumped out a small mound of the drug on an empty section of the pot-laden plate. It was mostly solid chunks with very little powder. He used a razor blade that had been on the table to chop at the coke. Then, when some was fairly fine, used the razor blade to set out four long, even lines. From somewhere he came up with a short, silver, metal straw. He bent and noisily inhaled a line. As I watched him vacuum up a second line, I debated whether I should refuse or not when he offered it. When he did, I didn't. Refuse, that is. Why I don't know.

He did more coke. Me not so much. I drank beer very slowly. We talked for hours about Susan Worthman, the Demons, the hoods from the North End, and everything else under the sun. I felt like we accomplished a lot. What the hell it was, I had no idea.

CHAPTER 9

THE NEXT DAY I still had no brilliant ideas on the Worthman case, just run-of-the-mill ones. I'd told Stoney to stay out of it—I didn't want to see him hurt again. I figured the first thing I needed to know was what the North End's connection to Susan Worthman was and why the hell they didn't want anyone nosing around after her. I had to also confirm my first thought that Susan might be a Demon's old lady. I wasn't as sure of that anymore.

I got to the office, twirled through my skimpy Rolodex, and pulled a card from it. I'd accumulated a small list of sources since I'd hung out my shingle. I called the phone number on the card. The man on the other end agreed to meet me that afternoon. I did a lot of nothing until it was time to leave for my meeting.

I drove my Karman Ghia across the bridge into Boston. My destination was the Combat Zone, Boston's semi-legal red-light district. Street spaces were a tough find, so I reluctantly paid to leave the car in a parking garage.

Walking along Washington Street the first smell that hit me was the pizza, strong and appealing. It came from a large joint up on the corner that I knew did a booming business. Later, after dark, there would be other odors, less appetizing than pizza, permeating the Zone.

Those businesses with liquor licenses had to close at one or two a.m., depending on the day of the week. It was afternoon now and everything was open for business. I passed a couple of cheap strip bars, rock music blaring from one. I stopped out of curiosity as I reached one of the area's numerous dirty bookstores. Signs in the windows offered sex toys, erotic paperbacks, skin mags, and peepshows—all featuring every imaginable kinkiness for your purchasing pleasure.

"Quarter, budsie?" I looked in the direction of the speaker. He stood there in a long topcoat buttoned up to his neck. He looked in worse shape than any Bowery bum.

I tried to get around him, but he'd planted himself in front of me and moved when I did. I could have shoved him out of the way, but I was afraid even the gentlest push might send him falling. I dug in for some money. After all, I guess he needed it more than I did. For heroin or booze, I wasn't sure which. Maybe both. If he was alive at the end of the year, it would be a miracle. I held the coins above his outstretched palm, dropped them in. He stepped out of my way.

A few more yards and I passed a dingy storefront. Above it a sign offered: "Live Models—Camera Rentals." There was a figure leaning back against the facade. I didn't turn my head, just my eyes, unable to resist watching as I passed. She or he—I couldn't be sure which—wore skin tight, fire engine-red hot pants with a cheap, stained white blouse knotted up against its chest. Black surrounded a pair of piercing eyes. I couldn't tell if it was makeup or not. Those eyes followed me, mouth open, tongue flicking in and out rapidly. At the same time one hand rubbed the crotch area fast enough to spark a flame. I could make out the tracks on that arm. I shuddered and walked on.

A fraction of a minute later, I reached my destination—The Burgundy Lounge. The place was on a corner and the words *Cocktails and Dancers* were painted on the window. I pulled open the door, walked in. The aroma hit me first—cigarette smoke and disinfectant. I hesitated, let my eyes become accustomed to the dim lighting, and when they did, I pushed on through the heavy cigarette smoke.

A black bar ran the length of the premises, from near the front door to the back wall—about fifty feet. Up two stairs was a slightly raised twin of the lower bar, also running the entire length of the room. The patrons on both sides faced each other and were separated by an area large enough for the bartenders to prowl back and forth, like tigers in a cage, and serve customers seated at both bars. Half the stools were already occupied even at this early time of day. There were men and women, almost all bikers, the rest a scattering of down-on-their-luck Zone denizens.

I'd only taken a few steps when I heard a shout from the far bar. "Hey, Mike. Up here."

I walked back, took the steps up, and proceeded halfway down the bar where I was greeted by my acquaintance—Tank Turner. He still sported the bushy salt-and-pepper beard that he'd had the last time I'd seen him. And it looked like he had on the same clothes I'd seen him in last time too—greasy black jeans, black T-shirt, motorcycle boots, and a leather vest decorated with various patches. I knew on the back of the vest was the logo of a full patch member of the Vipers Motorcycle Club. The man had a couple of inches and probably close to a hundred pounds on me. He grabbed me in a bear hug, and I mean a *bear* hug, pulled me close. I could smell grease, beer, and body odor as he adjusted my spine.

Finally Tank let me go, stepped back a bit, and slapped my back hard enough to rock me. "Mikey, brother. How the hell you been?" He pulled out a stool for me.

I sat. "Good." I hoped I'd be able to say that about my back in the morning.

Tank waved in the direction of a bartender who looked like he was an alumnus of Walpole State Prison. "Hit me again and . . ." Tank turned toward me. "Still drink that Schlitz shit, Mikey?" I nodded. The bartender heard it, nodded too.

Tank drained a bottle of Knickerbocker beer, slammed it down on the bar. "Jesus, it's good to see you, Mikey. How long's it been? Couple of years?"

"Less than a year, Tank."

The bartender dropped a Knick in front of Tank and a bottle of Schlitz along with a foul-looking glass for me. I shook my head, pushed the glass back. I wouldn't have used one here even if it had sparkled. "No thanks." The bartender sneered.

Tank rapped his knuckles on the bar. "Put that on my check."

The bartender stopped sneering.

Tank turned toward me. "So that's all it's been? You're shitting me?"

"Nope, that's all it's been." Tank had given me a hand on one of my first cases—supposedly stolen motorcycles. The bikes had all been insured by a small Massachusetts company. The insurer was being taken to the cleaners by some bikers with the assistance of some inside help. I'd gotten the case because more experienced PIs had been smart enough to stay away from it. I hadn't been. Besides, I had to start somewhere. One of the older PIs had told me about Tank. The man had worked with him before. And if it hadn't been for Tank, I would have probably gotten my head handed to me on a platter. Luckily, everything had turned out okay with even a modest fee paid. I'd passed on a generous piece of that fee to Tank. It had been worth it.

Tank stubbed out a butt in a cracked plastic ashtray. "Well, whatever the hell it's been, I like seein' ya, but I hope you come with some payin' work."

Just as he stopped speaking, I felt a thin arm loop around my shoulder. "Hi, handsome." I turned. She was a slim, washed-out blonde who might have looked pretty at one time but had seen better days. Her two-sizes-too-small dress was the only thing about her that didn't look cheap. "Wanna buy me a glass of champagne, honey?" She lifted her leg and rubbed her thigh against mine.

Before I could speak, Tank dragged the woman's arm from around my neck. "He's with me, wench. Whattaya blind?"

She put on a hurt little girl face. "How am I supposed to know that, Tank? I'm supposed to try all the guys."

Tank leaned back; his stool creaked. "Because I'm fuckin' talking to him. And ya don't hit on anyone with me. Got it?"

She nodded rapidly, her stringy hair shaking. "Sure, Tank, sure. No problem."

"Git," he said. She ambled down the bar to her next victim. Before she was out of earshot he added, "Skank."

Tank leaned back toward the bar, his large hairy forearms resting on the cheap black wood. "Christ, I just saved you from paying twenty bucks for a glass of ginger ale."

I'd heard rumors that the Burgundy was not only the Vipers hangout, but also that the Vipers were either hidden owners or muscle for the real owners. I could see that about half the males in the place, including Tank, wore colors, and all were Vipers and they all seemed to be paying for their drinks. I figured even if they owned the place, they probably had to—pay for their drinks, that is. Otherwise, with the amounts they drank they'd bankrupt the joint. Whatever—I could see now that Tank had some serious pull here. And there was probably more going on than the sale of real and fake booze. But none of that had any bearing on why I was there.

"Thanks, Tank. I don't like champagne or ginger ale." I took a pull on my Schlitz. Before I put it down, Tank had called for two more. That was fast even for me. I figured if I was going to get out of here sober enough to drive back to Cambridge, I better put my problem to him.

As soon as the bartender with the prison face dropped off our beers, I told Tank the story. Part of it anyway. The part concerning Susan Worthman and the Devil's Demons. I left out any mention of Stoney and the mob guys who stuck his head in the toilet.

When I was through, Tank banged his fist on the bar, startling a lot of people, including me. "Devil's Demons," he said, spitting the words out. "Shit. We call them the Devil's Dinks." He made no effort to keep his voice down. "So you want me to find out what gives between the Dinks and this Sparkle chick? That it?"

I shrugged, sipped Schlitz. "Yeah, that's it so far." I had to go easy giving assignments to a man with his reputation—it was like juggling nitroglycerin. He was known to have handled some things with more violence than necessary in the past.

On this job, I didn't want him to cause more trouble than his help was worth. And depending on what he came back with, maybe he could help with more later. As long as he didn't get out of hand, that is.

"Okay then." Tank gave me another slap on the back. This one rocked me like an earthquake. "Two more," he yelled at the bartender. To me, "The dancers are comin' on in another hour. You're gonna see some real sweet bitches then."

I hoped not. I didn't want to be here that long, but how was I going to get out quickly without offending Tank? That was a tricky question.

CHAPTER 10

I FINALLY MADE my escape from Tank and the Burgundy Lounge with just enough time to make it back to the Square and an early supper at O'Toole's. It wasn't crowded and Jake was behind the bar. I grabbed my customary stool and Jake presented me with my usual draft Schlitz.

"Someone was in looking for you," he said.

"Oh, yeah. Who?" I took a sip of the beer. It was very cold and very good.

"Julie." Jake wiped at imaginary spots on the bar with a dishrag as he looked at me. "She said she'll be back."

Julie. I sighed, took another swig of beer. "When?"

He kept moving the stupid rag around. "Didn't say. She looks good, Mike. Nothing to drink either."

I studied Jake's face. "Nothing?"

"Nothing."

We were both silent for a minute. I suddenly didn't feel as upbeat as I had when I'd come in. I thought for a moment of leaving, but where would I go? If it wasn't today that I saw her, it would be tomorrow or the day after that.

Jake finished with his imaginary cleaning job and said, "Usual?"

I nodded. "Yeah."

He ambled away to put my baked haddock order into the kitchen.

I took another pull on my beer. It wasn't as cold and it didn't taste as good anymore. I'd been crazy about Julie in my own warped way. Maybe I still was. I guess you could say she was the love of my life. I hadn't treated her that way though. Anything but. I hadn't seen her in almost six months now. And that last time hadn't been pretty. We'd been sitting here in O'Toole's, me on this same stool, she on the one beside me. I glanced at that stool—empty now—but I could remember it all like it was yesterday. Booze was what started it, of course. Not just what happened here either, but everything, everywhere. I drank a lot back then. She less. Ever since we'd first hooked up about a year earlier she'd tried to keep pace with me. I hadn't discouraged her. I felt guilty about that now. She'd rarely drank before she met me. I must've known I was the wrong person for her. She was one of those people who changed after that first drink. You could see it in her eyes, in her speech, in her face. Anyone that knew her could see it.

Jake had been the one to break it up that night. She was half-gone and had come at me with a steak knife. I was just as blitzed. Even still, I should have known better than to say the things I said. I could see her eyes after all. Or whoever the hell's eyes they were. They were the eyes of that other person—the sarcastic, cynical one who took over when she drank. I'd seen it plenty of times before, but never like that night. She'd have killed me if she could. And I probably would've deserved it. I was drunk and ignorant. Knew all the right buttons to push and I pushed them. Hard.

I'd just looked up to try to focus on the TV, when I felt the knife puncture my shoulder, the searing pain. I turned, she already had the blade out of me and raised over her shoulder, ready for another stab. I jumped off the stool and all of a sudden I could focus real good. I already told you about those eyes—it wasn't Julie standing there. At least not the Julie I loved.

She screamed something unintelligible and lunged at me again with the knife. I backed into the bar and she missed. She took a step toward me, raised the knife again . . .

I had nowhere to go, so I smashed her in the nose with my right fist. It was just drunken, blind instinct. The second it was over, I wished I'd let her stick me again. She was on the barroom floor, her face covered with blood. Jake was holding me as if he thought I was going to give her more. I don't think I would have, but who the hell knows. She rolled around on the worn wooden floor, spreading the blood like she was painting with it. There was so much blood. I looked down at my arm, saw the red dripping from it like a faucet. On the floor my blood pooled with Julie's. I was aware enough that I could see the accusing eyes of the crowd around us now, all staring at me as if I was a convicted child molester.

The cops came and ambulances took us to the hospital. My wound wasn't that bad; stitches fixed it. Julie's damage was worse. I'd shattered her nose and closed both her eyes. Jake told me that part. I never saw her again. She spent two days in the hospital. The police charged us both; I didn't push for self-defense. She took out a restraining order against me. My lawyer said I had to do the same. I did, reluctantly. She checked into rehab.

It went back and forth for a while with our lawyers and the cops, what was going to happen legally, to both of us.

Finally, after some strings were pulled, money shelled out, and some concessions on both our parts, we walked away from it.

After a while, I heard she'd gotten out of rehab. Soon, a friend of hers called, told me to stay away from her, she was making it and didn't need any temptations. That was funny because I didn't want to see her anyway. Well, not that I didn't want to see her—I couldn't. I didn't drink hard stuff anymore, but I still drank my beer—I had to sleep, didn't I? And maybe it *would* have been too tempting for her. And another reason I couldn't see her was how bad I felt every time I remembered that beautiful face covered in blood staring up at me from O'Toole's dirty floor. Knowing that I'd done that to her. I remembered it all. And that image had haunted me ever since, though on the guilt meter, the Julie thing only rated a seven, with the Vietnamese girl a solid ten. But together they were a seventeen.

I heard the heavy wooden door open, and glanced in the mirror. I knew it was her before I actually saw her in the mirror. She saw me, hesitated, and then walked my way.

"Hello, Mike."

Her voice was nasally. I turned to face her. Her nose was a bit off-center. This was going to be great. I offered her the stool beside me. The stool she'd had *that* night. "Hello, Julie."

We were both as uncomfortable as hell. There was no way around that. I tried to catch Jake's eye. He was pretending not to see me; he was probably as uncomfortable as we were. When they pushed my dinner through the little window from the kitchen, he was stuck. He brought the food over, said hello to Julie. I asked her if she was hungry. She said no. I wasn't either. I pushed my meal aside.

"Want something to drink?" I asked.

"Tonic water and lime please, Jake."

He scurried off to get the drink. The two of us sat there in silence. I wasn't playing it cozy. My heart was hammering and I honestly didn't know what to say.

When Jake brought me another beer along with Julie's tonic water, I tried to discreetly wave the beer off.

Julie caught me. She smiled. "That's all right, Mike. Leave the beer, Jake. It doesn't bother me."

Jake took the old empty, left the new. I didn't touch it.

"What are you watching?" She pointed toward the TV.

"Oh, I don't even know what it is." And I didn't. I was perspiring heavily and felt lightheaded. The smell of the baked haddock I hadn't eaten was strong. It was my favorite dish but for some reason it made my stomach queasy.

I turned my head toward her, said, "Julie, I want to tell you how sorry I am. I wanted to tell you before but . . ." I hoped she didn't hear the quiver in my voice.

I did hear the quiver in hers. "It wasn't your fault, Mike. It was mine. I could've killed you."

That's all we said for a while. We both stared at the television. I still had no idea what was on. I wondered if she did.

I kept glancing at her, couldn't help it. Every time I did, I flashed on that night again, remembered what I'd done. I saw the moisture in her blue eyes now; that hurt almost as bad. Her dusty blonde hair was shorter than it had been, and she was thinner. Her skin smooth—the booze hadn't damaged it a bit. She was still as beautiful as ever. She had on jeans, an expensive brown leather jacket, and a red blouse.

She lifted her drink, stirred the straw, set it back down. "How have you been?"

How have I been? I couldn't answer that truthfully. My God, for all I knew she was barely hanging on as it was. "Good. I've been doing pretty good."

She turned, looked at me. I kept my eyes glued to the TV. "I'm glad, Mike. I was worried about you."

Worried about me? I said to myself, then said the same thing to her.

"Yes, Mike, I was worried about you." She touched my arm, tugged a bit, forced me to look at her.

I did and wished right away that I'd broken her foot instead of her nose. At least I wouldn't have had to see it every time I looked at her.

I don't know why but I got indignant. "I'm doing good, Julie. There's nothing to worry about with me." I hesitated, then stupidly said, "You're the one who went away. How are *you?*"

She looked hurt for a moment. "I'm doing fine, Mike. I take it day by day."

She must have caught the flicker of my eyes toward her glass because she added, "I haven't had a drink . . . since the time . . . that time."

"That's good," I said.

"It is good. I still get tempted every so often, to tell you the truth. I guess it takes a while before that goes away." She leaned down, took the straw in her mouth, sipped at her tonic water. I watched her. Her lips were very full; I remembered them well. Even the taste.

"Do you ever think of . . ." she began, stopped in mid-sentence.

I answered with a lie so large it hurt coming out. "No!"

We were both silent. She stared at her tonic water. I stared at the TV, even though I still didn't know, or care, what the hell was on.

Finally, she said, "Don't you want your meal?"

Softer this time, "No."

She spoke again, softer too. "We have to talk, Mike." Hesitated, then, "At least I do."

I didn't say anything.

She asked Jake for a pen and a piece of paper. When he brought them, she wrote something, pushed the paper along the bar toward me. "Please call. For me."

She slid off her stool. "It was nice seeing you, Mike." She stood there looking at me for a long moment. I don't know what she saw.

I looked at her and again all I saw was that crooked little nose. The nose I'd adjusted for her. "Yeah, Julie, it was good to see you, too."

She turned, left. I was probably the only male in the bar who didn't watch her go.

I had the Schlitz up to my mouth before I heard her go out the door. The beer was warm. I drained it in one hoist. Waved to Jake to bring another . . . and another . . . and another.

CHAPTER 11

THE NEXT MORNING I was sick as a dog. I pulled myself together somehow and headed for the office. When I arrived at my building, I trudged up the stairs, feeling like my legs were two cement posts. I reached the landing and was surprised to see two visitors—Stoney and my landlord. I nodded to Stoney, glared at my landlord. I was in a foul mood. I unlocked the door, directed Stoney inside, told him I'd be right in and closed the door.

Before I could even turn the little weasel behind me had already started. "I need money, Malloy. I told you that. I haven't heard from you."

He was waving his hand in front of my face. On one finger was a large diamond ring. I wanted to tear that ring off, finger and all, and shove it down his throat. I had to fight not to. "I just told you the other day. You're going to get it and soon."

I guess I wasn't trying hard enough to keep it together because I bulled him right back against the bannister. He didn't like that. Not one bit. His eyes got wide and he glanced over his shoulder at the drop behind him, then looked back at me. I was right in his face now. He leaned his body back over the stairwell.

"Jesus Christ, Malloy." He pushed against my chest with his hands, the entire weight of his skinny body behind it. I eased up and he slid out of his precarious position, backpedaling away from me. "You can't treat me like that." His voice shook.

"Like what?" I roared. "You'll get your dough. All of it and soon."

He was at the stairs now. He waved a finger at me. "I'll get the cops after you."

I faked a lurch toward him. He was down the stairs like a shot.

I turned and went in the office. Stoney was in his usual chair, boots up on my desk. I glared at him. He put his feet on the floor.

"He was trying to pump me before you came, Mikey. Wanted to know if you had a case and when you were getting paid."

"I bet." I grabbed a beer from the fridge, plopped down behind my desk. I took the vial of percs from my pocket, shook out two, washed them down with beer.

"Rough night?" Stoney asked.

"I saw Julie at O'Toole's." Stoney knew Julie, knew our history.

"Oh." He looked suddenly uncomfortable. "How is she?"

"Except for a bent nose I had to look at all night, she's fine. Doesn't drink."

Stoney leaned toward me. "That wasn't your fault, Mikey. She stabbed you with a knife, for God's sake. You couldn't have done anything else."

"Thanks, Stoney. But it doesn't help."

I took another pull on my beer and we sat there in silence until Stoney pulled out *his* vial, held it up. "Maybe we both better have a taste of this before we get any more depressed."

I felt my bowels grumble. He nodded toward a glass-framed picture on the desk. It was a photo of myself with one of my favorite private eye novelists. It had been taken at an author signing over at a bookshop on Mass. Ave. I nodded back. I would have nodded if it had been a picture of my dead mother.

I watched as Stoney took the picture, set it flat on the desk, and laid four generous lines across the glass surface. No little boulders like last time. I figured he must chop his coke up before he put it in his personal vial. He handed me a cut-off straw. I did two of the lines like I'd been doing them for years, returned the straw to Stoney, and leaned back in my chair with my hands behind my head. I could hear him doing his, but I didn't watch. I felt better already.

"By the way, what the hell are you doing here? I thought I told you to stay out of this. I already got you in enough trouble." I realized my bad mood had lifted. And my hangover had disappeared.

Stoney was animated. "Mikey, you're going to need help on this. And Susie Sparkle? We can't leave her out there hanging with those types of characters. I'm not going to let a couple of guys like those two goombahs scare me away either. I do that, next thing they'll be coming for my business. Not to mention you're my friend. Besides, I can use the bread. And the front's nice too—Associate Private Investigator. I like that."

I sat forward in my chair, held up my hand, smiled. Damn, I did feel better. Even felt a little sorry now for almost throwing the landlord over the bannister. Maybe I'd apologize to him later. "Don't get carried away, Stoney. You don't have a license. This is kind of a gray area, you assisting me."

Stoney stood up. "Well, I'm here and I'm going to help you, Mikey. We'll get to the bottom of this, find that girl. Anything new by the way?"

As if on cue, the phone rang. It was Tank Turner. As I listened to him, I watched Stoney circle the room, perusing the various plaques, photos, and framed newspaper clippings I had on the walls. He'd read them all many times before.

When Tank was finished, I thanked him, hung up, and turned back to Stoney who was still engrossed in my wall decorations. "That was some info on the case. I had someone looking into the Demons. He couldn't be sure if the Demons had Susan Worthman or not, but I've got the address of their clubhouse. It's in Woburn. My source says our best bet is to stake the place out and see if we can spot her coming or going. Says if she's with them, she'll show up there sooner or later. They all do, all the members and their old ladies."

Stoney hurried back to his chair and sat down. "I'm in. Let's do it. What do you use? Binoculars?"

"Hold it a second. My man also mentioned they got a meth operation going. Said if we're caught, they'll figure that's why we're there. I don't have to tell you what that means."

Stoney gulped, hesitated. "They must be the ones that are flooding the Square with it. The garbage is ruining the area just like it did in Haight-Ashbury." After a few seconds, he shrugged. "Well, Mikey, I guess we'll have to be extra careful then, won't we? Another line?"

I didn't answer, didn't need to. It wasn't a question, just a figure of speech. He grabbed the framed photo and we indulged again.

CHAPTER 12

EVENTUALLY STONEY and I got it together enough to take a ride in the Karmann Ghia out to Woburn, a suburb of Boston. It was about ten miles away, but a thirty-minute drive. The address Tank had given me wasn't hard to find. The clubhouse was in an area called North Woburn, just off Main Street in a one-story cinderblock building. The clubhouse was at the end of a long gravel road that wound down a slight grade from Main Street. The area was populated by a junkyard, a car repair garage, and overgrown empty lots. We found ourselves an abandoned auto body shop about halfway down the road from the clubhouse. I drove around to the far side of the derelict body shop and backed the Karmann Ghia in between some junked cars. We had a good view of the clubhouse, yet we were inconspicuous to cars passing by on the main drag and also to any traffic that might come down the gravel road. There were no people about and the only sound was that of the vehicle traffic about fifty yards behind us on Main Street.

"They aren't trying to keep it a secret that they're here, that's for sure," Stoney said. He was referring to a large tin sign that adorned the front of the clubhouse. It had the Demons' name and their devil's head insignia emblazoned across it.

It was mid-afternoon and there were a half-dozen motorcycles parked near the clubhouse entrance. Stoney took out his vial and shared from the contents. We drank water and hunkered down for the duration. I really had no idea if there was any hope of locating Susan Worthman here. But I figured it was a start, and besides, I didn't have any other ideas.

A few hours passed and all we'd seen so far were the occasional bikers coming and going. We were both getting antsy. And I felt more impatient than usual. By the time the sun was beginning to set, I'd had it. Even with the coke, we'd run out of things to talk about.

"Let's go down and take a peek," I said, pointing in the direction of the clubhouse.

Stoney was hesitant. His voice cracked when he spoke. "You think that's a good idea?"

"Why not? We're not getting anywhere this way." I turned, looked at Stoney leaning against the passenger door. I wanted to say something else. I hesitated, thought, then said it. "Let's do a taste first." It was the first time I had ever asked for the white powder; Stoney had always offered.

He pulled out the coke. We tasted. We got out of the car.

We duckwalked over to the side of the auto body shop, keeping close to the wall. From the corner of the building we had to cross two empty lots, watching out for beer cans and other debris as we went. Finally, we made it to the clubhouse.

We went directly to the side of the building. There was a rectangular window there, open, about head-high. It was covered in chicken wire. I looked at Stoney. He was holding his knees, trying to catch his breath. Me? I felt fine.

I held my finger to my lips; Stoney nodded. I grabbed the sill, raised my face to the corner of the window. The first thing I noticed was the smell of marijuana—it was strong. Inside was a scattering of tables and chairs. Along one wall ran a makeshift bar. Behind it a biker/bartender. On the wall behind him was a large flag, again with the Demons' logo on it. There were about ten bikers lounging about, most at the bar, a few at a table. Also three women—none were Susan Worthman.

"What do you see?" Stoney was still crouched down, looking up at me.

"Shh. Nothing." At least nothing that was going to do us any good. All I could make out were a bunch of Demons with some women, drinking, passing joints, and talking. And they weren't saying anything that would help us either. The little I could pick up was no more than the usual bull you'd hear in any private club or bar. I did notice that two of my friends were present—JoJo and the sergeant at arms. Seeing them raised my blood pressure a bit.

Stoney came up to peer in the other side of the window. I gave him a minute. By then I'd figured we weren't going to get anywhere here. And besides, it was suddenly occurring to me how dangerous this was. My kidney had barely survived the last Demon assault. I jerked my head at Stoney in a signal to leave.

We were just about to go when the sound of an approaching car caught our attention. Stoney and I crouched low as a nondescript car came down the gravel drive in our direction. Fortunately, it circled around the opposite side of the clubhouse, headed toward its rear. I could hear the car stop and then the motor died. Car doors opened and closed.

I was frozen to the spot. If whoever it was walked this way, we'd be spotted for sure. I was just about to grab Stoney and make a dash for our car, when someone inside the clubhouse yelled out a greeting. A door inside slammed shut. I raised my face back up to the window.

When I looked in I was shocked to see Cummings and Dalton, the Cambridge cops who'd paid me a visit. They'd entered through a back door. Cummings was shaking hands with a well-built Demon sporting a waist-long ponytail. Beside the Demon stood the sergeant at arms. The four of them walked to a door, entered what looked like a small office, and closed the door behind them. That told me that the ponytailed Demon might be the club president.

I couldn't pass up the chance. I came away from the window, motioned for Stoney to stay put, and ran to the rear of the building. I glanced at the car the cops had come in—it was just a nothing civilian heap.

I made my way around to the other side of the building and found a window that I thought might belong to the room the four had gone into. I sidled up to it and looked in. I was right. The window was closed and I couldn't hear anything. But I could see plenty. Cummings was in the process of thumbing through a large stack of bills that I assumed the head Demon had just given him. When he was done, he put the money in the inside pocket of his sport coat. I watched as the cops shook hands with the two Demons.

I'd seen enough. I retraced my steps and got back to Stoney.

"We're done here," I whispered. "Let's get back to the car before they come out. If they drive around this side, we're dead."

CHAPTER 13

THE NEXT DAY I swallowed my pride and gave my cousin Billy Skinner a call. I didn't like doing it, but I wanted to feel him out about Cummings and Dalton. I knew what Billy thought of me and private detectives in general, but I also knew something else about Billy—he was one ambitious bastard. If there was a chance that this Worthman case was going to turn into something big, he'd want to get a piece of it. I could be his key to that. At least that's what I hoped he'd think.

Billy had wanted me to come to headquarters to discuss what I had on my mind. Considering what the topic was going to be, I thought that was unwise. I convinced him that a meeting somewhere else would be safer for both of us and possibly beneficial to him. He liked the beneficial part and the safer part got his curiosity piqued, so he finally agreed.

I didn't go to the office. Instead, I wasted time shuffling papers on the desk in my apartment. The next thing I knew, it was lunchtime and I found myself in a far end booth at O'Toole's with Billy sitting across from me.

"You're paying, right?" was the first thing he said. I nodded. He grabbed the lunch menu, perused it. I watched his Adam's apple go up and down.

We both had draft beers in front of us. I had barely started my probing when Billy waved me off. "Let's order. I could eat the freakin' table."

I looked around, caught the eye of Jen, our waitress. She came right over, order book in hand. "What can I get you today?" she said, looking at Billy. She was your stereotypical hippie chick. Long dark hair, no makeup (not that she needed it), a skirt down to the floor, and I could see no bra. She didn't need that either.

"Well, honey," Billy began, raising himself in his seat and looking directly at Jen's chest, "how are the clams today?"

"Small and tender," she answered, seeming to take no notice of his interest. I figured she was probably used to it, seeing how she looked and where she worked.

"Okay. I'll go with your fisherman's platter," Billy said, ordering the most expensive item on the lunch menu. He gave me a quick glance and then turned back to Jen as he handed her the menu and gave her his idea of an irresistible smile.

Jen looked at me, rolled her eyes. "Usual, Mike?" I nodded. She turned and left.

"Usual, huh?" Billy said. "What are they going to use, a dolly to bring the beer barrel over?" He let out a stupid little chuckle.

"Funny, Billy."

"It's Bill, Mike. Bill." His eyes narrowed as he looked at me; I almost laughed. But I didn't. I needed him.

We both drank our beer. I dropped some coins into the miniature jukebox. Before I could pick my first tune, Billy reached over and tapped out some numbers on the contraption. "*Smoke Gets In Your Eyes.* You know, the Platters." Yeah, I knew. That was dated, but it wasn't as bad as he could have chosen.

After I'd finished with the rest of the music selections, I waved for more beer. Jen delivered them. Billy leered again.

When she'd left he said, "All right. What's so important? What the hell did you drag me down to this dump for?"

I cleared my throat. "The Susan Worthman case."

He snickered. "I figured that. It's the only case ya got, isn't it?"

I felt my blood pressure spike, but I had to keep my emotions in check with this ignoramus. "Real comedian today, huh, Billy."

He shot me a dirty look. "I told you all we got on that chick."

I shook my head, took another sip of beer. I didn't relish telling him about two fellow detectives who might be crooked or that the gang I'd met in the alley was the Demons, but I couldn't fly blind into this any longer. I was afraid Stoney or I could end up hurt bad—or worse.

Still, I had to be very diplomatic. The blue brotherhood and all. "It's got to do with the bikers that I had that altercation with. They were Devil's Demons."

Billy spit out air. "Well, that doesn't surprise me any. When you get involved with someone, it's usually the lowest of the low."

Up, blood pressure, up. "Yeah, well, *this* may surprise you." My idea of being tactful had gone out the window. A man can only take so much. "I had the Demons' clubhouse staked out and two of your Cambridge detectives showed up."

He instantly got defensive, face colored. "So what? We deal with dirtbags all the time. They probably were questioning one of them or maybe they got stoolies in there. Ever think of that?"

I had him uncomfortable and I liked it. "Yeah, I thought of that, Billy. Until I saw them shake hands with the president of the club." I had decided to drag it out.

"Big deal. They're the best rats. They know everything."

It was then that Jen brought our meals. I could tell I'd gotten under my cousin's skin—he didn't even glance at Jen. I was sure she didn't miss the attention.

When she left, I didn't give him a chance to enjoy even one small, sweet, expensive clam. "That's not the end of it. They all went into an office, closed the door. I did a peeping Tom routine. And you know what I saw?"

He didn't answer, just scowled.

"One of the detectives counting a large stack of green and jamming it in his pocket." I took a forkful of my baked haddock, never taking my eyes off Billy, and shoved it in my mouth. Judging by the look he gave me you'd think I was the one who took the payoff.

I could tell he hated doing it, but he finally asked, "Who were they?"

"Cummings and Dalton. You know them?"

His scowl diminished a bit. "I know them. Where'd you say this supposedly took place?"

I finished a mouthful of string beans before I answered. "No supposedly about it. It was in Woburn. At the Demons' clubhouse."

"You know any of these scumbags' names?"

"Just the one who used me as a punching bag. JoJo. That's it."

Billy sat back on his bench, took a sip of beer, tried to act nonchalant. He didn't fool me. "It could've been a few other things," he said. "You'd be surprised the stuff detectives do to help people out sometimes. Could've been money the Demons ripped off from some straight citizen. Cummings and Dalton might've been just making things right. The victim gets their money back and the sleazeballs skate. Sometimes you just can't get enough for an arrest, let alone a conviction."

I munched on the ketchup-laden french fries; they were excellent. "And they might've been collecting for the police-man's ball too, but both scenarios are unlikely. And you know it." I watched him for a minute. Let him stew on what I'd just said. When he'd finally finished his first clam, I hit him again. "There's one more thing I should tell you."

He had his second clam hanging from a fork inches from his mouth. He stopped cold. "What?" he asked viciously.

I shrugged, took my time with another mouthful of had-dock. It was very good. "The same two cops—Cummings and Dalton. They came to my office, told me to lay off the Susan Worthman case. They weren't pleasant about it either. Threatened my license, not to mention my health. That was the same thing the Demons explained to me in an alleyway—drop the Worthman case. Of course, they were a bit more aggressive in their request."

Billy tossed the fork, clam and all, down on his plate. It bounced off, landed on the floor. Neither of us looked at it.

"Aren't you going to finish your clams?" I asked.

The scowl again. "You ruined my freakin' meal, Mike. You're always screwing up something. I should've known not to meet you. What the hell did you tell me this for? What were you thinking?"

Now it was my turn to get pissed. "Thinking? What the hell was I thinking? I was thinking that my cousin might be interested if a couple of fellow cops were on the payroll of one of the most vicious biker gangs in the country. You know, the gang that probably controls the meth trade in this area. The same area that includes the city you work for. The city you're supposed to serve and protect."

Billy grabbed the table with both hands, craned his thin head toward me. He was trying to look fierce but he wouldn't frighten anyone, let alone me. "Forget that moral bullshit. By telling me this, you've put me in a hell of a jackpot."

Now I moved my head toward his. We were nose to nose. He pulled back. "Tough," I spat out.

"That's easy for you to say." He was a bit more reserved now. "Not only do I have to work with these people, I gotta work with their friends and relatives. Between them they know a lot of people, in and out of the department. I could be the one who gets hurt out of this. I got a pension to worry about, not to mention my family. You wouldn't know about either of those things, genius."

I decided to take it a bit easier on him—he had a point after all. "You can't turn your back on something like this, Bill. That shit the Demons are pumping out is ruining a lot of people around here. You can't just ignore what I told you." I was thinking of Dottie, his daughter, as I spoke.

Maybe he was too. His shoulders sagged. "You sure know how to ruin a guy's appetite." He pushed the huge platter away from him.

I finished my meal. We ordered more beer. I debated boxing up the fisherman's platter and taking it with me, but I knew clams didn't travel well.

CHAPTER 14

ON THE WALK to my office from O'Toole's, I mulled over the Worthman case. Cousin Billy had grudgingly assured me he'd look into what I'd told him. He wasn't happy about it, that was for sure. It was more a love/hate type deal. He hated it because it looked like two of his brethren on the force could be involved with the Devil's Demons. He loved it because, like I said, he was one ambitious guy, and he could smell that this might turn out to be something big. So I expected that I would get some assistance from him now, but I assumed he'd pick and choose what he did. He didn't want to get burned. So he'd probably do just enough to get his name front and center in the newspapers if the case broke big, but not so much that he couldn't back out along the way if it looked like he'd get hurt. I was sure he wasn't worried about how things turned out for me.

And there was one more incentive for him to help—his daughter. He didn't like what hard drugs had done to her. Who would?

When I reached my building and trudged up to the second floor, I wasn't surprised to see I had a visitor. I *was* surprised to see it was George Worthman. Since his first visit to hire me to find his daughter, I'd only had a couple of phone conversations with the man, just to pretend to keep him up-to-date on my progress. I kept him in the dark about the Demons, the North End boys, and I'd do the same concerning the dirty cops. I didn't know what any of it meant yet, and I wasn't anxious for the man to go off half-cocked and approach one of these groups—I'd known irate family members to have done so in the past. If he did, it might turn out very bad for him. Until I knew what the hell was really going on, the less he knew, the better.

When I approached him, he was on me faster than my landlord after his rent. "Mr. Malloy, thank God you're here. I've been waiting all morning." He actually grabbed my arm and squeezed. "Please. I've got to talk to you. I don't know what to do. I'm sick with worry. I think . . ."

I waved my free arm like I was calling someone safe at home plate. "Not here. Inside." I could see that he was terrified. I hoped it was just an accumulation of worry over his daughter and not some new unwanted wrinkle. I opened the door, motioned him in, and closed it behind us. I pointed to one of the chairs in front of my desk. He almost made it. Three steps away, he started to go down and would have if I hadn't grabbed him around the shoulders. He was a tubby guy and a dead weight. Still, I got him in the chair okay. His face was as white as Stoney's cocaine. I held his shoulders, gave him a shake. It didn't do any good. I was just about ready to remove his horn-rimmed glasses and give him a bitch slap when he shook his head and came around. He brought his hands up, rubbed his face. I got him a glass of water from the bathroom and he drank it all, setting the glass on my desk.

I didn't like his look. Even the top of his bald head had an odd color. I guessed the strain was getting to him. In that case, water wouldn't be enough. I reached around my desk, took a bottle of Jack Daniel's from the bottom drawer. I didn't drink the stuff anymore—it was trouble for me. I filled the empty water glass almost halfway with the liquor and held it out toward Worthman.

He shook his head. "I don't drink." He kept staring at the glass though and something told me not to withdraw it. Finally he grabbed the glass with both hands, brought it up to his lips, and took a huge gulp. He sputtered, coughed, but he kept it down. I studied the bottle for a moment, then put it away.

George Worthman took another sip of the Jack and slowly composed himself. I didn't rush him. He put the glass down on my desk. After another few minutes, his color began to look more human.

"Oh, Mr. Malloy, it's terrible. I don't know what to do." He brought his hands up to his face.

I sat down. "Mr. Worthman, why don't you start by telling me what's happened?" I had a very bad feeling, and for a moment, my mind went to Stoney and his cocaine. I pushed the thought from my brain.

He lowered his hands, looked at me with a fear in his eyes so strong it shocked me. "You've got to get off my daughter's case now. Now, I tell you. Before it's too late. They'll kill my baby if you don't."

For a moment I thought he was going to come across the desk at me. "Who'll kill your ba . . . daughter, Mr. Worthman?" I demanded. "Tell me what the hell's happened?"

He opened his mouth but nothing came out except unintelligible gibberish. His hand moved toward his right breast.

For a moment I thought his ticker was on the blink and wondered if I remembered any lifesaving techniques. Fortunately, I didn't need to. Instead of reaching for his heart, he reached into his suit jacket's inside pocket and came out with a small white box. It looked like something that a watch might come in. He stared at the box, his eyes like red checkers, as he handed it to me.

I knew this couldn't be good. Nevertheless, I took the lid of the box off, placed it on my desk. Inside was a layer of cotton. I lifted it and my stomach flipped. Inside was a human finger. A woman's ring finger, judging by the size of the finger and the small turquoise ring on it. The finger appeared to have been severed near the bottom knuckle. It was a messy job. I had a feeling I knew whose finger this was, but still I asked Worthman to confirm it.

He nodded rapidly. "Yes. It's . . . it's Susan's. That's her . . . ring." It came out in gasps, like the man couldn't catch his breath. "Malloy . . . my Susan . . . my little . . . Susan. Her finger. Sweet . . . Jesus, her finger!"

"Get hold of yourself, Mr. Worthman. Snap out of it. Now!" I was being harsh, but the wild look in his eyes told me he was about to lose it. With shaking hands, he grabbed the glass off the desk and downed the last of the booze. He didn't gag this time, just stared into the empty glass.

I wondered if I should offer him more, but then realized I'd need him semi-coherent to find out what exactly we were dealing with. The man had just downed an amount that would have had most people taking a nap and he claimed he didn't drink. I believed him, too. It was just that he was so upset. I sat there, watched him for a while.

Soon he started to calm down a bit and I was glad I hadn't given him any more to drink. He set the empty glass down on the desk, leaned back in his chair. The amber liquid had done its work. Because of the high state of anxiety he'd been in, the liquor had just brought him back to near normal, like a junkie with a morning fix.

I covered the finger with the layer of cotton, replaced the cover, and pushed the box to the side of the desk. I then began talking, gently this time. "Mr. Worthman, can you tell me what happened now?"

He let out a sigh that seemed to rise from the bottom of his feet. "It came in the mail, Mr. Malloy. From the post office. I almost fainted when I opened it." He hesitated, eyes searching my face. "Thank God I got it instead of my wife. It would've killed her."

I pulled a yellow legal pad closer to me, grabbed a pen. "It came in that box?" I said, nodding toward the small box on the desk.

He shook his head very slowly. "No, a larger one. I left it at home. *That* was inside it." He pointed at the box, finger trembling.

I hurried along. "Was there a return address or postmark on the package?"

"No return address. A Boston postmark though."

I made a notation of all that he said. I wasn't sure what I'd remember later. I wasn't used to seeing a young girl's severed finger on my desk. "Was there anything else, Mr. Worthman?"

He reached into the same pocket he'd removed the box from and came out with a folded piece of paper. He handed it to me. The paper shook in his hand.

I opened it and read the following in big, black box letters:

TELL MALLOY TO STOP LOOKING FOR YOUR DAUGHTER OR YOU WILL NEVER SEE HER AGAIN. TELL THE COPS ABOUT ANY OF THIS AND WE WILL MAIL HER TO YOU PIECE BY PIECE.

It was crass but to the point. This note, along with the mailed gift, would be enough for any parent to hit the bottle.

I looked at Worthman; his eyes were dull now. When he spoke it was in a slow monotone. "You shee." He raised his arm slowly, pointed at the paper in my hand. "Thash why you have to stop looking for Susan. Stop now. Pleashh."

I ran my options through my head. There were really only two—stop the search like the note ordered and my employer seconded, or continue on the case. I wasn't sure of anything except that Susan Worthman, missing one finger or not, was in grave danger considering the cast of characters that were involved. Why the Demons would chop off the finger of one of their old ladies, if she was one, I had no idea. I was sure though, that if I just stopped looking for her she'd turn up dead, or as good as, sooner or later. Common sense told me that. So I made my decision right then. My only problem now was how to convince a distraught father that the only hope of getting his daughter back minus only one piece was for us to increase our efforts to find her.

I was just about to present my arguments when Worthman's eyes lowered to half-mast. I didn't breathe, just watched and prayed. Within minutes his eyes were closed and he was out cold. To make sure, I sat there for another five minutes until his deep snores became so irritating that I got up and half-dragged him to the couch. I laid him down and placed one of the end pillows under his head. I'd slept more than a few times on that cheap couch myself. I hoped he'd sleep better than I had.

I grabbed a Schlitz from the little fridge and returned to my chair. I took one glance at the small white box and knew the beer wouldn't be enough. I took out the prescription vial from my pocket, shook out two pills, and tossed them in my mouth. I quickly got the bottle of Jack and took a good-size plug to wash them down. I gagged, just like Worthman, but I held it down too. I opened the beer, took a big swig, and put out the fire in my throat.

I glanced over at Worthman. He was still snoring like a pig. That wouldn't last forever. I had to come up with something that would convince him to keep me on the case. There was no way I was going to abandon that girl. How I'd talk him into it, I didn't know. Nothing came to mind. Nothing except Stoney. Or more truthfully—Stoney's cocaine. I could have used some of that white powder now.

CHAPTER 15

WHEN GEORGE WORTHMAN finally woke, he was hungover and a mess. I checked him into a local hotel for the night. He agreed to head back to Maine in the morning and stay near the phone for my reports. There's no point in going through all the details of how I convinced him to keep me on the case. Enough said that I used every trick in the book, including lies, white lies I'd call them. I believed the ends justified the means to protect that girl and her father. I also believed a grief stricken, terrified father couldn't make an objective decision in the matter. I told him the best chance of his daughter's safe return was to keep me on the case. That wasn't a white lie or any kind of lie. It was the stone cold truth.

Two of the arguments I dropped on Mr. Worthman definitely were white lies though—that I'd be extremely discreet in any future inquiries and that I wouldn't notify the police. I knew there wasn't any way to be discreet in a mess like this one. It was too late for that. And as far as not notifying the police, I could do that, except where Cousin Billy was concerned. As much as I hated the idea, I was sure I'd need his assistance.

And the finger in the box? I wasn't sure if it was the Worthman girl's or not. It could have been anybody's finger. A ring didn't mean anything. It could have been slipped off Susan Worthman and put on another poor sap's digit. She'd never been arrested, so no fingerprints were on file. It really didn't make much difference whether she was simply a girl in grave danger or a girl with only nine fingers in grave danger. Still, I had no idea what my next step would be in trying to help her.

I returned to my office after getting George Worthman situated in his hotel room and started going through the mail that had been delivered while I was gone. Most of it was bills, as usual, but there was one envelope that stuck out. It was addressed to me here at the office, but there was no return address, no stamp, no postmark. Someone had just shoved the envelope in with the postal mail. I dumped the bills in a desk drawer with the mound of other unpaid obligations and opened the unstamped envelope.

Inside were several papers, xerox copies, all on Cambridge Police Department letterheads. I scanned them anxiously. They were more than very interesting. They were confidential files concerning an informant named William Connor, alias "JoJo." It seemed a few years earlier, Mr. Connor had fallen victim to a serious armed robbery arrest. He had agreed to cooperate with the Cambridge police. I figured out some of it by reading between the lines. In exchange for his assistance, a story about a faulty interrogation had been concocted so his release wouldn't look suspicious to his associates, and the charges had been dropped. Since then, JoJo had apparently been informing on the illegal activities of area criminals. He'd even dropped dimes the size of manhole covers on a couple of other Demons. I noticed there were no Demon speed arrests associated with him. It probably meant he didn't want to disrupt the goose that laid *his* golden egg—the meth trade.

One other item really caught my attention—the arrests of several members of the Vipers Motorcycle Club. The busts were instigated from information JoJo had supplied. Apparently these Vipers had been involved in a stolen goods operation and JoJo had put the finger on them. They were all doing long stretches. The Vipers was Tank's gang. He wouldn't be happy when I told him. That is *if* I told him. Anyway, it got me to thinking, to say the least. I needed a way forward helping George Worthman and maybe this could be it. I'd have to handle this info like it was dynamite, though. If I didn't, it could blow up in my face.

I folded the papers and put them in my rear pants pocket. I had no doubt who had sent them. It had to be Cousin Billy. He was just being very careful, sending them anonymously. He probably figured if this thing ended in a court case, I could honestly say I didn't know where the information had come from. And he was right—it was good thinking. I felt relieved now, knowing that my decision to open up with him was starting to pay off.

I wasn't sure exactly how I was going to play this, but I did know what my next step would be—call Tank Turner. So I did. When he got on the Burgundy's phone, I asked him if there was a pay phone somewhere he could call me back from. I was worried about the possible wiretapping of a Combat Zone bar's telephone. Tank agreed, acted like he received that request often. By the time he finally called me back on a pay phone, I had my idea all mapped out in my mind. Still, I was lucky to keep on track. I'd decided, for my plan to work, I had to tell Tank about JoJo's treachery. When I did, I was barely able to keep him from calling a *church* meeting to declare war on the Demons. I suggested there was a better way to handle it—a way where he could punish JoJo, the informer, and help me with the Worthman case. Also it could put some change in his pocket. We went back and forth and finally settled on the details. Mostly the ones I'd thought of. I hoped the plan would work. It felt right. But even if it wasn't, it was the only one I had. And I had Cousin Billy, of all people, to thank for it.

After I'd finished my conversation with Tank, I took my .38 from the drawer, placed it on the desk, and wondered who I could call for some coke. I had never bought the drug before. I had always gotten it free from Stoney. I'd been thinking about purchasing some for a while now. I didn't want Stoney to know I was buying it though. I wasn't really sure why. And yeah, money was tight, but not *that* tight. There was some serious stuff coming up. The coke could help me get through it, keep me sharp.

Then I remembered something. I thought I'd tossed a phone number in one of my drawers months ago. It had been given to me by a client who thought turning me on to a source for good cocaine was worth a chunk of my fee. Of course, it wasn't. At the time, the paper with the number was as valuable to me as used toilet paper. Now I started looking for that paper in the drawers. I was still rummaging through the desk an hour later, but I didn't give up. Eventually, I found it.

CHAPTER 16

THE NEXT NIGHT I found myself in the cellar of a Medford home owned by the man standing beside me—a member of the Vipers Motorcycle Club. His physique would put Arnold Schwarzenegger's to shame. Also present was Tank Turner. We were all standing in a semi-circle around another man who was anything but standing. He was strapped with duct tape to a wooden chair and he didn't look too happy about it. It was, of course, my old friend, the kidney puncher—JoJo.

We'd snatched him when he'd left his home just an hour before. Tank had come out from behind a bush and put a magnum to his head before JoJo could mount his Harley. I'd pushed him roughly into the backseat of a car. Then he was brought to this location, and hustled inside.

I didn't relish the thought of what was about to happen, but as long as nothing went overboard, I was okay with it. It was the only way I could see to find out where Susan Worthman was and have a chance to get her reunited with her father. I had made Tank promise that he wouldn't get too rough with JoJo and that there wouldn't be a fatal outcome.

He agreed not to kill the enemy biker but hedged on the part about going easy on him.

"After all," Tank had said, "some of my brothers are doing prison time because of the dirtbag."

I could understand that. I'd have to be on my toes and not let Tank and his associate get carried away.

We were in an unfinished cellar with water-stained concrete walls and two pull-string lightbulbs, one on each side of the room. Both lights were on and they gave off a harsh glare. The odor of mold was pervasive. Occasionally an old water heater in the corner would thump on and off. Tank was standing directly in front of JoJo. He was holding a wicked-looking .357 magnum in his left hand down by his side. I was to Tank's right. I had my .38 tucked in the rear of my waistband, covered by my sport coat. The unnamed Viper stood to the left of Tank. I didn't know if he was armed or not.

Tank began the interrogation. His free right hand came up in a club-like fist as he took one giant step toward the seated biker and swung. I had never realized a man Tank's size could move that fast. The fist struck JoJo's face with a sickening sound. JoJo grunted and flew backwards, chair and all. I prayed he wasn't dead.

Tank's biker brother walked over, picked JoJo and the chair up, and set them both back where they'd started. I was surprised to see that JoJo was still conscious. A good look at his face gave me a sensation of seasickness. His nose, or what used to be a nose, gushed dark red. There was probably mouth and jaw damage as well, but with all the blood I couldn't be sure how much. I just hoped the man would still be able to talk. If he couldn't, I was in trouble. I wondered for an instant if there was paper and pen upstairs if we needed him to write answers to our questions.

I jumped in quickly before Tank took another swing. "Let me talk to him for a minute."

Tank looked like an elephant ready to charge, but nonetheless he nodded.

I looked down at the bloody mess seated in front of me. I originally thought that I'd get in a few licks with this character myself. After all, he'd weakened my kidney considerably. And I hadn't forgotten that. But now I realized that whatever I could do to him would be laughable compared to what he'd already suffered, not to mention what might be coming. I shuddered and kept one eye on Tank. I didn't want to get involved in murder. I had enough trouble on my plate already.

"I want to know about Susan Worthman," I said.

JoJo tried to spit in my direction but all he did was lob a huge glob of congealed blood all over his blood-splattered T-shirt. Tank cocked his big first. JoJo saw it, too, and sputtered out something I guessed was, "Who? Who?"

"Susan Worthman. Maybe you know her as Susie Sparkle."

"I dunno any Sushi Shparkle."

He barely got the words out before Tank had the business end of the .357 jammed against Jojo's forehead. Jojo swallowed hard and his eyes bulged.

He gave me a desperate look and spoke. I translated what came out of his messed-up mouth as, "What do you want to know?"

Tank took the gun from JoJo's forehead. There was a deep round impression where the barrel had marked the flesh.

"Where is she?" I asked. "Where have the Demons got her?"

"We don't got the shick. Someone else doesh."

That caught me off guard. Would a man in a position like this lie? Especially with an armed gorilla like Tank in front of him? I had to doubt it. But if the Demons didn't have Susan Worthman, why in hell would they care so much that people were looking for her? I had to find out.

"Where is she then?"

JoJo smirked. Either the man wasn't too bright or he had big balls. Apparently Tank didn't care which because he didn't waste any time. He placed the end of the gun's barrel on JoJo's right knee. I hoped he was bluffing. I looked at Tank's face; I didn't think he was.

Apparently JoJo didn't think he was either. "If I shay anything, they'll kill me." His voice was cracking now.

Tank growled. "That's in the future. This is now. And I'll make you a fuckin' cripple."

To my surprise, JoJo shook his head. Apparently he was so frightened of someone else that he was willing to walk with a gimp or one leg for the rest of his life. Tank looked surprised too. But only for a moment. He put the gun on a pile of old boxes behind him. He turned to his muscle-bound friend and said, "There any lighter fluid around here?"

JoJo's eyes popped open. I think mine did too.

"Yeah, sure. In the garage."

Tank and I stared at JoJo and he stared back, his eyes the size of manhole covers. The other biker went upstairs. I silently prayed that JoJo'd talk before this went too far.

A few minutes later, the biker returned with a large white can of charcoal lighter fluid. Tank grabbed the can, opened the cap, and pointed it at JoJo. He squeezed the can with his huge hand and a steady stream of liquid shot out of the nozzle. The fluid saturated JoJo from the chest down. The odor was strong and JoJo had given up any attempt to act the tough guy. He thrashed around on the chair like a coked-up monkey.

When he'd finished, Tank put the can of lighter fluid on one of the boxes. Then he pulled a Zippo lighter from his dirty jeans, opened the top, and spun the wheel with his huge thumb. It ignited in an orange flame. Looked like I was going to have to jump in and stop him before we had nothing but a crispy corpse on our hands.

I didn't have to, though, thank God. JoJo started whimpering like a little girl. He'd tell us anything, anything we wanted to know, he said. "Mylesh. Mylesh Brogna. The broad's hish chick."

I knew the name, of course. Everyone in New England did. Myles Brogna was the boss of the number one criminal gang in South Boston, the Irish area of the city. He was involved in narcotics, loansharking, bookmaking, and supposedly anything else where he could make a buck. At least that's what the newspapers said. He was known to be ruthless and rumor had it that the bodies of people who ran afoul of him were buried throughout the Boston area.

Tank turned toward me, gave me a puzzled look. I shrugged, looked back at JoJo, and asked, "Are you talking about Susan Worthman? Susie Sparkle? She's involved with Myles Brogna?"

JoJo nodded his head rapidly, big drops of blood flying off his chin.

I didn't know whether to believe him or not. It didn't make any sense. But JoJo looked plenty scared. Matter of fact, I could smell something coming from his lower body and it wasn't lighter fluid.

"What's a guy like Brogna doing with a young girl like Susan Worthman?" I asked.

"Thash the way he likes 'em. The younger the better. We had her firsh, shtripping in the *Black Pearl*, until Brogna saw her. Now he's obshessed with the broad."

I still wasn't sure if I bought any of this. "Why did you want me off the case? What do the Demons care about Myles Brogna's girl?"

JoJo looked at me. I could see pure terror in his eyes. Still, he didn't answer. Not until Tank fired up the Zippo again. Then he couldn't talk fast enough. "Hesh our crank connection. We get our powder from Brogna. No way could we losh that— it's our biggest moneymaker. We do anything he needs done."

Tank put the lighter in the pocket of his leather vest, and motioned with his head. We walked to the far side of the room, out of JoJo's earshot.

"It makes sense, Mike," Tank said. He looked like a mountain standing in front of me. "I heard that Brogna's a pervert, loves underage chicks. He owns a few strip clubs and dirty book stores in the Zone. His stores are the only ones where you can buy kiddie porn under the counter. He probably carries it so he can jerk off to the garbage. He sure doesn't need the dough or the heat that it brings. When they made the Zone semi-legit, kiddie porn was one of the only things that was supposed to be taboo." Tank looked at JoJo, then back at me. "I know one of the stores—The First Amendment—is where his collectors bring the dough from all his bookies. Probably dope and protection money, too." Tank threw his shoulders back. "The Burgundy is one of the only joints down there that don't have to pay him or the guineas nothin'."

I didn't doubt that. "What about the meth?" I asked.

The mountain hesitated. I could almost see his brain churning. Tank obviously didn't like rats and I figured he didn't want to become one even if he was just giving up a lowlife like Brogna to a civilian like me. After he'd chewed on the matter for a minute, he said, "Would someone lie if they thought they were gonna be lit on fire if they didn't come clean? Especially someone like him?" He pointed at JoJo.

Of course not. So it was all true then. Myles Brogna had glommed onto beautiful young Susan Worthman. And Brogna, the Demons meth connection, had ordered them to stop me from poking around. I nodded at Tank.

"You might as well leave now, Mike," he said. "You can call a cab upstairs. You don't want to hang around and see this."

I had a couple more questions I wanted to ask JoJo and I told Tank that. I also said, "Remember you promised me. You're not going to get carried away? It'd be trouble for all of us."

Tank looked at me hard. "Trouble's my middle name, Mike. But I promised you, and besides, I don't want you gettin' in trouble. You lose that license of yours, who'd we use for discreet inquiries?" He chuckled like a rumbling volcano.

I laughed nervously. I just had to hope Tank would keep his word. There was nothing else I could do.

When we returned to JoJo, his head was hanging on his chest. I kicked his chair and he looked up. "I got a few more questions for you."

JoJo looked from me, to Tank, and back again. "Then you'll let me go? Right? You'll let me go?"

Tank growled before I could answer. "Where you gonna go, punk? You're a rat bastard and I'm gonna make sure the Demons and some others you squealed on see this." He took a copy of the informer papers out of his back jeans pocket and shook them at JoJo. Giving Tank a copy of JoJo's police file had been one of his demands. I had reluctantly agreed. I didn't tell him how I'd gotten it.

JoJo looked at me, his eyes wild. "I'll get outta Boshton. You'll never shee me again."

"I already figured that," I said. "But first I want to know where Brogna keeps the Worthman girl."

He shook his head. "I dunno."

Tank tapped the Zippo in his pocket.

JoJo's tongue licked his swollen and bloody lips. "I tell ya, I don't know. Why the hell would I care what I told ya now? I gotta get out of town fash as it is." He looked at me, his eyes pleading. "Maybe she livesh with him. Don't ask me where that ish—I don't know. They say he movesh around a lot."

I asked my next question. "Where's Brogna get his meth?"

JoJo shook his head. "I dunno, man. I'm being honesh with you. You think he'd let ush know where he wassh getting it from?"

He had a point there. Brogna probably only sold to these subhumans because they had a distribution channel and could move a lot of the stuff. He'd be dumb to let them know where it came from. And the little I'd picked up from following Brogna's career in the press told me he wasn't a stupid criminal.

I was sure I'd gotten all I was going to get out of JoJo. I turned to Tank and his friend, nodded good-bye. Then added to Tank, "Don't forget—you gave me your word."

Through gritted teeth, Tank answered, "Yeah, I did, didn't I." He sounded like he wished he hadn't.

As I headed for the stairs that led up from the cellar, JoJo hollered to me. "Malloy, aren't you gonna take me with you?"

Then almost in a whine he added, "You can't leave me alone with—"

I cut him off. "Don't worry, JoJo. You're in good hands. Better than I was. Remember?" I rubbed my side, turned, and walked up and out of the cellar.

CHAPTER 17

I SLEPT FITFULLY that night. I'd been up less than two minutes, and already I had my radio on and tuned to the big Boston news station. I was listening to hear if there were any unidentified bodies found overnight in the surrounding area. There hadn't been; that was good. Hopefully, Tank had kept his word and had not gotten overly rough with JoJo. I knew the world would be a better place without the man, but it still would have been murder and I didn't want to reap the consequences of being involved in that.

So now that I could breathe a temporary sigh of relief, I pondered what I should do next. It didn't take long; I didn't have many choices. In fact the *only* choice I had concerned the new name in the mix—Myles Brogna. So I decided to see the one man I figured must know more about Brogna than anyone else I knew—Jake O'Toole.

I glanced at the clock on my apartment wall and decided I should see him now, before his place loaded up with the lunch crowd and he was too busy to talk. At this time there would probably be only some morning drinkers. I decided to be one of them.

When I made it to O'Toole's, I saw I'd been correct—there were only two customers at the bar. They were seated side by side. I recognized them—retired guys who retirement hadn't been good to. It hadn't done much for them except increase their drinking time at O'Toole's. I nodded to them as I passed.

Jake must have seen me through the front window before I even reached the door, because he had a draft in hand and was racing me to my stool. He won. The frosted glass of beer was placed on a cocktail napkin in front of me as I sat. Jake leaned back against the back bar, arms folded across his chest.

He didn't speak. Instead, he waited while I took my first pull of beer for the day. God, was it good. I didn't even try to hide the sigh I let out.

"You look like you've been busy," Jake said.

I glanced at my reflection in the mirror behind him. I did look a little ragged. But I'd been working hard, I told myself. The Worthman case wasn't easy. I told Jake the same.

He nodded. "You sure you haven't been hanging out with Sundance too much?"

That comment surprised me. "It's Sundown, Jake. Sundown."

Jake made a face like he was sucking lemons. "Yeah. *Stoney* Sundown, ain't it?"

I ignored his emphasis on the first name. Instead, I changed the subject. I tilted my head, motioned him to come close.

He stepped toward me, put his hands on the bar. I looked to my right. The closest of the retired guys, about four stools away, turned quickly to look back at the overhead TV.

"It's the Susan Worthman case I told you about the other day," I said quietly. "You remember that?"

"'Course I do. I'm not that old, Mike."

I took a slow sip of beer. This wasn't going to be easy. "You still interested in helping out a little?"

He feigned indignation. "Of course I am. I got kids too, for Chrissake. I wouldn't want to see them running around the Square getting mixed up with dope."

We were both talking low. Still, I glanced toward the retiree again. And again, he quickly looked back at the TV. "I've got a line on where she is," I said.

He must have detected something in my voice because the grin disappeared. "Oh?"

I didn't know any other way to say it but straight out. I had no idea what his reaction would be. "I think she's living with Myles Brogna." Jake was not the type to show emotion. And even though he didn't say anything, I could still tell that he was turning my words over in his mind like an out-of-control Ferris wheel.

I decided to give him all the time he needed to respond but I was surprised at just how long that was. He left for a few minutes, refreshing the drinks of his two customers. He then returned with a beer for me, moved my empty glass below the bar, and resumed his position, hands on the bar in front of me.

He finally spoke, softly. "You know what you're getting into has about as much to do with a runaway case as terminal cancer does with the sniffles?"

"That means you'd rather not get involved? I don't blame you. You've got a business and a family. I understand."

Jake's face was dead serious now. "I didn't say that, Mike. I know all about Myles Brogna. I just want to make sure *you* do."

I nodded. "I've heard a lot about the man."

Jake's eyes narrowed and he spoke as if the words tasted bad. "He's the worst of the worst, Mike. A woman killer and a pedophile. He's been drowning my hometown in hard drugs for years. Claims he's got nothing to do with anything except bookmaking. Tries to portray himself as some kind of Robin Hood. Why most of the people in Southie don't see through that, I've never understood."

I was seeing Jake in a new light, a more serious light. "You'd help me then?"

Jake's tongue rolled the inside of his cheek before he spoke. "Yeah, I'll help you. Do what I can, within reason. The only thing I'd ask, Mike, and I'm sure I don't really have to say it, is that we're going to have to be very discreet about this. We're talking about something dangerous here, believe me. The man is a snake. You'll have to keep my name out of it."

I held my hands up. "That goes without saying, Jake."

He half smiled. "I know that. I just had to say it. Now tell me what you already know."

So I did. I told him almost everything—what I'd learned from JoJo, Stoney's involvement and the beating he'd taken from the Italians, the Demons and meth connection, the two shady Cambridge cops, and the gift George Worthman received in the mail. I left out the involvement of my cousin, Billy. Jake was leery of Stoney being in the mix, but I assured him Stoney was trustworthy. He accepted that halfheartedly.

When we were done with all that, he said, "So what do you think our first move should be?"

That was the million dollar question. I was flying by the seat of my pants on this, so I went with the obvious. "We find out where Susan Worthman is and get her out of there."

Still talking in a low voice, Jake said, "That first part shouldn't be too hard."

"I don't know. JoJo says Brogna moves around a lot. No set address."

Jake's eyes sparkled. "That'll be no problem. I can handle that. The scumbag moves around because he's got so many enemies on both sides of the law. Even so, he can't have more than a few places he uses. I can find out where they are."

I studied his face and didn't doubt for a minute he could do it, but how I didn't know. "All right. You handle that, I guess. I've got some other angles to work on." I almost asked him to give me a call when he had something, then remembered that I saw him almost every day anyhow. So instead, I just said, "Be careful, Jake. Remember what you said. The man's a snake."

"And I didn't tell you the half of it, Mike." He pushed away from the bar, walked toward the other end.

Before I left, I decided to cover all bases just in case Jake struck out. I used the pay phone in the rear of O'Toole's to call Cousin Billy. I didn't tell him much over the phone, just that I had a line on Susan Worthman and wanted to know if he could dig up an address for Myles Brogna. I could hear him spit out coffee before he hung up on me.

Before I left, I called to Jake, "Get one for the boys, on me." I nodded toward the two retired gents seated down the bar.

They looked in my direction. One held his glass up and said, "Thanks, Mike. You're a good man."

Yeah, a good man. I guess I even had one of my fellow bar flies fooled.

CHAPTER 18

WHEN I GOT back to the office, the newspapers had arrived. I tore through them. No mention of any bodies turning up that might have been JoJo's. It didn't really mean much though. It wasn't likely that if anything had happened to JoJo, it would have made the paper that fast. I still wouldn't have been shocked to see his ugly face in the next day's paper. Still, I felt a bit more confident that the man was alive somewhere, probably halfway across the country by now—if he was smart. I got up, grabbed a beer from the fridge. I never could stop once I started. And the starting time was a lot earlier, it seemed, every day.

I chugged the beer. It did nothing for me, just like the ones I'd already had at O'Toole's. It was going to take something stronger, something more powerful to get my mind off things I didn't want to think about. Things that had nothing to do with the Worthman case. It was the thoughts of two other girls that were troubling me. Well, a woman and a girl. Julie and what I'd done to her *that* night in O'Tooles. And before that, to the young girl in Vietnam that I'd . . .

I glared at the picture of Nixon on the wall. I didn't like the man. It was his fault. I threw the empty beer bottle. It missed the picture but shattered against the wall and fell to the floor. I dropped my hand to my pants pocket, touched something else I'd been thinking about a lot lately—cocaine. I'd called the number I'd found in my desk, visited the dealer and made a purchase. I hadn't used any yet. Why I don't know. Maybe proving to myself that I had willpower. I had none now.

I removed the small plastic baggie from my pocket. I took out the folded paper inside, put it on the desk, opened it. I dumped the small mound of white powder it held onto a yellow legal pad. I used my driver's license to scrape out two large equal lines of the cocaine. Chopped at them, like I'd seen Stoney do, even though they were nothing but fine powder, unlike Stoney's which was mostly what he called rocks.

I rolled a dollar bill and did what I'd been thinking of doing ever since I'd made this—my first cocaine purchase. The powder burned my nostrils. Stoney's was much gentler on my beak. Maybe the harshness meant it was good. I didn't know. It didn't take long to hit me, but that was different, too. Not euphoric like Stoney's, but it worked. My heart sped up, but to an unpleasant level.

I rushed over to the fridge and brought two beers back to the desk, opened them both quickly. I finished the first in three gulps. I was setting the bottle down when I heard someone bound up the stairs and come along the corridor outside my office. My heart jumped jaggedly. I pulled open the desk drawer, grabbed the .38, cocked it, and pointed it at the closed door. The gun shook in my hand.

Within seconds, with each one seeming like an hour, the knob turned and the door opened. Why I didn't shoot, I don't know. Thank God, I didn't. Standing there, his hand still on the doorknob, was Stoney. He looked from my face to the gun and back again.

"It's me, Mikey. Stoney."

I knew that. But what in the hell was the matter with me? I turned the gun away, lowered the hammer, and put it back in the drawer. My heart still hadn't slowed. I remembered the coke on the desk, but it was too late; Stoney saw it.

He walked over, sat, nodded toward the powder. "You been indulging, huh?"

"Just a little," I answered and felt my voice quivering. I hoped Stoney hadn't noticed.

"Mind if I check it out?"

I shook my head, held out the dollar bill. He refused it and pulled the legal pad with the powder on it close to him. He leaned over, examined it like a jeweler would when presented with new stones. He pressed the tip of his index finger into the corner of the powder and placed the small amount that stuck onto his tongue. He made a face like it was sour milk.

"Speed," he said. He wiped the few granules left on his finger onto his bell bottom jeans.

"What do you mean, speed?" I sputtered.

Stoney put his boots up on the desk, crossing his legs at the ankle. "Just what I said, Jack." He nodded toward the powder. "A bottle of Coca Cola has more cocaine in it than that stuff."

I didn't doubt him for a minute. It explained a lot—the jackhammer-like heart, the sweat running down my armpits, the paranoia filling the room, not to mention some very bizarre thoughts going through my head. "How long will it last?" I asked.

"Christ, you could still be buzzin' tomorrow." Stoney dug into his shirt pocket, pulled something out. "But lucky for you, I'm always prepared." He handed me a blue pill.

I took it, placed it in my palm. "What is it?" I asked. My voice sounded shakier—if that was possible.

"Valium. Ten milligrams, man. It would put most people to sleep, but looking at you, it probably will just calm you down a bit."

I trusted Stoney. Besides, I noticed perspiration on my hand and was frightened it would dissolve the pill. So I didn't bother to debate with myself. I opened the other beer and used a huge swig of it to down the pill.

"How long will it take?" Whatever his answer, it wouldn't be soon enough. I was still trying to ignore the wild thoughts in my mind and the strange sounds that I thought I heard every so often. I gulped more beer.

"Less than an hour." Stoney gave me a funny look before adding, "I hope."

"I'm all right. I'm all right." I hustled over to the fridge, grabbed two more beers, both for me, and raced back to my chair, hunkering down and praying for the pill to work quickly.

"Yeah, you're fine, Mikey," Stoney said. "Where the hell did you get that shit anyway?" He tipped his toe toward the speed.

I told him.

Stoney pulled his feet off the desk, placed them on the floor, and leaned toward me. That scared me for some reason, but I fought to control it. "I'm not looking to drum up business, Mikey. But if you're going to buy it anyway, get it from me. A lot of these characters around the Square see a guy like you coming and they'll give you anything. At least with me you know what you're getting."

I understood what he was saying. But I would never use any of it again anyhow. "I'll never touch this stuff again. Cocaine or speed. I've had it. It was just a spur of the moment thing anyway."

Stoney shrugged. "All right, Mikey. But if you change your mind and want the real thing, please don't get it from just anybody."

"Yeah, yeah, yeah. Thanks." I wondered when the damn pill would begin working. How long had it been? I wasn't sure. It would be a cold day in hell before I'd touch anything like this again.

We talked for a while. Mostly me, I think. I don't know for how long. Or about what. I did know I'd have to restock my fridge when this was all over. Eventually I noticed that I hadn't heard any strange sounds for a bit and that the bizarre thoughts had subsided. My heart slowed, not to its natural beat, but at least to a level where I stopped worrying about having a heart attack.

Stoney must have noticed a change in me too. "How you feeling now, Mikey?" he asked, a hopeful look on his face.

"Better," was all I said.

Stoney glanced up at the big plain office clock on the wall. "It's about time." He turned, pointed at my desk. "I thought I was going to have to make a beer run for you."

There were six empties and one half-full Schlitz bottle on the desk in front of me. I remembered Stoney hadn't had any.

"What are you going to do now, Mikey?"

I felt better, but only better enough to put an end to the day. "I'm going home."

Stoney smiled. "Good. I'll walk with you."

I got up, started to dispose of the empty beers. "I'm all right, Stoney. I've got to clean up a few things here first."

Stony stood up, a doubtful look on his face. "You sure you'll be okay, Mikey? You're going home, right?"

"I'll be fine. I'm going home." I wasn't lying; I was washed out. I couldn't have done much else even if I'd wanted to.

Stoney shrugged and his face relaxed. "All right then, man." He stepped up to me, and stuffed something into the pocket of my wrinkled white dress shirt. "Don't take that until you get home. Then go to bed. You'll sleep good."

"Thanks, Stoney." He was gone before I was back to my desk.

I didn't feel great, not with all the speed, beer, and tranquilizer in my system. But at least now that my mind had slowed down, I felt like I was going to live and that there would be a tomorrow. I sat at the desk, sipped the rest of my last beer very slowly, and gathered the courage for the short walk to my apartment.

CHAPTER 19

WHEN I TURNED the lock on my apartment door and stepped inside, I could see that the bathroom door on the other side of the living room was closed. I always left it open. It was enough to let the speed in my system override the tranquilizer and beer I'd consumed. My symptoms came roaring back to life like a freight train. I was attempting to keep my heart from popping out of my chest when the bathroom door opened and Julie walked out. She jumped when she saw me.

"Oh. Hello, Mike."

My mind was coming down from fight or flight, but my voice still shook when I asked, "How did you get in here?"

"My key still works. I guess you never changed the locks."

She hadn't changed much either I noticed as I stood there, staring at her like a dunce. Except for that damn nose. Even in my condition, I felt a yearning. The jeans and thin blouse she wore showed me that she hadn't been on the booze long enough to damage that figure. Her skin either.

She still wore only a touch of light makeup and didn't even need that. Her short, dusty-blonde hair was like parentheses around her face.

I still loved looking at her even as screwed up as I was. Until I started thinking about how she got that crooked little nose. Then I didn't like looking at her so much anymore.

I could tell she was waiting for me to say something. The condition I was in, I knew she'd have a long wait.

She took a couple of tentative steps toward me. "Are you all right, Mike?"

No, I wasn't all right, but I wasn't going to tell her that. "I'm fine." My voice wasn't quivering anymore, but it sounded about as solid as mashed potatoes.

I brushed past her, headed for the kitchen. I caught a whiff of her sweet scent; I remembered it well. I pulled a bottle of Schlitz from my banged-up fridge and almost grabbed her one too, before I remembered she didn't drink anymore. I returned to the living room.

"You want anything?"

She shook her head.

I sat in my easy chair. It didn't make me feel any easier.

She stood there for a minute looking down at me with the same concerned face Stoney had shown a little while ago. Then she went to the old couch, sat stiffly.

"I'm sorry I came in, Mike. Are you mad?"

Mad? Yeah, I was mad. Plenty mad. At myself though. "No. But what are you doing here?"

"I was worried about you. The other day when I saw you—"

I cut her off. "I was fine then. Stoney just called you?"

Her cheeks flushed lightly. "Don't tell him that you know, Mike. He was worried about you."

I sat up. "How did he know how to reach you?"

"I've talked to him. I can still be friends with him, you know."

My anxiety symptoms had receded a bit, but you couldn't say I was relaxed, that was for sure. I felt more like someone who'd just woken up from a three-day bender. Empty inside. Except for guilt. Plenty of guilt.

"So what do you want, Julie?" My eyes kept being pulled to that busted nose; I fought to focus on anything but that nose.

"I told you, I was worried about you." The concerned look again.

"I'm all right. You can see that."

She shook her head. Her blonde hair shimmied. "I don't see that. You need some sleep, Mike. Come on." She bounced up from the couch, grabbed my free hand. "I'm putting you to bed."

I didn't have the strength to fight her. Deep down I didn't really want to. I couldn't have fought anybody just then.

She led me into the bedroom. There wasn't much to it— bed, bureau, a couple of side tables. I sat on the bed, worked on my shirt. She removed my shoes, hoisted my legs onto the bed.

She leaned over me, pulled my shirt off. "Don't you want your pants and undershirt off, Mike?"

She came close to me, her hair almost brushed my cheek. I felt the stirring again. I couldn't help myself. I looked in her eyes, let myself go. I didn't have to raise my head, hers did the work, our tongues mingled. I remembered that taste; it was wonderful. Her breasts touched my chest. Some type of wicked tension I'd been holding was released through a slow breath. I just lay there as she first undressed me and then herself. She was as perfect as the day I first met her. Even her misshapen nose began to look good. She did everything; I couldn't do anything. The speed had made sure of that.

When we had both given up, she lay her head on my bare chest. I felt I had to say something. "I'm sorry, I . . ."

She held a finger up to my lips. Even her finger was something. "Don't say it. It's not your fault. It's just that stuff you took." She raised up, looked at me. "I shouldn't have started anything anyway. I know how you think you feel about me. And you probably will again tomorrow." She got up, went to my shirt she'd placed on a chair, and removed the blue pill Stoney had put in the pocket. He must have told her. She returned, placed it on my tongue, gently closed my mouth.

I swallowed the pill, then said, "No, no, I won't." I believed that, then.

It wasn't until the next morning I found out that I was wrong. And that, of course, she'd been right.

CHAPTER 20

THE NEXT MORNING I felt worse than shit on a stick. Julie was already up and puttering around in my small kitchen. I made my way to the bathroom, did my business, and stumbled out into the kitchen.

"Good morning," she said in a cheery voice. She waved her hand in the direction of the Formica table. "It's not much, but you didn't have much to work with."

She had on the same clothes as last night, but you wouldn't know it by how they looked—there wasn't a wrinkle to be seen. She looked the same, too. She stared at my face, not the underpants and white T-shirt I was wearing. On the table was one setting—orange juice, toast, cereal with a chopped-up banana on it, a half-empty gallon of milk.

I pulled out the chair in front of what was apparently my spot, sat down heavily. I felt as jovial as someone contemplating suicide. "You already ate?" I tried to perk up my speech but the words hit the floor as fast as they came out of my mouth.

"I had to." She looked at her dainty little watch. "I'm already late for work. But I wasn't leaving until you got up." She gave me that concerned look again. I'd seen it more times in the past twenty-four hours than in my entire lifetime.

She came closer, but didn't touch me; I was glad of that. "Mike, I know you're involved in something. I just want you to know if I can help you in any way, I want to."

I turned to the food, picked at it like a fussy kid. Her scent was light in the air. Even it couldn't break through my blackness though. "Stoney, again, huh?"

She folded her arms, looked down at me. "I told you, he's just worried, Mike. He didn't tell me anything more. He's a good friend to have."

I looked up at her and there was that smashed nose again; it didn't look so cute anymore. I knew I couldn't handle anything heavy in my condition so I said, "Yeah, I know."

She continued to look at me. I went back to playing with the food. Neither of us spoke for more than a minute, finally she said, "I have to go. Remember what I said—I want to help you with whatever's going on. I know you think it's impossible for us to be together after what happened, Mike, but I don't. And for a little while last night you thought that way, too. You did and that's how you feel deep down. I know it. If we could just be friends, we'd see . . . you'd see. Please call me." I already had it somewhere, but still she dropped a paper with her phone number toward the table. It floated down and landed on my buttered toast.

I didn't say anything, just watched as she left the apartment and closed the door behind her. I was up and over to the fridge before I heard her open the main door to the street. I grabbed a Schlitz and drank it down quickly. The liquid was so cold it hurt my throat. I opened a second and returned to my seat at the kitchen table.

I had no idea what I was going to do. Not only about Julie, but about the Worthman case, too. Even a drug and booze hangover couldn't get that out of my mind. And the way I felt right now, it wouldn't have surprised me any if I just threw the whole mess out the window with me right after it. Of course, that wouldn't have done any good. A two-story fall would probably only break an ankle. I suddenly had dark visions of the revolver in the bedroom. I looked in that direction. It frightened me and for a long black moment I was afraid I couldn't fight it. I jumped up, went to the phone, and with shaky fingers, dialed.

"Stoney," I said, "do you mind if I come by?"

I listened as he told me to come on over. Then I hung up. On my way to the bedroom to get ready for the trip to Stoney's, I saw the slip of paper Julie had left. It was stained with butter. I snatched it, brought it with me. In the bedroom I put it in my wallet. Why I didn't know. After all, I didn't think I'd ever need it.

CHAPTER 21

WHEN I GOT to Stoney's apartment, relief was just a sniff away. And that's what I did; more than one, too. The depression and hangover subsided, and I got down to business. I told Stoney about Myles Brogna, his meth operation, and brought him up to speed on Susan Worthman. I had no idea how he'd react. He answered quickly and didn't disappoint me.

"You know what I think of that speed shit, Mike," he said. "I'm still in."

Stoney and I tossed it around a bit and finally came up with what we thought was a reasonable idea to find out where Susan Worthman was being kept. We decided to head into the First Amendment Bookstore and see if we could get a line on where Brogna actually lived in case Jake had no luck. Tank had told me that money from some bookies, drug dealers, and semi-legitimate Zone businesses was dropped at the bookstore. It followed—I believed—that the money would then be shipped to Brogna wherever he was located. A dirty bookstore in Boston's Combat Zone certainly wasn't where anyone, including Myles Brogna, would want to warehouse a large amount of cash overnight.

When we reached the heart of downtown Boston, I parked the Karmann Ghia in a lot on Washington Street, down near the Jordan Marsh department store. We were planning on walking the couple extra blocks into the Zone. We must have looked like an unlikely pair as we passed the first strip joint—Stoney, looking like he was a resident of a hippie crash pad; me, looking like an office worker from the financial district out for some early titillation.

It was around noon and the first thing I noticed about the Zone, in addition to the interesting sights, of course, were the odors. The smell of cheap pizza was strong. It mixed with the powerful odors from trash bins located behind the buildings. And the stink of disinfectant as you passed the open doors of some establishments was noticeable. I coughed on the fumes of cars, slowly circling the blocks that contained the sex trade area, their drivers searching for early rising hookers plying their trade.

"I've never been in the Combat Zone before," Stoney said as we passed a storefront with a sign that proclaimed, *Hardcore Gay Peepshows—XXX*. "Have you, Mikey?"

"Ahh, no," I answered. Then quickly added, "Except for the other day. It was business." I was talking about the visit I'd made to see Tank at the Burgundy Lounge.

We were in front of a bar with a window that read: *Girls! Girls! Girls! ALL NUDE!* I raised my hand just a bit to signal Stoney to stop. I nodded across the street in the direction of a neon sign which resembled an American flag. It announced the name of the business as First Amendment Bookstore. Pasted to the plate glass windows, blocking any view to the inside, were about a dozen posters—"Fetish Clothes," "Hardcore Books & Mags," "XXX Movies," "Hot

Sex Toys," "Peep Booths," "Smoking Accessories," and others of a similar vein.

The two of us stood looking across Washington Street at the sex emporium. Suddenly, a black man with the filthiest shirt and pants I had ever seen stumbled into us. I stepped back; so did Stoney. The man had his hand held out, a gnarled claw, covered with burn marks. One of his bloodshot eyes stared off to the side. He opened his mouth. What teeth were left were worse than rotten. He spoke; it was gibberish. He came in closer, hand still outstretched. I backed up quickly. I knew his breath was probably dangerous. He began yelling. Again, just gibberish. Before he attracted attention to us, I pulled a buck from my wallet and handed it to him. He shoved it in the pocket of his dirty pants. I could smell shit. He staggered away, bouncing off the plate glass window of a gay movie theatre, somehow not crashing through.

"Jesus Christ," Stoney said. I could see that he was nervous. That wasn't like him. He usually took most things calmly or even as a joke. Then again, the Zone typically was a shock to newcomers.

Before I could tap down his worry, a man who'd been leaning against the front of the gay movie house sauntered towards us. He had a cigarette dangling from his lips. He looked about as shifty as a used car salesman behind on his bills. "Don't mind that fuckin' bum," he said. "Bums like him give this area a bad name."

Stoney and I quickly turned away from Cigarette Man before he could continue.

He stepped up beside us. "You guys look like you want something. You want some nice pussy?"

I glanced at him. Stoney didn't. Cigarette Man took the burning butt out of his mouth with fingers that looked like they were permanently stained a dark Dijon mustard color. He grinned like he should have been locked away somewhere and then glanced up and down Washington Street. "I can get you sweet pussy. Young pussy. You like pussy?"

I told him we weren't interested.

"Cock? You want cock then? I know where there's hot cock."

I felt Stoney tug at my arm. "Mike, let's get out of here."

To Stoney, I said, "We got a job to do." Then, lowering my voice, "These people are harmless." I turned to Cigarette Man. "We're all set, pal. We don't want anything."

He nodded and smiled like he'd just been released from an asylum that morning. "Dope? You like dope? What you want? Grass? I get good grass." When I shook my head, he said, "Cocaine then. You fuck good on cocaine." He jerked the hand with the cigarette in it back and forth rapidly.

"No!" I noticed he had very strong body odor. "Come on," I said to Stoney. "Let's get in there and see what we see." I motioned toward the First Amendment Bookstore.

Stoney was more than a little anxious to get away from Cigarette Man, so he didn't hesitate to follow me across the street. Behind us I could hear Cigarette Man saying, "Heroin, speed, whatever. I get the best. You remember me."

I hoped I wouldn't.

Once inside the bookstore, I noticed the lights—the place had rows and rows of long florescent bulbs along the ceiling. The place was lit up like a cathedral and the light was harsh. Just inside the door was a checkout counter that was chest high. Beside it was a long glass display case full of dildos, handcuffs, leather masks, butyl nitrate to sniff, and various other bizarre sex-related products. Up high, behind the counter, with a cash register beside him, was the clerk. If I hadn't known better, I would have thought that somehow Cigarette Man had gotten in ahead of us and taken the seat up there. They could have been brothers. The clerk's snake eyes followed us as we moved past him into the shop.

There were aisles loaded with magazines and paperback books. Each section had a placard that stated its offerings— "Gay," "Bondage," "Black Studs," "Girl on Girl," and other variations I wasn't aware anyone was interested in. There were patrons scattered about, perusing the books and mags. I tried not to get too close to any of them. I didn't want another new friend like Cigarette Man.

Stoney and I had already agreed that this was just a re-connaissance mission and that we were there only to scope out the place. We headed in different directions as agreed. I pretended to examine some of the books and mags. Most were in sealed plastic bags so the covers were all that could be investigated. Eventually, I got sick of looking at covers.

I'd noticed pretty quickly that some men seemed to gravitate toward the back of the establishment. Eventually, I followed the parade. An arrow on the wall, with the words *Peep Shows* stenciled on it, told me what the big attraction was. I had to climb a short flight of stairs to enter the rear area. It was walled in except for an entranceway covered in black velvet drapes. When I pushed through, I found myself in an area of semi-darkness. It took a long minute before my eyes adjusted to the lack of light.

When I could finally see where the hell I was, I found that I was standing in front of a large display of still photos advertising XXX rated movies. Each photo had a corresponding 1– 40 number. Beyond that were several skinny aisles, lined with doors on each side. Each door had a number that apparently matched one of the photo numbers. Looking at the photos I saw that they ran the gamut of sexual diversity. Fortunately, I saw no child pornography. Still, I felt like I was standing there in a trench coat with the collar pulled up.

Other men were also looking at the photo display. At first, I thought it was my imagination, but as more than a couple of them inched toward me and brushed my body more than once, I realized it was anything but imagination. Panicked, I moved down the closest aisle. It was dark except for a small nightlight on each door, illuminating a number stenciled there. A photo, matching the corresponding one up front, was taped below the number. Apparently the clientele didn't have the best of memories.

I needed a minute to figure out my next move, so I tried the door of a stall that appeared to show reasonably straight sex. It was open. I went into the little cubicle. You couldn't stretch your arms out all the way in any direction without both of them touching a wall. I plopped down on a tiny stool. The door was to my left.

I was facing a small screen about the size of one on a 13" TV. Below the screen was a coin box for depositing quarters. The door started to inch open. I shifted my body on the stool a bit and put my toes against the door, closing it. I left my foot there. Whoever was on the other side kept giving it repetitive shoves. After a minute they stopped trying to gain entrance.

What the hell was I doing here? Being in this room didn't have much to do with research on Myles Brogna and where he kept Susan Worthman. I dropped my hand down to the stool and felt something sticky. That was it. It was time to get Stoney and get the hell out. I wiped my hand on my pants.

Before I could rise, there was a sudden tapping at the door, soft at first, then becoming more aggressive. It continued. I didn't like it. My hands started sweating and my leg shook faster than a rabbit in heat. Whether it was the coke I'd ingested at Stoney's or the bizarre situation I was in, I didn't know. But I imagined it might be the police on the other side and remembered the gram of coke I'd purchased from Stoney before we'd left his apartment. I'd used a bit of it, but not much.

I had visions of a newspaper article about a private detective being arrested in a Combat Zone peep show booth with cocaine in his pocket. My mind was conjuring up what the possible headline would be while I hastily pulled the tiny square paper that held the drug from my pants pocket. I don't know why I did it, paranoia probably, but with my hands shaking I opened the paper and tipped the entire contents into my mouth, followed by the piece of paper itself.

Not only did my mouth go numb, my entire throat froze. The medicinal taste was potent. I guess I figured I had destroyed the evidence. What I didn't know was how fast the drug would hit me. I didn't move.

I don't know how long I sat there, but it was long enough for the coke to kick in. Occasionally, the tapping would sound again, but I swore it was more like banging now. I thought I saw the thin plywood door shake on its hinges.

By now my brain was aflame with paranoia and it told me to put coins in the slot if I didn't want to attract the police who I was convinced were just outside the door. I dropped in a quarter and the images of copulating men and women instantly came on the small screen. I forgot about the door and leered at the movie like I'd just been released from a straitjacket. My heart was going like a beatnik's bongos. I stared at the sex tape and felt a raw sexual arousal. My hands dropped to my lap.

I don't know where I was going with this, but just then my eye caught something moving shoulder high off to my right against the booth's wall. Either because of the dark or my condition or both, I couldn't make out exactly what it was. My hand snaked out, touched it tentatively. Still not knowing what it was I grabbed the object gently, pulled. It was then that it dawned on me that it was a penis poked through a hole in the wall. I pulled my hand back in horror.

I thought I could hear someone calling, "Mike. Mike." I looked at the door. Was it Stoney? Or was it a police trick? My mind latched onto the latter.

When I turned back to the hole, the foul object was gone. That's when a banging started on my stall door that shook the whole booth. It wasn't paranoia this time. There was a shove against the door but my foot was still braced against it and it held.

"Boston Police. Boston Police. Open the fuckin' door, pervert."

I knew what I heard was real but I was frozen with fear. I didn't move.

Someone rammed the door so hard, it flew in and my knee was shoved up toward my chest. Otherwise, my leg would have snapped like a dry twig. Numerous arms reached in, pulled me out. Someone shouted, "Turn the damn lights on." I was slammed up against the aisle wall face first. Then my arms were pulled behind me and handcuffs put on my wrists so tight they might as well have been torture devices. The lights came on; they were blinding. I could see men scampering out of booths and heading for the exits.

I looked over my shoulder and saw two burly men who looked like a cross between street bums and working class longhairs. The one with long, matted brown hair and a beard jerked the cuffs like he meant to hurt me; he did. He pulled me off the wall, yanking me close to him. "Fuckin' pervert. You thought my finger was a cock when it came through that Glory Hole, didn't ya? You like cock, don't ya?"

He pushed me roughly along the aisle toward the entrance. "This is a mistake," I said. "I'm . . . a . . . a . . . PI. I'm . . . I'm investigating." My voice shook like there was an earthquake going on.

"I don't give a fuck who you are, pervert. You're under arrest for disorderly conduct and lewd acts."

When we burst out of the peep booth area into the main store, there was a small group of patrons observing my perp walk. Among them was Stoney. He had on a face I'd never seen him wear before. He spoke to the cops as we passed. "What are you doing? What did he do?"

The other cop, a homeless person look-alike, gave Stoney a push in the chest. Stoney stumbled backwards into another man. "Shut the fuck up, ya stinkin' hippie, or you're going with him," the cop bellowed.

As they rushed me through the dirty bookstore toward the front door, I managed to shout over my shoulder, "Get Cousin Billy." I hated to say it, but the way I felt I was already on a death dive anyway. So I had nothing to lose.

CHAPTER 22

"WHERE'S YOUR RAINCOAT, diddler."

I never thought I'd be happy to see Cousin Billy's face. But sitting there on a steel bed in that filthy cell in a Boston police lockup, I knew, even with my jacked-up mind, that he was the only one who might be able to get me out of this jam before there were even worse consequences. I was still strung out bad from the coke, my mind going a mile a minute, barely holding myself together. I knew if I didn't get out of there soon, anything could happen.

Billy was standing on the other side of the cell door, looking at me with a smirk that made my face flush. Beside him was the turnkey; his look was just as disturbing.

"So this lowlife is actually a relative of yours?" he asked Billy. Billy was in his standard plainclothes detective outfit. The turnkey was old and had on dark slacks and a light blue, short-sleeved police issue shirt.

"He's the black sheep of the family," Billy said. "But keep it quiet and there's a sawbuck in it for you." They both had a good laugh over that crummy joke.

Billy motioned toward the lock, and the turnkey opened the cell door. It needed oil, along with a room deodorizer for the cell. Billy stepped in, stood over me. I didn't move from the hard bed, dropped my face in my hands. The turnkey left.

"You really went off the deep end this time, Mike. Not having a sexual outlet can get to anyone sooner or later."

I looked up at his face. He had a grin on his skinny puss as wide as the Callahan Tunnel. I jumped up. Now I was looking down at him. "I could fuck you up good before they could even get in here."

I must have looked wild because Cousin Billy's grin dropped like a dead bird. "Easy, Mike, easy. I'm just joking with you."

"I don't need any joking. I had a rough night. Get me out of here."

He jammed his hand into the inside pocket of his sport coat, came out with something, handed it to me. "Your hippie friend sent this. Felt me out first. Wanted to be sure I wouldn't bust him. Made you sound in such bad shape, I was almost crying." It was a blue valium; I swallowed it dry.

"Why don't you tell me what happened?" Billy asked. I must have scared him. He was using a very syrupy tone now.

I moved back, sat down on the rock-hard bed. "I was with Stoney. We . . ."

Billy interrupted. "Stoney?"

"Yeah, Stoney. Stoney Sundown. The hippie who told you I was here."

Billy scowled. "He gave me some other name. Where do you meet these people, anyway?"

I waved my hand. "I live in Harvard Square, for Chrissake. But forget that, will you? We were in the Zone checking out a line we had on Myles Brogna."

Billy looked at me like I was simple. "I'd hoped you were kidding when you mentioned his name over the phone. And you were looking for him in a dirty bookstore? You sure you didn't just want some reading material?" The grin started again, but he lost it fast when he saw the look on my face.

I ran my hand through my hair, rubbed my face. It didn't even feel like mine. "I was told that's where Brogna gets a lot of his action money dropped off. I figured I might be able to follow the dough to Brogna and that way find the Worthman girl."

Billy sighed. "Well, I got to admit you got balls. But you're dumb, too."

I almost went at him right then and there. Billy took a giant step back. "What I mean is, didn't you stop to think that Brogna might have protection against idiots like you who come poking around?"

"Protection? Who?" I asked stupidly.

Billy came close, bent over, lowered his voice. "Boston cops. Who else? You think there's ever any morals busts at a Myles Brogna smut joint? I'll bet yours was the first."

My mind was working like I'd lost a million brain cells, which I probably had. "But how the hell . . .?"

"Jesus, if you want to be a PI, you should know this stuff, Mike. Some Cambridge cops are plugged in pretty good with the Boston blue boys."

I was waking up. "You mean Cummings and Dalton? But how the hell would they know I was going to be there?"

Billy shrugged. "I don't know. Could be a tap or a source. Christ, when you called me you mentioned Brogna's name. Why the hell do you think I hung up? Those phones are about as secure as . . . where'd ya call from anyway?"

"O'Toole's," I answered sheepishly.

Billy rolled his eyes. "There's two possibles right there. Anyway, you better be careful. You got a leak somewhere."

It made sense, but I told myself I'd figure it out later. Right now, I wanted out of this lockup. "Can you get me out of here?" I asked.

"What's it worth to you?" As I started to get up, Billy quickly added, "Jesus, I'm only kidding. Let me see what I can do." I sat down.

Billy turned, walked to the cell door. He shouted for the turnkey, then said to me, "This isn't going to be easy. I'll have to reel in some markers." He stood there, staring at me, waiting for a response.

I hated to do it, but I said, "I'll owe you one."

Billy's big grin came back. "Yes, you will," he said as the turnkey walked up, let him out, and left me in.

Billy returned in about an hour. It seemed like ten.

He looked at me through the bars. "I worked something out. Your charges have been reduced to just the disorderly conduct." He pressed his face against the bars, lowered his voice. "The two who busted you didn't put up any stink, but that's no surprise. They wanted to deliver a message from Brogna, Mike. And it looks like you got it."

I nodded. Billy signaled for the turnkey who came down and let me out. Stoney had taken my car back to Cambridge, so I rode along with my cousin. The valium had kicked in and, along with that and the coke overdose finally wearing off, I felt a little better. On the guilt and shame scale, I'd dropped from a ten to a nine and a half.

"I've found out some things about Brogna," Billy said as we drove across the Mass. Ave. bridge into Cambridge. "You up to hearing them?"

"Barely," I answered.

"Remember, Mike, none of this came from me."

I nodded. My head felt like a cerebral hemorrhage was imminent.

Billy's hand was white on the steering wheel. "The man's behind most of the meth in Greater Boston."

I turned toward him. "I already know that."

Billy glanced toward me, then back at the road in front of him. He raised his chin and put a smug look on his face. "You didn't know he's got a lab though, did you? And it's a big one. One of the biggest in the country."

"How do you know?" I asked.

Billy looked at me like I'd just been released from a grade school instead of the police lockup. "Let's just say I peeked at some paperwork from another agency."

Federal, state, or local—I didn't care. I was beginning to see a little more clearly what was going on. "So that's why they want me off the Worthman case. The Demons are protecting their connection—Brogna. And Brogna's protecting his meth source—his own lab. They all think if I keep on looking for the girl, I might stumble onto something that'll screw up their operation."

"Bingo!"

Then another question came out of the fog called my mind. "And the North End boys who gave Stoney the thumping? What's their angle?"

"That's easy, Mike. I could figure that out on my own." He raised his thin shoulders and graced me with his famous smug look again. "Even Brogna has to give Prince Street a piece of the pie every month to operate. A street tax."

That made sense too. Brogna had to pay off the Boston Mafia so he could operate in their territory. "So the big boys wouldn't want me disrupting Brogna's life, either. They're making money with him."

"Of course. The man's probably a cash cow to them. Not only the meth. Christ, he's involved in lots of shit besides meth and dirty bookstores. And he probably has to pay big every month. We could probably both retire on just a year's worth of those envelopes."

It was that simple. Brogna was not only a gangster and a pervert, he was also a big source of income for the mob and the bikers. It explained a lot. Except . . .

I hesitated, then asked. "Cummings and Dalton?"

"Yeah. They're dirty, too. Both on Brogna's payroll."

So that was it. It was me against Brogna, the Devil's Demons, the Boston Mafia, a couple of crooked Cambridge cops, and maybe others I wasn't even aware of yet. There were only two things I could do concerning this apparent suicide mission I was on—get out now or even the odds somehow. But, like I said before, there was no way I could drop the case and that hadn't changed. So that left making the sides a little more equal my only option. I figured I might as well start right now.

"Billy, I'm not getting out of this. I'm going to find this girl and if that means Brogna's business gets hurt, so be it."

Billy pulled the car in front of a fire hydrant across from my apartment building. "You're going to need help, Mike." He shifted in his seat, looked at me in a way he never had. "I don't know how much you know about Dottie?" Dottie was his daughter and I instantly knew what was coming. I didn't answer; he didn't want me to. "You heard it's drugs. But did you know it's meth?" I didn't know. No one had ever told me. There were half a dozen drugs the poor kid could've been strung out on. When I'd first heard the story, it really didn't matter which. But I wasn't surprised.

He continued. "*Now* I know it's probably Brogna's dope. I want to see that cocksucker out of business, Mike. And it looks like the law can't touch him yet. And by the time it does, if ever, a lot of kids'll end up like Dottie."

For a moment it looked like he was tearing up.

"Billy, she'll be okay." It sounded lame, but what else could I say?

He shook his head vigorously. "No, she won't. But maybe some other kids won't get into it if this waste product Brogna is brought down." He hesitated, added, "And maybe *you* can do it, Mike. With some help that is."

He used his keys to open the glove box, removed a sheaf of papers, handed them to me. I perused them quickly. They were confidential police files on the drug activities of Myles Brogna. The agency's name had been cut from the top of the sheets, but I guessed they were federal or possibly state police reports.

"There's a lot of information there," he said. "I can't touch it. I'm not even supposed to see it. Do you think you can use it? Put something together?"

Apparently he didn't care anymore if I knew the files came from him. He was beyond that. And so was I. I was determined to 'put something together.' Brogna was as low as a human being could get. And then there was Susan. And besides, it was personal now. I'd been beaten, tossed in the clink, humiliated, and who knew what else might come my way. Yeah, I could put something together. Damn right I could. And I would, I promised myself.

"I need a little time, but yeah, I can do it." I looked at Billy in a new light. "How far can I count on you, Bill?"

"It's my daughter they fucked up, Mike."

That was all I had to hear. The next step was up to me.

CHAPTER 23

I SPENT THAT night going over the police intelligence reports Billy had given me. I even stayed away from the Schlitz. There was a lot of information. I could see why a major case hadn't been made on Myles Brogna yet. He kept himself well insulated—both from his product and from associates who might put a finger on him. He saw very few people. And on the rare occasions when someone did try to incriminate him, the poor slob was usually put to sleep permanently.

I kept reading over the same pages, trying to come up with something. I didn't have any luck. After what had happened, The First Amendment Bookstore was a dead end as far as tracking down Susan Worthman. And I wasn't digging anything out of these papers that could help me either. Eventually, I fell asleep in my chair.

You know the old saying—sleep on it and you'll come up with something? Well, it actually worked for me. Sometime during the night I made it to bed, and when I woke early in the morning, I had a plan. Most of it anyway. And it was crystal clear in my mind. I'd need a team to make the plan work, but I had that—Stoney, Billy, Jake, and Tank. I needed a woman, too. And that part worried me.

As soon as the hour was decent, I made some phone calls. I asked everyone to meet me at my office that afternoon. I told them who would be there and the bare bones of what it was about. To my surprise, no one objected. Maybe because of their dislike for Brogna and what he was doing. I kept Cousin Billy out of it; he wouldn't have come anyway. It was too dangerous for him in his position. Besides, his help—if needed—would be more valuable from behind the scenes, a fact he'd already proven. I was beginning to like that man a little more every day.

It was just after two o'clock when all of us settled in my office. I was behind my desk, of course. Seated in front of me in the two guest chairs and two foldouts I'd put out for the meet were Tank, who looked like he was seated in a chair meant for a first grader; Jake, in a white shirt with the sleeves rolled up, a butt in his mouth, and minus his usual white apron; Stoney, who looked reasonably straight today; and beside him, Julie, beautiful, of course, even with that damn crooked nose.

Everyone knew each other to one degree or another, even Jake and Tank. I'd brought Tank into O'Toole's a couple of times, treated him to a meal. Still, the two men seemed a little uncomfortable with each other. And Jake and Stoney were from different generations. I tried to ease the tension in the room.

"First off, I'm glad everyone agreed to come." No reactions. "Second, I want to say that I trust all of you all the way, or I wouldn't have asked you here." I looked at Tank, then Jake, then Stoney, and back again. I couldn't tell if my endorsement reassured them but I hoped it had. "You all know what I want to talk about—Myles Brogna and Susan Worthman.

Susan's the girl I'm trying to find for her dad. As I've told some of you—she's underage and Brogna's got her all strung out on meth and is using her for his sex toy."

Julie let out a little gasp.

"Fuckin' pervert," Jake muttered, then turned red. "Pardon my French, Julie. That snake gives Southie and all Irishmen a bad name."

I continued. "I've been trying to get a line on where Brogna might be staying."

Stoney suddenly became animated. "Yeah, we tried to track him through a dirty bookstore he's got in the Combat Zone, but Mikey got mixed up with some weird shit in one of those peep booth things and he got . . ."

I waved my hand. "No need to get into that," I said. Julie gave me a quizzical look. There was no reaction from Tank or Jake. I had no idea if they were aware of the unpleasant incident. I got us back on track. "Anyway, I think I've come up with something. A way to find the Worthman girl and maybe even bring down Myles Brogna as a bonus. First, I want to make sure you're all interested and that you realize how dangerous this could be. You all know Brogna's reputation, but what you might not all know is that there are others just as heavy as him involved. The Devil's Demons, the Mafia, even a couple of crooked cops." I looked from face to face; there was no reaction.

"I wouldn't blame anyone if you wanted to leave now. We could be walking into big trouble." Still no reaction. "I'm willing to split my fee five ways if it works out. Unfortunately, that won't be much. So if anyone wants to back out, now's the time to leave. And no hard feelings."

Silence.

Suddenly, Tank's big fist crashed down like an anvil on my desk. Everything bounced around, including a cup of coffee I'd been working on. I snatched the intelligence reports from the desk just before they took a bath. I made a mental note to wipe up the spill later.

"I don't want no damn money, Mike," Tank bellowed. He stretched his massive body halfway across the desk toward me. His breath came with him, all cigarette smoke, stale beer, and poor dental hygiene. I didn't dare back away.

"Brogna's been trying to muscle into the Burgundy for a long time now. Me and my brothers been looking for a way to stick it to him. As far as the Demons go, they're on our shit list, too. And we ain't afraid of no guineas." He eased back into his chair; it creaked ominously.

I turned to look at Jake. "You know how I feel, Mike. The man's a child molester. Not to mention the poison he's spreading all through South Boston. Used to be a nice family area until he took over the rackets and started selling the hard stuff to his own people. A little old lady can't even walk the streets there anymore without being mugged by some goddamn speed freak. So I'd like to help get rid of him. And I don't have to get paid to do it either." His blue eyes looked like they were on fire.

Stoney was looking off into space.

"Stoney."

Nothing.

"Stoney," I repeated.

Jake scowled. "Ahh, the kid's loaded again."

"Wake up, shit for brains," Tank growled.

Stoney finally spoke up. "I'm not loaded and I'm not asleep. I'm trying to come up with an idea to help Mikey here. Sometimes if I meditate a little, my mind becomes clearer."

Jake folded his arms across his chest. "For Chrissake. That's all we need on this—one of them Hare Krishna characters. All you need's a shaved head."

Tank leaned over, looked at Stoney. "Where's your orange robe, fruitcake?" Both he and Jake laughed loudly.

At least this exchange seemed to have brought Jake and Tank closer together, but I had to get us back to business. "I appreciate the effort, Stoney. But I've already got an idea. I want to try it first before we look elsewhere. But I take it you're in?"

"Of course I'm in," Stoney said indignantly, raising himself in his chair. "Besides getting my hair washed in a toilet, I don't like what's happening to the Square. Used to be just pot and psychedelics. A real groovy scene. Now with that speed shit all over the place, it's starting to go the way of Haight Ashbury. Ripoffs, OD's, junkies with rotten teeth. Instead of peace and love, it's Paranoia City. I want it back the way it was."

I looked at Julie, tried to ignore her nose. She just stared back at me.

"Julie?"

"Yes, Mike." Everyone was silent. The other three seemed to be inspecting the ceiling.

Finally, I said, "As some of you already know, Myles Brogna is the largest source of meth in this area."

"No surprise there, Mike," Tank said.

"But did you know he has his own lab? And I think that's his Achilles heel."

Jake shook his head vigorously. "We can't even find *him*, Mike. He'll guard the location of that place like it's a gold mine. How you gonna find it?"

"I don't intend to, Jake. I think you're right about the lab being impossible to find. Besides, I've come up with a better way. I've found out who his chemist is. His *cook*. He's an MIT grad student." I lifted the papers Cousin Billy had given me, gave them a little shake.

"So *we* follow him to the laboratory?" Julie said. I didn't miss that she emphasized the word we.

"I don't think that would work either, unless we were awful lucky. For all we know he only goes to the lab every six months. By that time Susan Worthman could be dead. Besides, we don't have the time or the manpower to keep the kid under twenty-four-hour surveillance for who knows how long."

"What've you got in mind?" Jake asked.

I took a breath, set my palms on the desk. I didn't know how they'd take what I was about to say. "We snatch Mr. MIT. Hold him in exchange for the Worthman girl." I looked from face to face; I could see the wheels spinning.

Jake was the first to speak. "Kidnapping? That's a federal rap."

I was ready for that. "Only if someone files a report. I don't think the kid will complain to anyone. He won't want the feds to find out what he's involved in. By the time he got out of prison, he'd be wearing a dress and lipstick."

"Brogna ain't gonna call the cops, that's for sure," Tank growled.

I turned to Stoney. "So no one's going to get hurt?" he asked. "I don't like violence, man."

"Freakin' hippies," Tank muttered.

I tried to set Stoney's mind at ease. "No, of course not. A good job for you—if you want it —is to babysit this character wherever we decide to hold him."

"I could do that," Stoney said, bobbing his head.

I turned to Tank. "Tank, how about if you and I grab the kid?" We'd already had experience with JoJo, but there was no need to tell the others. "You all right with that?"

Tank adjusted himself in his chair; it creaked again. "Damn straight I am. How we gonna do it? When he comes out of his apartment? I can get the twerp into the backseat of a car faster than a twenty-buck whore can get out of her panties." He let out a laugh; his belly shook.

"No, no, no," I said. "Too much can go wrong if we grab him out in public like that." I turned, looked at Julie.

"What do you want me to do, Mike?" was all she said.

My heart sped up a bit. I didn't like this for more than one reason. But somehow it seemed the only way to go. What her reaction would be, I didn't know. "If you could . . . ahh . . . maybe . . . say, just bump into this kid somewhere. A bar, say, or wherever the hell we find out he goes . . . maybe . . ."

She held up her hand. A look crossed her face, telling me she already knew what I was thinking. "I could lure him to the place you want to hold him at. I've never done anything like that but I'd give it a try. I don't know if it'd work or not."

"You serious?" Tank said. "With a head like yours, Julie, you won't have any trouble."

Julie's cheeks flushed. I knew she wouldn't be in danger if the only person she came in contact with was the student. At least one of us would be watching her at all times. "That's how we'll do it then," I said.

"Hey, what am I black?" Jake asked.

Stoney muttered something unintelligible and scowled.

"I didn't forget you, Jake," I said. "How would you like to handle communications with Brogna? I don't know how you'd get in touch with him. I'd leave that up to you. Through someone you trust, for sure. You're the only one who has the connections to reach out to him and open up negotiations to swap the cook for Susan."

Jake didn't hesitate. "I'll do it. I'll come up with something. I want to make this prick squeal."

"Like a pig," Tank chimed in. "Oink, oink, oink."

Everyone laughed.

"Okay then," I said, "we're all in?"

Nods right down the line.

"Good. Now all we have to do is figure out the particulars." I pointed toward my little fridge. "Anyone want a beer?"

CHAPTER 24

AFTER THE OTHERS left, I pulled out a gram of coke I'd buttonholed Stoney for just before he'd left. I know—I said I'd never do it again. But I'd convinced myself, conveniently maybe, that I'd never get through the next few days without it. Anyway, I grabbed an empty manila folder, dumped the white drug on it. It sparkled. It wasn't dull looking like the speed-laced stuff I had the bad experience with. That had been a nightmare. It had been meth. And meth was a bad drug. Kids were all strung out on it. It was a poison. Not like cocaine. At least not real cocaine. The kind of coke honest dealers like Stoney had. And what about my Zone experience? Well sure, that had been cocaine, but I'd taken too much at once. I wouldn't do that again.

And cocaine would come in handy. It seemed to make my thinking much clearer. And I'd need clear thinking to put this scheme into play. Didn't cocaine help Sherlock Holmes? Of course, he was a fictional character, but the author must've known what he was talking about. Besides none of the literature I'd read said coke was dangerous or addictive. Just had to use it in moderation. From now on I'd use it just to help me do my work.

I took my driver's license, chopped at the little boulders, and spread out two equal lines. I rolled up a one dollar bill, vacuumed one of the lines into my right nostril. It was nothing like that speed crap I'd been fooled into using. This was nice. My nose wasn't on fire and the medicinal taste in the back of my mouth was pleasant. I repeated the process, funneling the remaining line up my other nostril.

I popped up out of the chair, retrieved a Schlitz from the fridge. Back at my desk I tipped the bottle to my lips. The liquid was ice cold and tasted like my first of the day, even though it wasn't.

I started going over what I'd need for the plan to work. The police intelligence papers had already told me where the suspected cook lived. It was a Cambridge address. Once we found out where this cook spent his drinking hours—and I was confident a kid that age *did* go out somewhere to drink, at least occasionally—it would be time for step two.

That's where Julie came in. She'd visit the bar and hopefully lure the cook to wherever we were going to hold him. And like Tank had said, Julie wouldn't have much trouble with that assignment.

Sure, I had reservations about using Julie, but she'd be in no danger. She'd only be coming in contact with the MIT student, and I hadn't seen one yet that wasn't a full-blown nerd. Besides, she'd said she wanted to help with the Worthman case. And I didn't like admitting it to myself, but I couldn't get her out of mind. I guess I wanted to have her around.

I put out two more lines, did both quickly. I hadn't touched my beer since that first cold swig. I didn't now, either.

I wasn't sure yet where we were going to hold the cook until the exchange for Susan Worthman could be made. It couldn't be anywhere that could be tied to me or Stoney. Those were the first places Brogna and his boys would check. Ditto for Jake if they learned he was involved. Anyplace connected with Tank would be too hot under even normal circumstances. Julie's apartment was out—I didn't want her at risk. Wherever it ended up being, Tank and I would be there to surprise the cook when Julie brought him back to what he thought was going to be his lucky night. Tank and I had easily handled JoJo, so I didn't foresee any difficulty with an MIT student. We could keep him tied up, if we had to, so even Stoney wouldn't have any trouble babysitting him.

That left Jake to reach out to Brogna after we had the cook secured. He said he could do it and I had absolutely no doubt that he could. Jake was from Southie and he had a hatred for Brogna.

My plan was coming together nicely. Still, I had one more little itch in my brain—what a nice bonus it would be if somehow I could knock a dirtbag like Myles Brogna out of the picture at the same time we rescued Susan Worthman. A double-play! Wouldn't that be great.

I placed out another two lines of the powder, longer this time and inhaled. That would be a wonderful thing—Myles Brogna going down in flames. I sat there, my mind going round and round over the same things. I still hadn't touched the half-filled bottle of beer on the desk since that first sip. I didn't need it. At least not yet.

CHAPTER 25

IT DIDN'T TAKE long to find out where the MIT cook did his drinking. It was a little hole-in-the-wall just off the Square, a college-age drinking hangout. So when Julie walked in late that afternoon, and plunked herself down at the bar beside the cook, wearing a black wig and decked out like a high-class call girl, it was a done deal how the evening was going to end. On the first try, too. I kept watch from a corner table just to make sure nothing went wrong, but Julie handled it nicely, pumping the cook with drinks and holding back on her own.

Two hours later, I followed them out of the bar, ducking back to my car as they climbed in Julie's. Mine was parked a few cars behind it. I followed them through Cambridge to Medford, where we picked up Route 93, which led to 128 and then Route 95. We were headed for a house in Hampton Beach, New Hampshire—about an hour away. The house belonged to a customer of Stoney's who was on a ganja vacation to Jamaica, whatever that was. He'd be gone for another two weeks. We'd have the place to ourselves until then. I hoped we wouldn't need that much time.

The closer we got to the beach, the farther back I dropped, confident that there was no trouble in Julie's car and that it was headed where it was supposed to go. After we crossed the bridge into Hampton, Julie's car traveled a short distance further and then turned right onto the street I'd expected. I pulled over to the side of Ocean Boulevard, Hampton's main strip.

I gave them five minutes, then pulled down the street and parked a block short of the house. Julie's car was in front of it. I got out of my car and walked in that direction. Tank's car, I knew, was parked on a nearby street. The house itself was really just a small cottage, one of the few occupied during the off-season. It was evening and some lights were on inside. Nothing looked amiss. I decided to go right in.

Once I'd gone up the rickety stairs, I gave a coded tap on the door. Julie opened it, a smile on her face; I was relieved. Inside, the scene was as I had hoped. Tank was busy binding the cook to a straight-back wooden chair with duct tape. The cook looked like he was all of nineteen, even though I knew he was a graduate student. Then it dawned on me that MIT probably had some geniuses who were quite young. It didn't matter.

"Any trouble?" I asked Tank.

"Easy as pie. I'd be damned embarrassed if there had been."

The kid looked terrified. And who wouldn't be with Tank looming over them. I studied the cook. He was a nerd all right. Brown frame glasses; black curly hair, unusually short for someone his age nowadays; new jeans, again unusual; a shirt with *MIT* stenciled on the left breast; and a very poor complexion. If he hadn't been so young, I would have worried his heart might give out from fear. He looked at me, then at Julie, then at Tank, and then back at me again.

"How are you?" I asked Julie. She looked so good I couldn't blame the kid for coming with her. The only way that wouldn't have worked was if he'd been gay.

"Fine. He's a nice kid."

That's what she said but I detected some nervousness in her voice. She wasn't used to this kind of thing. "You can go now," I said gently.

She shook her head slowly. Her fake black hair swayed. "I'll stay a while if you don't mind."

No, I didn't mind. In fact, I had to force myself to look away from her and back at the seated figure. She was a special woman. I'd forgotten that somewhere along the line.

"What's your name?" I said in a tone I hoped was firm, but not one that would frighten him further. I already knew this info from the reports, but I had to make sure. I also wanted to find out quickly if he'd be any trouble.

"Elliot. Elliot Spencer," he told me. His voice shook; I noticed his body did too. "What's . . . what's . . . going on?"

Tank finished securing him and stood back, big arms folded across his chest.

"Well, Elliot, we know all about you," I began. "You're a big methamphetamine chemist. Right?"

"Who are you? What do you want?" He turned his head around, glanced nervously at Tank. "You can't be cops."

Tank and I both chuckled. "Good guess." I tried to keep my voice relaxed. Everything would be a lot easier if this kid wasn't too scared. "We're going to be holding you here for a while."

"M . . . me? Here? Why? Is it money you want? I can get you money. I've got some put away. You can have it all. Please, just don't hurt me."

At that moment, he looked like he'd give up his mother to get out of there. I didn't want him to flip out. That wouldn't be good. So I had to calm him down.

"Elliot, look at me." He didn't—he was looking at the duct tape that bound him. Probably doing a mathematical equation on his odds of escape.

"Elliot, look at me," I said much louder. His eyes lasered in on me. "Now listen to what I'm going to tell you."

I proceeded to explain what was going on—the parts that pertained to him. When I finished, his nerves seemed to have calmed just a bit.

"Brogna won't care about me." Elliot shook his head. "He can get someone else."

"Not like you, Elliot," I said. I'd read comments about his superior drug-cooking skill in the confidential reports. I didn't tell him that though. I thought it best he didn't know about the papers Billy had given me. "The speed you make is top-notch. It'd be hard for Brogna to find someone else who would, and could, do it as well as you."

"But his girlfriend," Elliott said, voice shaking. "He won't give her to you."

I guffawed. "Even you can't be that naive, Elliot. You must know enough about Brogna to know he doesn't give a shit about anything but him and his money. If it comes down to his wallet, he'll give us the girl wrapped up in ribbons and bows."

"But if he doesn't . . ." The kid glanced back over his shoulder at Tank again. "You'll . . . kill me?"

Like I said, I didn't want him too afraid. So I told him the truth. "I think he'll come through, Elliot. But even if he doesn't, we'll let you go. You can't go to the police."

"But wouldn't . . ." he began, then caught himself.

"But wouldn't what?" I asked.

He didn't answer until Tank gave him a hard slap upside the head. I winced.

"Wouldn't you be worried that I'd tell Brogna who you are?" Elliot asked.

It *was* a legitimate concern. But I'd already thought about that not-so-little issue. And I had to make Elliot believe I wasn't worried about him telling Brogna who we were, otherwise he'd think he was going to be killed. And that would make him a much more difficult hostage to handle. "By the time this is over, Brogna will realize I'm behind it anyway. But by then I should have plenty of incriminating information on him. Information he wouldn't want the feds to get ahold of. And I'm going to make sure he knows that if any harm comes to me or my friends that's exactly where the info will go—to the feds." I folded my arms across my chest, looked down at Elliot. "So, you see, we have no reason not to let you go as soon as this is over. As long as you cooperate, that is."

The kid seemed to be mulling it over in his mind. As he did I could actually see the tension melt from his thin face. Then his body relaxed. And that's how I wanted him—relaxed. At least as relaxed as a kid who had just been kidnapped and strapped to a chair with Tank standing behind him could be.

"If you don't cause us any trouble, we might actually take the duct tape off," I said. Elliot smiled tentatively. "We'll see how you act."

I turned toward Julie. She'd been standing there, watching and listening. "I'll walk you to your car," I said. "Let me just hit the head first."

As I passed Tank, I said, "Great job. I'll call Stoney. Get him up here to relieve you." He just nodded.

I didn't go into the bathroom to do any business. Bathroom business, that is. I'd bought a gram from Stoney a couple of days earlier, chopped it fine, and transferred it to my vial. The second I had the bathroom door closed behind me, I snatched the vial out my pocket and finished up the coke with a healthy toot up each nostril. I instantly felt better, more confident. And I needed that confidence. It wasn't going to be easy dealing with a man like Myles Brogna. The man was as devious as they came. He wouldn't have gotten where he was in the Boston underworld if he hadn't been. Caution had to be the watchword. I was on alert.

I checked my nose in the mirror for any telltale white powder and returned to the front room. I said goodbye to Tank and my new friend Elliot, then followed Julie out the front door. It was a cloudy night but no rain. Her car was parked in front. She offered to give me a lift the short distance to my car. I accepted; I don't know why.

As she turned the car around and headed toward mine, we were both silent. With her black wig, trashy clothes, and thick makeup, I don't think I would've known the woman sitting beside me was Julie if I hadn't been in on the secret. I was sure Elliot would never be able to identify her. She looked like another woman, but still hot as hell. I noticed her tight skirt, the one she'd worn to seduce Elliot, was high on her thigh, showing off her smooth skin. I tried not to look, but whether it was the cocaine or Julie's beauty or both, I felt myself getting hard. I didn't want this again. At least I didn't think I did. But I couldn't help myself. In the time it took us to reach my car, I knew what I was going to do.

She pulled the car in front of mine, turned to speak, but I didn't let her. I just slid closer, held that gorgeous face in my hands. I don't think I even noticed her nose. If I did, it wasn't as the one I'd broken. Now it was just sexily crooked.

She offered me her neck; I put my lips against it. Her scent was so familiar, it seemed like we had never separated. I kissed her neck, ran my tongue along it. I could taste the salt in her skin mixed with something sweet. I pulled my face away so I was inches from hers. I stared into her eyes. Either they told me nothing or I didn't care what they had to say.

My fingers shook as I slowly unbuttoned her blouse, saw those round breasts held in her frilly bra. Somehow I got them free, kissed each nipple, licked them into hardness. That's when she dropped her hand to my pants, undid the belt and unzipped me. Then she pulled me free. I gasped, used one thumb on her nipple, moved my other hand up her skirt, got my fingers inside her panties and beyond. Her hand that felt soft and hot at the same time, stroked me slowly, maddeningly. Her other hand ran through my hair as she said my name over and over. All the time we stared into each other's eyes, our faces inches apart. Neither one of us made a move to go farther; we didn't have to. It was as good as it got. Right to the end.

CHAPTER 26

WHEN I GOT back to Cambridge, I parked as close to the office as I could get. I stopped at a pay phone on the walk there and called Jake, told him we had the kid and that he could go ahead and reach out to Brogna. I told him nothing else. I was worried about O'Toole's phone. In addition, I was going to let Cousin Billy know where we stood. Eventually, he'd probably want to become more visible, get some of the glory—*if* things turned out all right. But visible or not, we needed him for his information and maybe even to pull our chestnuts out of the fire if things went south.

Walking the last block to my office I could hear drums and whistles off in the direction of the Square. Probably either a protest march or a concert. They sprang up all the time around the Square. So I didn't pay the racket much mind.

Even though it was dark, I had no problem seeing the two figures up ahead, slouched in the doorway just before mine. I hesitated, but it was too late to walk away. I had to fake it and hope it was nothing, that my queasy gut was wrong. It wasn't; they were waiting for me.

Two men I didn't recognize stepped out in front of me before I could pass, blocking my way. I took one look at them and would have placed a large bet that they were the two hoods who had given Stoney his toilet shampoo. They looked like low-level mobsters—gold chains, shirts open low at the chest, pumped-up torsos, jet black hair gelled and styled. They both had hard faces and I guessed that if they didn't like their work, it was probably all they could do anyway. I didn't relish this confrontation; most men wouldn't.

The shorter of the two opened his black leather coat enough for me to see a hand cannon in a shoulder holster. "You're coming with us, Malloy. And don't try anything." He motioned with his head for me to keep walking in the direction I had been. I did. They fell in behind me.

The tall one gave me a jab in the back. "Who the hell do you think you are anyway? Mike Hammer? You got the message from your flunky, didn't you? You were supposed to lay off the broad. You don't seem to understand too good. Pretty soon you will though." He let out a chuckle. It chilled my spine.

We passed my building, heading toward the Square. I assumed they had a car up ahead and I was going to be taken for the proverbial ride. Whether it would be fatal or just a beating, I wasn't sure. But either way, I wasn't looking forward to it. My mind spun like a pinwheel, trying to think of a way out.

In front of me, I could see the lights of the Square. The noises were louder now and there was shouting along with the occasional sounds of muffled explosions, like cars backfiring. It was when I saw gray smoke curling into the air up ahead and realized it was tear gas, that it dawned on me what was happening. It had to be one of the many anti-war demonstrations that the area was famous for. And this one had turned violent.

That gave me an idea. I might just survive—if I lost these two jokers in the mob of rioters. If I didn't, they'd beat me senseless for trying. But that was probably going to happen anyway.

I took a few more strides, sucked in a deep breath, and bolted. The goons shouted in unison. I was betting that they wouldn't pull out guns in an area like this. They did come pounding after me, though, screaming threats as they ran.

As I neared the Square, I ran into a horde of college-age kids and hippies, moving backwards toward me. A few were hurling beer bottles, stones, anything they could get their hands on toward the Square at what looked like a phalanx of tactical cops. The air was thick with fumes. I gagged and my eyes teared. But I didn't stop. As I ran by one kid, he used a gloved hand to grab a smoking canister from the pavement and hurl it back in the direction of the cops. I was moving fast toward the cops, too; everyone else was moving away. Except the two hoods, I realized as I glanced over my shoulder and saw them just breaking free of the rioters. Maybe they didn't want to go back empty handed to their boss.

Reaching the Square, I could see a bank building was on fire, flames shooting from its shattered plate glass windows. Much closer, a group of about two dozen rioters, faces hidden by bandanas, charged out of an alley to my right. Many wore football helmets and carried clubs of some type. One waved a red-and-blue Viet Cong flag. Because I was desperate for anything that might discourage my pursuers, I was happier to see that flag than Old Glory.

The rioters moved in a wedge formation toward the tactical unit, who pulled their numbers tighter to confront them. That left room for me to run to one side of the police ranks.

Lungs burning, I poured on the steam and headed for the unoccupied area before the cops straightened out their formation again. Out of the corner of my eye I saw the rioters halt yards from the cops. A few of them pulled out sling shots and started launching what must have been rocks or large ball bearings. The police line buckled, but it held and then regrouped. A few cops stepped out from the line and returned fire with more tear gas. I raced around the side of the police line and was now behind them. I found myself in the middle of a Harvard Square that was like the eye of a hurricane. Calm.

No one was there. I could see the backs of different tactical units heading down side streets away from the Square. Apparently they'd just cleared the Square proper by forcing the demonstrators down various streets and were now pushing them farther and farther away from the Square.

I stopped for a moment, bent, put my hands on my knees. Whether it was the exertion from running, the tear gas, the fear I felt, or all three, I gave up my lunch. At the same time I glanced behind me, assuming that the hoods chasing me had given up. I was wrong. They were trying to sidestep the police ranks just as I had done. I was ready to resume my mad dash when I realized they wouldn't make it. A few of the tactical cops raced to extend their lines.

I watched as the hoods threw up their hands and shouted something they probably hoped would convince the cops they were patriotic citizens and not part of the rioting rabble. It wouldn't do any good with these men; I knew that. Cops had probably been hurt, maybe badly. And Cambridge cops were known not to be sympathetic creatures, even during peaceful protests.

One of the tactical cops who looked like he weighed 300 pounds caught the smaller of the two hoods with a brutal baton blow that glanced off the hood's shoulder. He was lucky. If that baton had found his head, he'd probably be dead. Still, he went down. Another cop was using his long baton to jab viciously at the tall hood's genital area. The hood was successfully blocking the thrusts until another tactical cop came up behind him and clocked him in the back of the head. As he was going down, the other cop finally got in a series of body blows with his club.

Now both hoods were down, writhing on the pavement. Other cops began beating and kicking the two fallen men. I don't think the cops had had much luck catching many, if any, of the young, swift demonstrators, so the two gangsters were the focus of all their frustration and revenge. Finally, a ranking officer came over and dragged his men off the bodies on the ground. The hoods weren't moving.

I turned and ran in the direction I'd initially been heading. There wasn't any action that way, except a few fire trucks and a horde of firefighters trying to save the bank building. The heat of the fire felt as hot as a bad sunburn as I ran past. The smoke was darker, but not as noxious as the dose of gas I'd gotten earlier. My eyes still burned and my throat felt constricted. Still, I felt a sense of relief. I'd seen a lot of crazy happenings in Harvard Square in the past, but this was the first time one of them had saved my life.

CHAPTER 27

I'D HEADED TOWARD Stoney's to escape the goons. Now that I was there, I had a couple of other things I wanted to take care of, one of which was to tell him to head up to Hampton to babysit Elliot. When he buzzed me into the building, I bounded up the stairs. He had the door open, waiting for me.

When he saw me, his mouth fell open. "What happened to you, Mikey? You look like a wet joint."

"I feel like one too," I said as I walked past him and got myself uncomfortable on the red beanbag chair. The room smelled of weed.

He walked over, stood near me. "You want a beer?"

I shook my head. "How about a taste?" I said. I could feel myself flush, but after what I'd just been through, I deserved it, didn't I?

He looked at me for a long moment. Then he went into his bedroom and came out with a large polished stone that had a pile of the powder on it. We indulged. I told Stoney what had happened.

Stoney's eyes sparkled. "Yep, that sounds like the two who shoved my head in the toilet." He shuddered. "Sounds like they got what they deserved."

My heart was still beating fast, but now it was from the coke rather than the crazy pursuit and it was a pleasant sensation. Confident, I felt back in the driver's seat. "It looked like they could've been hurt bad though. Real bad."

Stoney shook his head slowly, then looked down. Hair fell in front of his face. "I don't like seeing anyone get hurt bad."

"The cops were like wild animals, clubbing and kicking the two goons while they were on the ground."

Stoney's voice quivered. "Yeah, they can sure get carried away. The only thing they hate worse than dealers are radicals. That's why I stay away from the demonstrations. What I do is heavy enough." He glanced at the entrance door. I did, too.

"I didn't like seeing even them get hurt *that* bad," I said. "They could be dead."

Stoney leaned forward, put four more large lines out. "It wasn't your fault, Mike. Those two might've killed you. Besides, sometimes those cop thumpings look worse than they are. They use special clubs that aren't supposed to kill people."

I'd never heard of that before, but I hoped it was true. I watched anxiously as Stoney held the metal straw in his hand and talked on. *Shut up*, I said to myself, *and do the coke*. Finally he did; then I did.

We sat there for a while taking turns, while I filled Stoney in on how Elliot the meth cook's abduction had gone down. He agreed to go and relieve Tank. Stoney's main job would be to entertain Elliot and make sure he didn't get away. I was sure he would have no problem, even without a weapon.

Elliot had looked like he couldn't fight his way out of a wet paper bag.

As we discussed his role in the plan, the rest of it suddenly seemed crystal clear in my mind. I was convinced nothing could go wrong.

"We should have this all wrapped up in a few days," I said. Then I added, looking at the small pile of cocaine, "That's really some good coke."

Stoney smiled, straightened his back. "Yeah, it is."

"Maybe I ought to get some to take with me." I hesitated, then added, "In case you don't get any that good again." I hoped I sounded nonchalant. Of course, it was just an excuse to get more coke.

"It's the same as I always have, Mikey."

I didn't want to contradict him, but now that I had started the ridiculous gambit, I had to continue. "I dunno, Stoney. Seems a little better. I think I should get some. Might not come around again for a long time." Excitement coursed through my body; I hoped Stoney couldn't see it.

There was no reaction on Stoney's face. I didn't know if he accepted my lame fib or if he'd heard it so many times in his line of work it was just old hat. "Sure, Mikey," he said. "Gram?"

I tried to remain relaxed. "Better make it an eight-ball." Three and a half grams. Yeah, that's what I wanted.

Stoney looked at me like I'd just asked for a pound. "An eight-ball? You even know the lingo now."

I shrugged, flushed again. "That stuff's awfully good and it will last me forever."

He had a doubtful look on his face. "I dunno about that. But, yeah, sure." He went into his bedroom, left the door open.

I couldn't see much, just him fooling around with a scale on the dresser and what I assumed to be the coke. When he returned, he handed me a small corner of a plastic baggie secured with a yellow tie. The white drug was inside. I shoved it in my inside jacket pocket, felt it a couple more times to make sure it hadn't gone anywhere. I asked how much and paid up. Now I couldn't wait to get out of there but I couldn't let him know that.

He asked about our next steps in the Susan Worthman project. I told him quickly. I wanted to leave. And besides, I just couldn't sit still.

He stared at me. Did he know what I was really thinking?

I said as calmly as I could, "Well, I better get going. I've got things to do. You're going to get up to Hampton, right?"

"Sure, Mikey. I'll leave right away." Then he furrowed his brows. "You all right?"

"Yeah, yeah, yeah, I'm going to use your head before I go. Gotta take a leak." I heard him say something as I headed for the bathroom.

Inside, I quietly locked the door behind me and removed the coke from my jacket pocket. It was the largest amount I'd ever held. My hands shook and my heart pounded. I dumped a small amount of it on the back of the toilet. I was smart enough to close the seat first. Little rocks came out in the mixture. I retied the baggie and put it back in my pocket. I took a coin from my pocket, tried to crush the tiny rocks. When I'd done the best I could, I rolled a bill and inhaled the powder as quietly as possible. The lines were double what I was used to doing. I brushed off the back of the toilet, flushed it, and inspected my nose in the mirror.

I stepped back into the room trying to look casual even though I felt like a street bum on a modeling runway. Stoney was standing in the middle of the room, looking at me strangely.

"Are you sure you're okay, man?"

"Yeah, fine. How about a beer for the road?"

Stoney nodded, headed for the little kitchen.

"Better make it two," I called after him. "It's a long way to my place. And can you loosen the caps?" I didn't like the sound of my voice, but it was the only one I had right now.

Stoney returned with two beers, their caps askew. "Sorry, this is all I have." He handed them to me. They were some kind of import; I didn't care if they were panther piss. They'd work. I held them by their necks in one hand.

I turned in the direction of the door, said, "Okay, gotta go, see you later."

"For Chrissake, take these. You might need them." He placed five or six blue Valiums in my palm. I put them in my shirt pocket.

"Thanks, Stoney, talk to you later."

He chased me to the door. "You sure you're okay, Mike?"

"I'm fine," I yelled over my shoulder as I raced down the stairs.

I heard him call, "Be careful, Mike," just as I went out the building's main door into the night.

CHAPTER 28

I STOOD ON the front stoop of Stoney's building and chugged one of the two beers he'd just given me. When it was empty, I flipped the bottle into some evergreen bushes. I walked down the last couple of steps to the sidewalk, looked around. Traffic was light. I studied each passing car. I wasn't going back to my apartment like I'd told Stoney. My mind was fixated on one spot—The Combat Zone.

I tried to flag down the first empty cab I saw. The cab sped up. Maybe I didn't look too good. I took a swig of the second beer and slipped the bottle under my jacket. The next cab I attempted to stop, did.

I opened the rear door, hopped in.

"Where ya wanna go, mistah?" the driver asked with a heavy Boston accent. He turned his head, stared at me over the seat.

"Boston. Washington Street." My voice still sounded shaky. Whether it really was or not, I couldn't be sure.

"Where abouts? The Zone?"

"Yeah."

He gave me a knowing look. "Can you put that beer out? I can't be driving around with an open beer."

Apparently, I hadn't concealed it well enough. I put the bottle up to my lips, drained it. I opened the door, set the bottle on the street against the curb. When I closed the door, he turned back to the wheel with a sigh, let his dispatcher know where he was going, and drove.

On the ride there, I had thoughts that should have been illegal. I was excited and nervous at the same time. It didn't help that the driver kept glancing at me in the rear view for the entire trip. At least I think he was.

I had some crazy ideas on the way. One minute I wondered if I could do some coke without the driver seeing me. The next I'd be ready to throw the coke out the window before the cops, who I was sure were following us, pulled the cab over. Fortunately, I did neither.

When we finally reached Washington Street, he pulled over to the curb a block short of the beginning of the Combat Zone proper.

"Here okay?" he asked in a tone that meant it wasn't really a question. "I don't want to go in there. The freakin' hookers will be trying to get me to take them and their johns somewhere. I don't want to get involved with that shit."

Up ahead I could see the blinking neon lights of the porno theaters and the strip bars. The lights seemed to shimmer. Hordes of humanity filled both sidewalks of Washington Street for as far as I could see. I paid the driver what he asked, plus a generous tip, and slid out.

Behind me the cabbie shouted, "Watch your wallet, pal."

I moved rapidly into the Combat Zone. A mugger couldn't have caught up with me. I had two things on my mind—sex and cocaine. The sex wasn't anything like what I usually thought about either. There were new fantasies going through my head like high speed movies on a screen. Every so often the thought of cocaine would stop the projector. I had to find somewhere to do it.

The Zone was bustling, lit up with garish signs selling every perversion that was legal and hinting at some that probably weren't. Even though I was interested in some of them— God, was I interested—it all took a momentary back seat to finding a place to do my drug. The large flashing sign *Peep Booths—Private* on a storefront caught my eye. You'd think after my last experience, I'd stay away from these places even though it was a different location. That wasn't why I made a beeline towards it though. My mind was locked on cocaine and sex and nothing else mattered. I could kill two birds with one stone in a place like this. Even if it had been the one I'd been arrested in, I probably would have gone in anyway.

I went right up to the counter; there was that man again. Or one that looked like him anyway, sitting behind it on a stool up high.

"Whataya want?" he asked, like I was no better than the worst who came through the door.

I fumbled a five out of my wallet, handed it to him. "Quarters," I answered.

I swear he gave me a little sneer as he released the coins from a metal change chute on the counter beside him and passed them to me. I shoved them in my pocket and hurried down one of the aisles in the direction of a sign that announced *Booths*. On both sides of the aisle were long racks of magazines exposing every sexual preference possible. I barely glanced at them, less at the men standing there staring at them.

When I reached the back, I pushed through a swinging wood door and entered a dark hall that ran to my left and right. When my eyes adjusted, I saw a display of dozens of pictures on the wall directly in front of me. Each picture represented a movie available for viewing and they all displayed a number that matched which booth they could be seen in. It was a twin of the peep show I'd been arrested in.

I had a flash of paranoia. What if the cops had been tipped off again that I was coming to the Zone just like they had been before? What if they'd followed me here? I'd thought that in the cab. Or were they already waiting for me? No, I told myself. No one could know I was here. Could they? I wasn't 100 percent sure, but I didn't give a damn. I stepped up to the rows of photos. My eyes flicked from picture to picture. Each was a still photo from the offered movie. There were other men standing there; I could feel eyes on me. I didn't dare look at anyone. I zeroed in on one display that caught my eye. 23A. I found the correct corridor and walked down it. It was dark and lined with booths on each side with the only illumination a soft red bulb showcasing the number of each booth. In front of a few of the booths, single men lounged. They reminded me of huge praying mantises. I had an idea what they were about. I didn't make eye contact with any of them as I hurried past, but I felt their stares boring into me. One muttered something unintelligible.

Number 23A was at the end on the right. I went in, latched the door behind me, and put one foot against it. Extra security. Before I could get the cocaine out of my pocket, someone on the other side pushed against the door. I stiffened my leg and froze. Whoever it was shoved the door a few more times and then finally gave up. I relaxed my leg just a bit, removed the clear plastic baggie of cocaine, and carefully opened it. My hands shook. I think my heart was shaking, too. I set the tiny baggie down on a small wooden shelf below the coin deposit machine. I tore a bill from my wallet, formed a funnel with it, and shoved it into the coke. I didn't bother to chop it. I knew I probably couldn't have done the job anyway. I inhaled deeply and the top of my head almost came off. I did the other nostril, snorted the powder up, little rocks and all. I looked in the bag, saw a rock bigger than the others, one maybe Stoney had put in just because it was me. I snatched the rock with my fingers, threw it in my mouth, chewed, and swallowed.

I sealed the bag of coke with the yellow tie and shoved it back in my coat pocket. I pulled out a fistful of quarters and put them on the shelf. I tried to jam one of the coins into the slot; it fell on the floor. I didn't go for it, just grabbed another. The small screen flickered and came to life right in the middle of the action. No preliminaries with these things. I watched the figures involved in something I'd never seen before. And it got me going. Christ, did it get me going. It was like mainlining sex.

The rest of the night was a blur, racing from one peep show to the next and back again. I hit lots of other spots too—XXX movie theaters, strip joints, and places I don't want to talk about. Not caring about anything in the world except the next stop and the cocaine in my pocket. I was a reckless man in a dangerous place—the Combat Zone. I'd heard some people hadn't survived nights like this. Would I? I'd find that out tomorrow, if there was one.

CHAPTER 29

THERE WAS A tomorrow. It wasn't a good one though. When I woke, it was early afternoon. I couldn't remember how or when I'd gotten there, but at least I was in my own apartment. Fully dressed, passed out on the bed. I lay there for a bit. The nausea and headache were as bad as I'd ever had, but I could deal with that. I'd done it before. Plenty of times. But there was more. The minute I opened my eyes I was engulfed with depression and guilt so strong I knew it would dog me for a lot longer than a usual one-day hangover did. I tried not to think. But that was impossible. I did think. And the second I did, painful recollections of the previous night surfaced, one after the other, like bursting boils. I couldn't stop them; they were too strong. No matter how sick I felt, I had to do something, anything to get my mind off them. I sat up, felt for my wallet. Except that it contained only a few dollar bills, everything else was there. I looked for the coke. I wasn't surprised that I couldn't find it. I'd probably done the whole thing. Three and a half grams! I pushed that frightening realization from my mind.

I got up, stumbled for the bathroom, checked myself in the mirror, and grabbed three aspirins. In the kitchen, I swallowed them with water and kept drinking long after they were gone. I plopped down in my easy chair. It didn't feel very easy. More like what it really was—just an old piece of cheap furniture that'd come with the apartment. I felt in my shirt pocket for the blue Valiums Stoney had given me. There were only three of the five or six left. So that was how I was able to sleep with all the cocaine in my system. I'd gotten carried away for sure. But at least I'd gotten home okay. Nothing too bad had happened or I'd remember. The instant I thought that, visions of the night before began to bubble up in my brain again. The guilt and depression returned. A guilt and depression stronger than any I'd ever felt before, even during the worst of my drinking bouts. They were the kind of feelings they medicate you for if you have them too long.

But last night was just a one-shot thing, I told myself. That was all. I was sure of it. Could've happened to anybody. I'd stay away from the cocaine. Never do it again. I felt a little better, barely.

I thought of Stoney and Tank, babysitting Elliot. Jake, maybe wanting to let me know what, if any, luck he'd had with Brogna. They were all waiting on me, and I'd fallen apart the night before. I may have put them in danger, worse danger than they were already in. And Jesus, they'd come into this thing because they trusted me. I could have done something really stupid last night and then where would they be?

And Julie?

I shook that off quick. Last night was just a one-time thing, I told myself again. No one has to know. I felt a sense of dread—of what I didn't know—settle over me along with the guilt and depression. Never again, I swore. Never again.

I lurched up from the chair. I had to get myself together. I couldn't let everyone down. I placed two bottles of Schlitz in the freezer, told myself that's all I'd have. Two beers were nothing compared to the amount I must have consumed the night before. Hopefully, they'd act like medicine. I forced myself into the shower and began an attempt to look human. Feeling human would take a lot longer.

When I was dressed, I grabbed both beers from the freezer, sat at my desk and sipped them, one after the other. They were ice cold, and under other circumstances, they would have tasted awful good. Right now, they were for medicinal purposes and medicine never tasted good. Just ask any kid.

Jake was the first person I had to get in touch with. He'd probably be concerned, and maybe angry, that I hadn't called yet. He was risking a lot, and I'd almost blown it. But it was okay now. I'd put everything back on track and no one would ever know how close I'd come to screwing everything up.

I could've used one of Stoney's blue pills right then, but I shoved that notion quickly out of my mind. I wasn't sure the effect it would have on me. Maybe put me to sleep. Halfway through the second bottle of beer, I felt that I could at least talk to Jake without my voice sounding like a skipping record. I removed the telephone from the refrigerator, where I'd apparently put it when I'd come in so I wouldn't hear it ring. The hand piece was cold. I dialed O'Toole's number.

"Where the hell have you been, Mike?" was the first thing he said.

I rambled out some inane excuse.

"I been tryin' to reach you. Can you get down here? Three o'clock—when it's slowed down?"

I agreed. He hung up, didn't say good-bye. I looked at the clock. It was one forty-five. I drained the second beer.

CHAPTER 30

I TIMED IT so I'd arrive at O'Toole's at exactly three o'clock. When I walked in, one of the other bartenders was working the spigots. Jake was in a back booth looking my way, a *Boston Herald* in his hands. I slid in opposite him, tried to impersonate a respectable person, the exact opposite of what I felt like.

He closed the newspaper, pushed it aside. "What the hell happened to you? I've been trying to reach you since yesterday."

"Nothing. Been working on some details." I hoped Jake would buy that, but I doubted it. It didn't sound convincing even to me.

His eyes scanned my face, every inch of it. "You look like shit. I'm not your father, Mike, but Jesus Christ, we're involved in something very heavy here."

Jake had been in the bar business a long time and had seen more people after a bad night than a bail bondsman. I hadn't fooled him for an instant. I just prayed he never found out how far it had really gone.

"Stevie," Jake shouted, holding up two fingers in the direction of the bartender. Then to me, "You want something to eat?"

"No, no thanks."

"You sure?" he said.

"I'm sure."

"All right. How'd it go then?"

I told him how it had gone with the meth cook and that Julie and Tank had done a good job. I let him know that Stoney was there now. Maybe Tank too. I tried to sound relaxed, but I don't think I pulled it off. When the beers came, I immediately raised mine to my lips; my hand shook.

Jake scowled. "I wish you'd told me some of these details when you called. It would've saved me a lot of worry."

"Sorry about that." I set the glass down and changed the subject. "Have you had any luck?"

He nodded vigorously, white wispy hair dancing. "Yeah, I've had luck." He hadn't touched his beer. "I reached out to a guy I've known for years. He's in awful tight with Brogna. Probably because he pays him large every month. This guy just makes book, I *think*, but anyway, he's pretty big in Boston. One of the biggest. We was kids together. We also got a family relationship, but I don't want to talk about any of that. Thing is you're gonna have to call this guy direct. He's expecting to hear from you."

"I can do that." I finished the beer, glanced toward the bartender, caught his eye, and turned back again.

"You sure?" Jake said. He gave me the once-over again.

"Of course." Then I thought of something else. "You get any hint if Brogna knows Elliot's missing yet?"

"No, but Elliot?"

Steve delivered my beer, walked back to the bar. Jake had still barely touched his. "That's the cook's name," I said.

"First name basis all ready? Gettin' kind of chummy, aren't you?" Jake shook his head. "That might not be a good idea, Mike. Especially if it don't go right. I pray to Jesus it don't come to it, but we might have to threaten him, slap him around a little to keep him quiet."

I was surprised to hear Jake speak of violence, even if it was only slapping. "Nothing's going wrong. And nobody's going to get hurt."

"We might *have* to throw a scare into him. And if you're his best buddy, we'll probably have to get a little more rough than a couple of slaps or he won't take us serious."

"Oh, come on. He's just a nerdy MIT kid for Chrissake."

"He's a fuckin' meth maker," Jake spit out. "Don't forget that. And when this is all over he can put the finger on you." He looked at me, his blue eyes hard, then added quickly, "And if you don't care about yourself anymore, what about your buddies, the biker and pothead?" Before I could answer, he said, "And Julie? What about her? She's an awful sweet girl. This *Elliot* saw her?"

Yes, he had. And I hadn't forgotten that. But she'd been in disguise. I hoped I had it all figured out. "It's all going to work, Jake."

"And if it doesn't?"

"You don't have to worry. Nobody is going to get by me. No matter what. Not even Myles Brogna. You got my word on that." And I meant it.

"All right, Mike. I hope you know what you're doing."

Jake removed a piece of paper from the pocket of his white dress shirt. Both the shirt and paper were wrinkled. He placed the paper on the table in front of me. "Here's a number and a first name. Not real . . . the name, that is. You're going to have to use your name though. He insisted."

I picked up the paper, looked at a Boston telephone number along with a time of day.

"It's a pay phone," Jake said. "Call that number on any of the next three days at that time. He'll answer. Don't screw up. Miss it, and we'll have to start all over."

"I won't miss it." I put the paper in my jacket pocket, drained the beer.

"Want another one?" he asked.

God, did I want another one. But I couldn't tell him that. He was suspicious enough. I shook my head, pointed at the one he'd barely touched. "Aren't you going to finish that?"

"Nah, too early for me." He started to push it with one finger in my direction. "You want it?"

Of course I did. Not in circumstances like this, though. He could already read me like a book. Neither of us was fooling the other. But I wasn't going to admit anything to him. I just shook my head again.

He withdrew his finger. "So you'll keep me posted this time? Remember, I got a lot invested in this, too."

"I'll let you know as soon as something solid happens." I pushed myself up and out of the booth. I had to get the hell out of there.

Jake's hand flew across the table, grabbed my wrist. "Mike, if there's anything I can do, *for you*, you know I'm here."

I did know it. And I also knew there was nothing he could do for me. Only I could help myself. The question was— would I?

CHAPTER 31

AFTER I LEFT O'Toole's, I gave Stoney a call at the cottage. Tank was scheduled to drop by to give him sleep time. So far Elliot hadn't given them any problems.

That was about all I could do for the day. I'd had hangovers before, but this was more than a simple hangover. Along with the aftereffects of the coke, booze, and pills, Guilt sat on my shoulders like two blacksmith anvils. The only reason I wasn't considering putting the business end of a .38 into my mouth was that the unpleasantness would end eventually—I hoped.

I stopped at the little liquor store down the street, bought two six-packs of Schlitz. I thought I had plenty left in the apartment, but I hadn't counted. And I wasn't taking any chances. Not today.

When I was back in the apartment, I sat in my chair, sipped beer, and stared at the TV. Hours passed before I'd finally had enough that I could sleep.

When I woke the next morning, I was consumed by a mood fouler than a gambler's on a losing streak. It was a dangerous mood. I tried to direct my thoughts elsewhere. I took out the paper Jake had given me for calling the go-between. The first day listed was today. The time—later this afternoon. I was determined to make that call and soldier through the day. So I ate, showered, and headed for the office.

I reached my building, went inside. The landlord was coming down the stairs as I was going up. He stopped, looked at me, started to speak, then pinned himself against the wall as I lurched past him. I guess he was smarter than I'd thought.

At my desk, I leaned back in the wooden swivel chair. I tried to go over what I was going to say to the go-between and how I was going to say it. I'd have to play it by ear, so except for the general idea there wasn't much point in re-hashing it. What I was really trying to do was keep my mind occupied and off the painful thoughts of the other night. I couldn't though. My mind was drawn back to what I'd done like lemmings going over a cliff. And I deserved it.

Little bits and pieces of the escapades I'd been involved in that night kept coming back to me. At least I thought I'd been involved in them—I couldn't even be sure of that. Maybe some of the visions were just dreams. Nightmares more accurately. I couldn't fool myself with bullshit like that though. The only solace I had was that something worse hadn't happened—at least I hoped it hadn't.

Thinking about that night was getting me nothing except a lot of pain. Maybe that was the idea. You paid for stuff like that for a long time before you began to feel semi-normal again. I knew that from the booze. And I had a feeling that this one would take a lot longer than usual to get over.

I considered having my first beer of the day, but decided not to. My mood was so dark, I wasn't sure if beer would help me or push me down the hole a little further. I remembered someone had once told me Percodans helped with a hang-over. I didn't have a hangover. And I didn't know whether they'd help with guilt and depression or not, but I was desperate. I still had some of the pills prescribed at the hospital after the Demon's beating. I went to the bathroom, returned with a glass of water, and washed two of the pills down.

I sat at my desk, staring at the picture of Nixon on the wall. One minute hating the man in a rage, the next feeling a deep sadness that he was the President. I don't know how much time passed before I grabbed the water glass and threw it toward his ugly face. I missed; the glass shattered on the wall to the picture's left, water running down the wall.

That did it; the rage facet of the depression was on top now, the despair buried below it. I got two beers from the fridge and was almost done with the second when I heard footsteps on the staircase outside the office. It couldn't be anyone good, so I opened the desk's top drawer on my right, flicked on the tape recorder switch, left the drawer slightly ajar. Then slid open, just a bit, the shallow drawer directly in front of me, glanced at the black .38 lying there. The foot-steps came closer. I heard the doorknob turn, the door opened, and in stepped the cop, Dalton. He closed the door behind him, started across the small room toward me. He hesitated when shards of broken glass crunched under his feet.

"You need a cleaning lady, Dick Tracy," he said as he resumed walking in my direction. He dropped into one of the two client chairs and put his feet on the desk, crossing them at the ankles.

"What the hell do you want?" To say I wasn't in the mood for this piece of human garbage was an understatement.

"Got up on the wrong side of the bed, huh?" He smirked at me.

Everything about the man was sleazy—his suit, his haircut, the stink of his cheap cologne. "I asked you what you want." I glanced down toward the drawer with the .38.

His little black snake eyes shifted around the room. "I got a little proposition for you, Malloy. It's something you'll be plenty interested in." Sounded like he thought I should've been thrilled to see him. I wasn't. I wouldn't have been thrilled to see anybody.

His small ugly eyes bored in on me. He waited for me to respond; I didn't. "The Worthman girl," he continued, "you're looking for her. I can tell you where she is."

"Go on."

He shifted his body just a bit. "It'll cost you five grand."

I guffawed. "Where the hell would I get that kind of money? Look around." I waved my hand at the walls.

He didn't look. "You can get it from her old man. He'd pay that to get his precious daughter back."

"You're right, he probably would've . . . a few days ago. But now you're a day late and a dollar short." I drained the beer, slammed the bottle on the desk. It startled him.

"Whaddaya mean?" he asked suspiciously.

"Is your boss in on this, too?" I asked referring to his partner Cummings.

It wouldn't have surprised me if he was, but he answered, "This is just between you and me. No one else gotta know."

The smell of his cheap cologne was so strong I could taste it. "I already told you. You're too late. Now get out of my office." I had the sudden urge to hurt him.

"You're bluffing, shithead." He put on that tough guy face, the one he'd worn on his previous visit. "Five grand's what I want. Nothing less."

I leaned across the desk toward him. He still had his feet up on the desk, but he leaned back in the chair.

"Get out of here while you still can." I was breathing heavily, but for the first time today I had something else on my mind other than what I'd done the other night. I liked that.

He didn't look so sure of himself anymore. "So that must mean you found out where she is?"

I didn't answer, just ground my teeth.

I could see him trying to screw up his courage just as if there was a sign around his neck announcing it. "Maybe you did, but you don't get out that easy. I still want that dough. And you're gonna pay it."

"Why?"

"'Cause I said so."

My eyes were burning, obscuring my vision. "Or *what?*" I growled. My breathing was shallow and I was clenching my right fist behind the desk.

He looked at me smugly. "You could lose your snoop license. Or your friends might start having some legal troubles. Or maybe even physical problems. All sorts of things could happen."

He waited for me to say something, maybe show I was afraid or intimidated. I wasn't. But I was so hot, I couldn't have talked anyway. I had to fight not to come across the desk at him.

Then he threw a match on the gasoline he'd just poured. "Your old girlfriend there. Julie what's-her-name? The one I heard you're seeing again. You busted her nose that time. Jeez, whaddaya do to people who ain't your friend?" He let out a slimy little snicker. "She's still awful pretty though.

I'd hate to see her get sent to jail on some dope rap. Those dykes'd love to get their hands on her. They'd probably have her wearing a . . ."

I grabbed his feet with both hands, flipped him backwards. The chair tumbled over, and he went down hard on his side. I came around the desk, kicking the other chair out of my way. He struggled to get up, a look like he was about to be tossed in a wood chipper on his face. I couldn't enjoy his fear though. I was too far gone. He rolled up on one knee and went for his shoulder holster. I reached down, grabbed his hand just before it latched onto his revolver. I held his wrist with my other hand. Then I pulled his index finger back until it cracked like a gunshot, and he howled like a wounded dog. He wouldn't use that trigger finger for a while.

I grabbed his shirt with both hands, pulled him to his feet. He blubbered something, but it was meaningless to me. I wanted blood. His face had gone white, a picture of shock. I let go of his shirt and pushed him back a bit. I knew the sight of *his* nose would never bother me, so I let him have it. And it felt good when his nose collapsed under my fist. He crashed against the wall like a rag doll, oozing down to the floor.

I came closer, looked at him. I couldn't have done a better job if I'd used a baseball bat. He went for the shoulder holster again, but this time it was in slow motion and with a mangled finger. I let him get his gun out and struggle with it as he tried to figure out what finger to put around the trigger. When I got sick of watching, I kicked the gun out of his hand. He cried out like a wounded animal again. It made me feel good.

I pulled him to his feet. He started to beg, splattering blood all over my shirt as he tried to find words that would stop me. I hit him in the right eye. He went down hard again, but his survival instinct must have kicked into high gear. As soon as he was down, he made a mad crawl for the door.

He didn't get far; my foot caught him hard in the side. He deflated like a popped balloon. I dragged him up again, let him have it again. I connected near his left eye. He went down, didn't make a break for it this time. I don't think he could see the door. I hauled him up and smashed him in the mouth. Teeth gave, maybe his jaw. I wasn't sure but it was an ugly sound and he went down hard.

I bent and picked up his service revolver. I jammed the barrel roughly into his mouth, past what was left of his teeth. He was still conscious, but his face was like something out of a horror movie. I cocked the hammer. Just before I changed my life forever, a vision of Julie came into my mind. I stopped.

"If anything ever happens to her . . ." I hissed, "or to any of my friends, I'll kill you, you dirty bastard. You hear me?"

I didn't think he could see me too well, but he could hear me. He nodded his head, the gun barrel banging against his jagged teeth.

I dragged him over to the desk. I bent him over it backwards, kept the gun in his mouth, pushed the barrel hard against the back of his throat. He was gagging now. With my other hand, I reached across the desk, opened the drawer with the tape player in it. "And if you ever get any ideas, this'll be going to the newspapers." I rewound the machine, pressed play. I let enough of it run so that he knew the score.

I pulled the gun from his mouth. The barrel was slick with blood. I didn't bother cleaning it. I released the cartridges from the cylinder, let them fall on the desk before returning the piece to his holster. I dragged him over to the door.

Once I'd looked out and seen the hallway was empty, I towed him behind me down the back stairs and out the rear door. I sat him up against a brick wall, behind a dumpster where he couldn't be seen from the street.

He was awake, but in bad shape. I'd rearranged his face nicely. I went back to the office, cleaned up, changed my bloody shirt, drank beer, and waited until it was time to call the go-between.

CHAPTER 32

FINALLY THE TIME on the piece of paper Jake had given me came. I made the call to the go-between, gave him my name and phone number. It didn't matter. I was sure Brogna was already well aware of who I was—the detective nosing around looking for Susan Worthman—so he probably would've figured it was me behind the kidnapping anyway. Now my job was to keep everybody else safe. The go-between told me to sit tight, wait for a call. I didn't wait long. When the office phone rang, I answered on the first ring.

"You motherfucker, I'll cut off your cock and shove it down your throat." Those were the first words that came screaming through the phone at me after I answered it. I tried to get a word in. It was no use. Brogna went on ranting and spewing filth. I let him tire himself out. Finally he said, "Don't say my name, asshole, but you know who I am, right?" He spoke with a Southie accent, like Jake.

I was still in a foul mood, but I answered pretty politely considering. "I know who you are."

"Then you spring that kid yesterday or you and whoever else is involved in this . . ."

He trailed off. I could tell he wanted to say more, but even though I assumed he was on a pay phone, he was reported to rarely use any phone, period. He probably didn't like using one now. He'd already lost his temper once. Made a threat. Didn't want to repeat the mistake.

"You done?" was all I said.

"If you're letting the kid go, I'm done."

"The kid's not going anywhere until you and I talk."

"I ain't talking to you, asshole. I'm telling."

It was time to play hard ball. "If you want your money-maker back, you'll talk to me. *Or* I could hand him over to the feds along with a little info I've picked up. With twenty years hanging over his head, they'd have to slap him to get him to stop talking. I could arrange that. Easy."

Except for the heavy breathing the line was silent. I studied Nixon's face on the wall near the door. He seemed to be smirking.

"You can meet with one of my associates," Brogna finally said.

"You and you alone," I shot back.

He started with the filthy mouth again until the operator broke in and asked for more money. I smiled as I heard him sputter and drop coins in. When he was done, he seemed to have calmed down a bit.

"All right, Malloy. But I'll pick when and where."

"Shoot and we'll see."

He named a restaurant up on Route 1. And a time: tomorrow.

"I'm all right with that," I said.

He tried to do a little face saving. "You'd better be."

"And don't forget," I said, "come by yourself." I felt good popping his balloon.

"Same goes for you, Malloy." He spit the words out. "Remember, the Irish got hot tempers. And I'm one hundred percent Irish."

"So am I."

The operator broke in, asking for more money and he slammed down the phone. I hung up.

I sat there congratulating myself on how I'd handled the call. In less than a minute the phone rang. It was the operator. The party I'd been talking to owed fifty-five cents. Did I know who it was? "No, operator," I said. "It was a salesman I couldn't get rid of."

I wondered what she would have thought if I'd told her who it really was—Myles Brogna, the most dangerous man in Boston. The same man I was meeting tomorrow.

CHAPTER 33

I CALLED STONEY at the Hampton cottage from an out-side pay phone. I was now as leery of phones as Brogna. The way I had it figured, with his connections, it would be easy for him to have my telephone tapped. I told Stoney I was on my way to Hampton, that I wanted to go over some things. I did, but I had something more in mind.

My mood was still as dark as a death row inmate's. So dark in fact, it was starting to scare me. I didn't feel any remorse about what I'd done to Dalton, and I didn't have second thoughts about the cocky way I'd handled Brogna, but it got me to wondering what else would I do before this was over. Next time it might be something I'd wish later that I hadn't done. I needed something to mellow my mood just a bit. There was only one thing that could brighten me up—cocaine. I know I said I would never do it again, but this time it would be for a positive reason. I'd be more in control of my actions. I'd be able to make the right decisions, something I wasn't sure I was capable of right now. Not with the mood I was in. Getting rid of my ugly state of mind would help protect my friends. So I'd decided to see if Stoney had some with him, just a little.

I rationalized all the way to Hampton Beach and my mood even seemed to lighten a little. I actually didn't feel like careening head on into an approaching car. The ride took double the time it usually would have. I went a roundabout way and stopped often, making sure no one was following me. During one stop I made a phone call to Cousin Billy and let him know about my meeting with Brogna the next day. When I finally sped over the Hampton Bridge, turned down the side street, and pulled into the driveway, I couldn't park and get out of the car fast enough.

I noticed the smell of salt in the air as I bounded up the cottage stairs and gave our signal knock. The lock unlatched and the door swung open. Stoney let me in.

"Where is he?" I asked anxiously.

He pointed in the direction of the kitchen. "He's right out there, Mikey. No problem, man."

I brushed past Stoney, hurried to the kitchen, and yes, Elliot was there. He was seated at the kitchen table. A chessboard was in front of him; a game was in play.

He looked up at me from behind those nerdy glasses. "Hi, Mike."

I remembered what Jake had said about being too close to our guest. "We're getting pretty friendly, aren't we?" I said, pointing at the chessboard.

Stoney had followed me into the kitchen. "Look, Mikey. You said we might be here a while. I figured we might as well relax a little. Elliot promised me he won't try anything."

"He promised you?" I said.

Elliot chimed in. "I did, Mike. It's only logical that I wouldn't be anxious to leave here. Stoney's assured me that I'm not going to be hurt no matter how this turns out. I believe him. And besides, if I did run, my employer could be waiting for me in Cambridge. He's a paranoid individual. Might have doubts when I tell him I've told you nothing. Then he might look at me as a possible debit in his account book and no longer a credit. He'd most likely want to erase me like any other debit. He's all business. So you see, Mike, I feel much safer staying right here for now."

"Yeah, I see," I said. I wasn't sure I believed him, though. "Who's winning?" I nodded toward the chessboard.

"He's doing respectably well," Elliot acknowledged. "Considering."

Stoney hopped into the chair opposite Elliot. "Yeah, Mike. Considering he's been the Vice-President of the MIT chess team for two years now."

"Three," Elliot corrected.

"You behave, maybe someday you'll be president," I said.

Then I asked Stoney to join me in the other room. No matter how much a member of the family Elliot was becoming, I didn't want him to know everything. Before we left the kitchen, I glanced at the back door and then at Elliot. I agreed that Elliot was unlikely to make a break for it. What might be waiting for him out there was undoubtedly less pleasant than a gentlemanly game of chess.

We stepped into the front room. The walls were adorned with nautical knickknacks and cheap seascape paintings. The furniture was what you'd expect to see in a beach cottage—inexpensive and heavily used. I motioned Stoney to sit on the worn couch beside me so we could talk privately.

"I'm meeting Brogna tomorrow," I said.

Stoney breathed out loudly. "Whoa, that's heavy, man. Who are you going to take with you?"

I shook my head. "No one. He's coming alone, too."

He raised his eyebrows. "I wouldn't trust him, Mikey. He might kidnap *you*."

I told him where we were meeting.

He chuckled nervously. "Yeah, I guess that's about as public as you can get. Still, what if he grabs you coming or going?"

"I don't think he will. I've already told him," I nodded toward the kitchen, "we'll turn Elliot over to the feds if any harm comes to us. He doesn't want that."

"Be careful." He glanced down at my hands. My knuckles were cut. He pointed. "What happened?"

"Nothing."

He looked quizzically at me. "You all right, Mikey?"

That question again. "Of course I'm all right. Why the fuck is everyone asking me that lately?"

Stoney shifted uneasily on the couch.

"I wanted to ask you something," I said. I hadn't felt nervous up until this moment. The exact opposite as a matter of fact. But oddly, my voice shook. I hoped Stoney didn't notice it. "I was wondering if you got any coke on you?"

He gave me a suspicious look. "You're out?" I didn't answer. What could I have said? After a few long seconds that seemed like minutes, Stoney said, "I got a little, Mikey. I brought it to keep me on my toes with Elliot."

I waited for him to continue. Finally, I said, "Well? Can I buy some?" It came out louder than it should have and my voice sounded even shakier.

"Yeah, sure. I guess I can give you half. I got a little over a gram. You got anything to put it in?"

I whipped out a new glass vial I'd bought in the Zone. He removed a twin from his shirt pocket. Little spoons dangled from both black caps. His vial held white powder; mine was empty. Stony began transferring coke from his vial to mine. I watched him intently. He seemed pretty fair, although he should have put in a little more in mine, but I didn't say anything. When he was done, we both put or vials away. I noticed that my bowels were churning.

Then I paid Stoney and told him I'd be in touch. Let him know what happened with my Brogna meeting and what our next move would be. Before he could get up from the couch, I made a beeline for the bathroom. Even the coke had to wait as I took a violent crap. When that was done, I took two healthy jolts of the drug. I felt better instantly. Even felt a little bad about beating Dalton so badly.

When I left the bathroom, I said goodbye to Stoney and Elliot. They were both bent over the chessboard. They grunted; neither looked up.

CHAPTER 34

I WAS GOOD that night, believe it or not. I finished the half-gram Stoney had given me and had a few beers to get me to sleep. I slept decently considering everything. Maybe it was because I didn't have anyone to worry about, at least for a bit, except myself. Julie had wisely taken my advice to stay at a girlfriend's place until this was resolved. I didn't think there was any way Brogna could've known about her involvement. Still, better safe than sorry. Stoney was at the safe house with Elliot. I'd been extra careful about tails when I'd gone there. I was confident there'd been none. So I was sure Brogna couldn't have located it. I'd let both Tank and Jake know that I'd made contact with Brogna. Maybe they'd even make themselves scarce for a bit, too. Although knowing them both as well as I did, I doubted it. But I wasn't concerned. They could take care of themselves.

I arrived at the Hilltop Steak House, on busy Route 1, just before noon. It was in Saugus, about ten miles north of Boston. I was a few minutes early. Brogna wasn't there yet. I took a booth in the back of one of the large dining rooms, near a window that looked out over the highway and the life-size plastic cows grazing on the front lawn. I ordered, my first beer of the day, and went over what I was going to say to the man. I didn't feel quite as cheerful and perky as the previous day when I'd blown those first two lines in the cottage bathroom. Instead, I found myself back in a dark, aggressive frame of mind. Maybe that's the attitude I'd need facing a man like Brogna.

He was right on time, not a second late—if that was possible. I noticed him coming across the dining room in my direction. You couldn't miss him. He looked just like his newspaper pictures. He wore a flat-as-a-pancake scally cap topping off a dark blue designer track suit and strutted toward me like a cocky bantam rooster. He wasn't a big man, but you could see he took care of himself and he was solid. A young-looking sixty, maybe. A few other patrons recognized him and quickly turned away.

He sat down ramrod straight opposite me in the booth. He took off his scally cap, placed it on the table, and looked at me. He had white hair combed backwards and Irish blue eyes.

"So you're Malloy, the private dick who's causing me all these problems?"

I nodded.

The waitress came over, took one look at Brogna, and said in a quivering voice, "Can I get you anything from the bar?"

He didn't seem surprised at her reaction. He probably got it all the time.

"Soda water, no fruit," he answered.

She couldn't get away from the table fast enough, and I had to shout my request for another beer after her.

He said, "Restroom," and pointed with his chin in that direction.

I wasn't worried. I didn't think he'd try anything here. The restaurant was as crowded as a cattle show. When we got to the men's room, there were a couple of patrons inside. We had to wash our hands a couple of times waiting for them to leave. As Brogna washed his hands at the sink beside me, I noticed he wore a large Irish Claddagh ring on his right hand. Finally, Brogna gave the last person a look and the man left. Brogna gave me a thorough pat down. I knew it wasn't a gun he was worried about, but some kind of wire or recording device. When he was satisfied I was clean, we returned to our booth.

The waitress was just dropping off our drinks. "Would you like to order?" Again with the shaky voice.

"Give us a few minutes, will ya?" Brogna said. "I'll let you know when we're ready, honey?"

She nodded rapidly and hurried away.

Brogna took a sip from his soda. I remembered reading somewhere that he was a health nut who neither drank nor smoked. When he set the soft drink down, he said, "All right, genius, why don't you start? You called this meet. Talk to me."

I took a plug of my beer. I wasn't nervous at all. I had a job to do and I felt mean enough to do it. "Susan Worthman," I began. "I'm working for her father. He wants his daughter back."

He leaned toward me. "First of all, keep your voice down. Second, I figured all that. Third, she don't want to go back."

"She's underage."

"Age is in the eye of the beholder, sport."

I looked at his face; it was a hard face. That, and the reputation that went along with the face, made it quite intimidating. Even so, it didn't frighten me much. Sure, I had a healthy respect for the danger the man sitting across from me represented, but I remembered why I was really there. That was more important. And my dark mood was a plus in this situation. "We still want her back, Brogna."

I saw a flicker of anger in his eyes. I imagined he wasn't used to anyone telling him what he had to do. "Call me Myles, sport. And what are you gonna do if you don't get her back—spell it out for me."

Before I could start, he signaled for the waitress. She flew over. Her voice wasn't any more relaxed.

"What can I get you gentlemen?" She kept her eyes on me. Didn't look at Brogna.

He went first. "I'll have the large salad with grilled chicken and any kind of low-fat dressing you got, honey."

She nodded.

"Good."

"I'll have a well-done cheeseburger with fries," I said. "Very well done."

When the waitress was gone, Brogna made a face. "That shit'll kill you, sport." Then he made little circles with his index finger in the air. "You were going to answer my question."

"Elliot'll . . ."

He interrupted. "Elliot? You're on a first-name basis?"

At this point I figured anything that might make Brogna wary was good. "Yeah, we've become good friends. And wouldn't you like to get him back before he's knocked out of the picture one way or another?"

He made a face, shrugged his shoulders. "So what do I care? Kids like him are a dime a dozen." He was acting cozy, playing the long-shot that I didn't realize just how valuable Elliot was to him.

Of course, I did know. "He's one of the best cooks in the country, Brogna. It won't be easy finding someone who can make crank as good as he does, if at all." I stopped, looked at him. There was no reaction but he knew it was true. "And if the feds get Elliot handed to them all wrapped up with a pretty bow, they'll hit him with twenty years. You think he'll stand up to that without rolling over on you?"

Brogna leaned in closer and stared at me. "What if you and your friends end up dead, real quick-like. Whaddaya think of that, smart guy?"

"I don't think you'd be that stupid over one girl, Brogna. First of all, I don't care what happens to me." Since my recent escapades in the Combat Zone, that was almost the truth. "As far as any other people go—and I'm not saying there are any, but if there were—you know I'd have them protected by now. It's too late for you to do anything, anyway. I've got things arranged so Elliot and a lot of info I've gathered will be delivered to the feds if anything happens to me or anyone I know."

"Thought of everything, huh, Shamus?" Brogna leaned back in his seat. "And I agree with one part of it . . . one broad ain't worth the headaches she's causing me."

The waitress returned, plunked down our meals, and hurried away.

Brogna blessed himself with his right hand and went at the salad like it was an expensive delicacy. "So let me get this straight," he said after a couple of bites. "I give you the girl, you give me my employee, and that's the end of it?" He moved his hands like an umpire calling someone out at home plate. "*And* you forget about anything you've learned during your little investigation. If you don't, I'll kill you and everyone you love. I promise you that, sport."

"All I want is the girl," I lied.

"All right then," he said. "I'll get in touch with you about a time and place for the exchange."

I bit into the cheeseburger. It was rare and my stomach lurched. "No, I'm going to pick the time and place."

Brogna's eyes narrowed. "Okay, Malloy, but it better pass the smell test." He put down his fork, put both hands on the table, leaned in toward me again, and lowered his voice even more. "You remember what I said on the phone yesterday?"

"Some of it."

"About what I was going to feed you. Don't forget it. Because if you try anything, that's what you'll be dining on. And if you gagged on that . . ." he pointed at the uneaten cheeseburger on my plate, "I'd love to see how hard the meal I'll feed ya goes down." He let out a wicked little laugh.

Brogna got up, threw his napkin on the table, placed the scally cap back on his head. He took out his wallet, pulled out a card, tossed it to me. I caught it. "When you're ready, call that. Tell 'em you want Ed, that's me, and just give 'em your first name and a number. From a pay phone. I'll get right back to ya. And don't take long to call, sport." He pulled a few bills from his wallet, dropped them on the table, turned and left.

I watched him walk from the dining room, noticed heads turning to watch him pass. When he was gone, the waitress returned.

"Anything wrong with the burger?" Her voice was rock steady now that Brogna was gone.

"I'm just not hungry." I looked down at the rare burger and realized I wouldn't have been able to eat it even if it had looked like a hockey puck. My stomach was in a knot. And that was the truth.

CHAPTER 35

AFTER MY LUNCH with Myles Brogna, I made a quick call to Cousin Billy. I told him it was important that I see him. We agreed to meet at Cambridge police headquarters. On the drive there, I mulled over my face-to-face with Brogna and how it had gone.

I'd done as well as could be expected. Brogna hadn't gone ballistic on me, which is one of the things I'd been concerned about, especially after our phone conversation. Matter of fact, the man had been almost gentlemanly. I wasn't naive though; I realized that it was all an act. I knew if he was given the opportunity to feed me my penis for dinner with no repercussions, he'd do it and laugh. I had to very careful. Watch the man like I was dealing with a genuine psychopath.

By the time I reached Cambridge I was convinced that, as long as I didn't make any mistakes, we could pull this off. Brogna was, above all, a businessman. A criminal business-man, but still, a businessman. As long as he couldn't read minds, the plan should work.

When I reached Cousin Billy's cubicle, I found him behind his desk, shuffling papers. He looked up, motioned me to sit. "How did it go?"

"I met with him. He's agreed to swap the cook for the Worthman girl."

For the second time that day, I was told to keep my voice down. "There's more snoops around here than at a PTA meeting. What else did he say?"

The ashtray on the desk was jammed with butts and the cubicle smelled it. "Just that he'll swap the girl for Elliot."

"Elliot? What are you two, best friends now?"

"Never mind that," I said irritably. "We'll get the girl. That's what we wanted."

Billy looked at me like I was stupid. "You think you can trust a man like Brogna?"

"He wants the cook, Billy. He doesn't give a shit about the Worthman girl. She was just a sex toy to him. Christ, he's got a store full of those in Boston."

He smirked. "Yeah, you'd know about that wouldn't you?"

"Ha, ha. Very funny. But I think as long as we're careful we'll get her back fine. Right now I'm trying to figure out something else."

"What might that be?"

"How are we going to put Brogna out of business as an added bonus?"

"It's not going to be easy."

"That's a given." I said. "We also have to make certain that bringing down Brogna doesn't bounce back on my friends."

"What about you?"

"He already knows all about me. I'll take my chances."

"I can believe that. You like taking chances."

"What do you mean?"

Billy folded his hands on the desk like he was praying. "What happened to Dalton. Goddamn, is he fucked up. You could have killed him, for Chrissake."

I tried to feign shock. "I don't know what you're talking about."

He waved like he was batting at a fly. "Bullshit. I put two and two together the minute I heard the meat wagon picked him up behind your building, and it added up to four. But you're a lucky suck. I guess you scared him good, 'cause he's claiming he was beaten by some anonymous drug dealers he stumbled on."

"Yeah?"

"Yeah. But you still better watch your ass. His partner, Cummings, is an amateur mathematician, too. He'll know two and two equals four, just like I did. Whether Dalton tells him or not."

Cummings didn't worry me. I didn't have time for it. He'd have to get in line behind everyone else that wanted a piece of me. I was bothered though by the fact that I knew I'd gone too far that day. The beating I'd given Dalton had bothered me since shortly after it had happened. I'd lost control. Why, I didn't know. But I couldn't dwell on it. Not now. Not with everything else that was going down. So I told Billy the same thing I'd been telling myself since it had happened. "Forget it. What about nailing Brogna?"

Billy smiled, fired up a smoke. He blew bluish rings toward the ceiling. "Like I told ya, you're a lucky suck. Your friend Elliot isn't."

"What do you mean?"

Billy leaned in close, lowered his voice. I had to move even closer to hear him. "I got a friend, a fed."

"A narc?"

"I'm not saying. Now let me finish." He placed the burning cig in the crowded ashtray. "Your friend Elliot will be indicted soon. They've had enough evidence on him for a while now."

I couldn't help it—I got excited. "So we better move fast. He gets indicted, or if Brogna gets wind it's coming down, we'll lose our leverage."

"That's only part of it, Sherlock. I've got more interesting info than just that." We were almost nose to nose. He was making me sweat. I could tell he liked it. I had to restrain myself from wiping the smirk off his face.

Finally, he started again. "So like I said, they've got all they need on the cook. They've been holding off, hoping to get their hooks into Brogna. They haven't been able to, though. Of course, when they pull your friend Elliot in, they're going to squeeze him hard and they figure he'll roll over pretty easy. I think they're right. Christ, a college kid like him? He wouldn't be in the federal pen more than a week before he'd be the girlfriend of some big black buck." He chuckled; I didn't.

"So Brogna'll go down, too?"

Billy sat back, shrugged. "My friend isn't sure the cook's testimony alone will be enough to make it stick. Brogna's got the best lawyers in Boston. They might be able to come up with a way out for him. That's why they were hoping to get something on Brogna in addition to the cook flipping." He hesitated, then added, "He thinks that if Brogna was caught holding his own product, that would be the icing on the cake as far as getting a conviction."

I thought for a minute, watched Billy light up again and resume his smoke ring exhibition. That's when a gruff voice said from behind me, "If it isn't, Dick Tracy. Who let you in?"

I turned in my chair. It was Cummings, Dalton's partner.

"He's visiting me, Bob."

Cummings snickered. "You got the shit end of the stick as far as relatives go, Skinner."

I stared up at him. He looked even bigger from my angle. "You got a problem, Sergeant?"

He looked at me like he wanted to kill me. "Yeah, I got a big problem with you, jerk-off. But we'll discuss it sometime when it's a little more private."

I started to rise. Billy grabbed my arm. "Get the hell out of here, Cummings. You're stinking up my cube."

Cummings looked at the overflowing ashtray, snickered. "I'll talk to you later, Malloy." He jabbed me in the shoulder with an index finger that felt like an iron spike. Billy held onto my arm. Cummings' eyes narrowed as he gave me a last look before he walked away.

I turned back to Billy, rubbed my shoulder. "I guess you were right about him thinking I had something to do with Dalton getting worked over."

"Of course that's what he thinks. I don't know how the hell you thought you were going to get away with it."

"He'll let Brogna know I was here."

Billy pointed his chin in the direction Cummings had gone. "He knows we're family. I'm hoping that's all he thinks we got going."

I got back to the discussion we were having before Cummings interrupted. "So we have to find a way to get him arrested while holding his own product?"

Billy scowled. "Yeah. And that'll be tough. I'm sure the man never touches it himself."

"There's got to be a way," I said.

Billy looked up at the ceiling. It was dirty white with rows of tubular fluorescent lights. It lit the place up like daylight. "We have to put on our thinking caps."

"They better be extra large." We were both silent for a couple of minutes. Finally, I spoke. "If Brogna never handles the drugs himself, I only see one option. And there's two major problems with it. One—where do we get some meth? Two—how do we get it into Brogna's possession?"

Billy put his elbows on the desk, steepled his hands under his chin. "Those problems are a little too delicate for me to get involved in, Mike. That'd be up to you. Matter of fact, don't tell me any more. But my friend did say if I ever got wind Brogna was holding, they'd be willing to move in for a federal bust quickly. I've known him a long time, and if he says he'll do something, he'll do it. So there is a possibility there."

Yes, there was. But could I take advantage of it? I just sat there, mulled it over in my mind. I couldn't come up with a thing.

"Don't forget Brogna'll get suspicious if you take too long to call him. When did you say you would?"

"I didn't. But he said to make it soon."

"Soon means soon."

"That's a third problem. Not only do I have to come up with something, I have to make it fast."

"Yes, you do. Now I got to get back to work." Billy made that motion with his hand again like he was a king dismissing a subject. I didn't like it. Made me feel like a peasant.

I told him I'd keep in touch, then left his cubicle. The chatter from police radios, clack of typewriters, and male voices filled my head as I walked through the building. When I got outside I stopped on the sidewalk, tried to think. I couldn't. My mind was foggy. I felt like someone who might go off half-cocked and make a mistake. There was only one thing I could do.

I stopped at the first pay phone I saw, called Stoney at the beach, spoke meaningless chitchat for a minute. When I finally asked, in coded language, about the real reason I'd called, he gave me the number of someone else he said was reliable. Within an hour, I had a gram of cocaine along with a blue Valium to add to my collection and was back in my apartment. I sat in my chair, snorting the coke, drinking beer, and going over the Brogna conundrum. The TV was on with the sound low, and I discarded different ideas as they rolled through my brain.

It was just before dawn when my thoughts finally jelled.

CHAPTER 36

WHEN I WOKE late the next morning, I didn't feel great. In addition to a moderate hangover, I hadn't had enough sleep. Still, I was ready to put my brainchild from the night before into motion. I wolfed down a little food, showered, dressed. I left the apartment and went to a pay phone in front of my favorite liquor store. Inside the booth, I watched as a few patrons entered and left the store. Finally, I called Stoney. I asked him to buy our guest a change of clothes somewhere—a couple of pairs of everything—the next time Tank came to relieve him. He asked what was up. I just said that Elliot must be getting ripe.

"Now that you mention it," Stoney said.

My next move was to track down Tank. That wasn't hard. He took my call at the Burgundy Lounge. Even the threat of retaliation from Myles Brogna hadn't had Tank change his routine. I guess he lived in a world of danger. He agreed to meet me there at one o'clock.

Walking through the Zone on my way to the Burgundy, I had a flashback to the last night I'd been in the area. It was the smell of cheap pizza mixed with disinfectant that triggered it. That and the garish facades of businesses I thought I might have seen from the inside. I tried to push the thoughts from my mind. Still, there was something about the place. Not any real attraction, of course. It had just been the cocaine that had brought me here that night. Nothing more. I wouldn't be caught dead here otherwise. Unless, it was for business, like I was on now. I couldn't understand what had gotten into me, except probably too much of the drug. I wouldn't let that happen again.

When I entered the lounge and my eyes had adjusted to the dim light, I saw Tank sitting in the upper level exactly where he'd been the last time we'd met here. I made my way toward him. Colored lights flashed, rock music throbbed with heavy bass, and a scantily clad go-go dancer gyrated wildly in a cage above the bar. Again there was a battle between cigarette smoke and some type of cleaning product to be the dominant aroma. I knew the smoke would win eventually.

When I reached Tank, he gave a light shove to a man wearing a business suit seated beside him at the bar, motioned him to move over so I could sit down. The businessman, probably there for a three-martini lunch and some ogling, glanced at Tank and moved quickly over.

When I sat, Tank gave me a back slap that would have gotten a dead man breathing. "How goes it, Mikey?" Then he waved at a tough-looking female bartender. "Hey, sweetheart, a Schlitz for my compadre. Do me, too."

We both studied the semi-nude gyrating blonde in the cage while we waited for the beers. The dancer looked bored. I didn't blame her. I looked around the bar. Half the stools were occupied. At this time of the day, except for me, Tank and some bikers, there were only a few businessmen, probably on lunch break, who looked like they were capable of tipping the dancers. The rest of the faces had desolation written on them. Most were street people, losers in one way or another, getting a cheap drink before the prices went up in the late afternoon when the after-work commuter crowd came in. The street people would leave then. And they'd leave no tips behind for anyone—bartender or dancers. That's just the way it was. The way it had always been.

The waitress brought our beers. We both took a healthy swig. Tank wiped his beard with his hairy arm.

"So how's it going?" he asked.

I leaned toward him. "Good." I lowered my voice. "I had a meet . . ."

"Talk louder," Tank interrupted. "I can't hear ya with the fuckin' music. Don't worry, no one else can either."

I raised my voice a notch. "I had a meet with our friend." I could tell he was still struggling to hear me. He moved closer. His leather vest smelled like oil. I raised my voice a bit more. "We're going to do the swap."

"Good." He took another plug on his beer, thumped the bottle down on the bar. A few heads looked towards us, then quickly turned the other way.

I didn't say anything else, but I must have given myself away because Tank eyed me suspiciously. "There's something else," he said. "Isn't there?"

I watched the go-go girl. "Remember what I said about maybe making our friend go down big time? How would you feel about that?"

He guffawed. "You kiddin'? About as good as a junkie after their first fix of the day. The man's a sleaze bag, a damn pervert. And I told ya, he's still tryin' to muscle in here. Not to mention the Demons are number one on our shit list, and he's the one who's feeding them all their dough. Without him, they'd be nothing. Just like they should be."

I ran the basics of my plan past him. I had to leave a couple of things out, including Cousin Billy's involvement. I was vague about the fed, just that things had been arranged. He didn't press me on that point; I think he trusted me.

He smiled behind that bushy beard. "Let's do it then. The prick deserves it if anyone does."

I nodded. "There's one problem though—the speed."

"What's the problem there?"

I think he knew, but he wanted me to say it. "We need to get hold of a good amount of meth, Tank."

"That ain't no problem," he said. Then took it partially back. "Well, it might be a little problem, but *we* can get it."

I didn't mind him emphasizing the *we*. I couldn't expect him to take care of the problem by himself.

I could see that he was raking over something in his mind. He drank his beer gingerly, set it down carefully this time. I did the same.

Finally, he said, "It'd be plenty . . . what do they call it?"

"Ironic?" I answered, having an idea what he meant.

He nodded his big head. His long greasy hair shook. "Yeah, ironic . . . that's it." He pointed a finger at me. "Listen to this."

He told me that his club knew who some of the large scale dealers for the Demons were and where they lived. "We never made a move on any of them because it would've started a war. But I'm thinking if they're going to be losing their main source of bread—and maybe some of them'll get busted heavy too—they might have more on their minds than trying to figure out who ripped off one of their dealers."

It was good reasoning and it *would* be very ironic, that was for sure. Myles Brogna getting caught with some of his very own product. How fitting and well deserved that would be. "I think there's a good chance some of the Devil's Demons will get caught up in the investigation," I finally said. "I can't promise, though."

"That's all right. Even if they just lose that source of dough, that'll be it for them. They'll fall apart. Everybody'll defect. That's all they got goin' for them." He turned, looked at me warily. "One thing, Mikey."

"What?"

"The rip-off. There's no way I can disguise myself." He looked down at his body. "No matter what I'd do, my size'd give me away. A couple of words from the dealer and I'd be right at the top of the Demons' suspect list."

The man was one hundred percent right. If he was going along, he might just as well go unmasked, his size made him that recognizable. "I can do it alone," I said.

"You sure, Mikey? I can help with everything except going inside. You can do that?"

"I did okay the last time," I said, referring to our snatching of JoJo.

"Yeah, you did. But look who the hell you had for back-up." He looked at me with a straight face that held for more than a few seconds before he broke into a roar of laughter. A few heads at the bar turned.

"You can get me the info I'll need?"

"I can get it. I still think you might need someone to do the heavy work with you. I can't ask any of my brothers though. Some of them might not like our idea, so I'd like to keep them in the dark about this."

I did too. Maybe not for the same reason though. Just because I trusted this biker didn't mean I trusted every biker. "We don't want anyone else knowing about this anyway. Like I said, I'll do it myself."

"You got a piece you can use?" Tank asked. "Not traceable?"

I thought of my .38. "Only a registered one. But I won't be using it, so it doesn't matter. It'll just be for show."

Tank looked down at his beer. "You never know. I'll get you one that's clean."

That made me uneasy, but I said, "All right. But we have to move fast on this."

"The piece is no problem—I can get that quick. I'll have the skinny on who's holding, where, and how much by tomorrow. How about if I give you a call then?"

"That'll do." I stood up from my stool.

"You don't want another? I'm buying."

"No, thanks. I gotta go."

"All right then. I'll call ya." Tank stood and I glanced up at him as he gave me one of his infamous bear hugs that did a more extensive back adjustment than a chiropractor could. When he was done, he threw in a back slap that almost sent me to my knees.

I walked through the Burgundy, a little twinge of back pain with every step I took. Outside the sun was bright. It didn't make the Zone look any less dingy.

CHAPTER 37

I WAS SURE Tank would come through for me. He wasn't the type who just bragged. If he said he could find out which of the Demons' dealers was holding speed, I had no doubt he was telling the truth. The one thing I did have doubt about was whether I could hold up my end of the plan. I wasn't a professional stickup man, after all. Matter of fact, the last thing I'd stolen was a few bills from my old man's wallet when I was a kid. And that still bothered me.

Then I suddenly remembered that hadn't been the last time I'd stolen something. I'd done it at Stoney's apartment just recently. He'd gone into the bathroom and I'd helped myself to a tiny portion of the coke he'd left on the table. I took it with me when I left. It was a stupid thing to do; he would have given it to me if I'd asked. I'd felt horrible about it later. Stealing from a friend was pretty low. But I'd needed extra coke that night to help me with my plans for the Worthman case. So maybe I'd had an honorable reason to take it. At least that's what I'd told myself.

And I was going to need a little something extra again if I was going to handle this speed rip-off. Just to give me the confidence that I could do it. That was the main thing in something like this—having the confidence you could do it. If you had that confidence, you were halfway home.

When I got back to my apartment, I decided to call the coke dealer Stoney had turned me on to earlier. His product didn't seem quite as good as Stoney's, but it had been decent. Besides, I didn't want Stoney to know I was using as much as I was. Not that I was using all that much, but you know the ideas people can get.

I had no trouble reaching the other dealer. I arranged to purchase a gram. I'd learned my lesson on what could happen with larger amounts.

I did two small lines at the dealer's apartment. When I left, I felt better, more confident. I had the coke in my pocket and promised myself I'd wait until tomorrow to use more. This was for business, not pleasure. I drove, parked my car near my apartment. Instead of going in, I decided to go to O'Toole's. I'd told myself earlier it was best to stay away from the bar. But I couldn't and I knew why. Julie.

Just before I reached my destination, I stepped into a pay phone booth, called Julie at her girlfriend's. I knew I shouldn't have, but I had to. When I was done, I walked to O'Toole's, went in. I nodded to a couple of the regulars as I made my way toward the rear and claimed my customary stool. It was late afternoon and the place was moderately crowded with workers stopping in for a pop after their stint in the salt mine.

Wally was behind the bar. He was the opposite of Jake— young, hip, with moderately long dark hair. He had my Schlitz draft in front of me before I had time to figure out what was on the TV. It turned out to be an inane talk show.

"No Jake?" I asked.

"Somethin' came up. He's taking the day off."

I wondered if it had anything to do with our project, then realized that Jake wasn't as wrapped up in this thing as I was, and that he probably had a normal life with normal day-to-day problems.

"How's the PI business going, Mike?" Wally kept his eyes on the customers farther down the bar as he spoke to me. He had his ass resting against the back bar, his arms folded across his chest.

"Quiet," I lied.

He turned to look at me. "Any dough in that racket—if you don't mind me asking?"

I shook my head, set my beer down after a slow sip. "No, I don't mind you asking." Then I answered, "There's less dough in it than in an out-of-business bakery."

Wally sighed. "I'm looking for something else for myself. I was wondering . . . but if there's no money in it, what's the point?"

"Not only is there not much money in it, it's chock-full of aggravation."

He held up one hand, waved. "I don't need any more of that. I got more aggravation than someone in line at a sold-out rock concert."

I took another swig, glanced toward the door. "Believe me, you're better off here."

He stood up straight. "I'm happy here. It's just I could use more money. Kids are damn expensive, let me tell you."

"I've heard. But there's no easy money anymore."

"I guess you're right." He sighed again. "But if you hear of any, let me know, will you?"

I laughed. "Of course, I will. Same goes for you."

We went around like that for a while. Us talking about the economy and how bad it was. Him bringing me a couple more beers, occasionally peeling himself away from our conversation to attend to other customers.

The idle chitchat only faltered when the door opened and in the back bar mirror I could see Julie come in and start walking in my direction. Wally knew who she was, of course. But he looked at her a little longer than he did most customers who entered O'Toole's. Most men who saw her did. Sometimes even a woman or two.

I pushed the stool beside me out, and she slipped onto it. She was dressed as usual—jeans, soft brown leather coat, and this time a light-blue blouse, silk maybe? There was a thin gold chain around her neck. The blouse wasn't cut low. Still, I could see the rise at the top of her breasts, they weren't large or small, and the way her nipples pushed at the soft material. I tried not to look at her nose.

Wally stepped up to Julie, put a cocktail napkin on the bar in front of her. "Hi, Julie. What can I get you?"

"Soda with lime," she said.

When he'd left to get Julie's drink, she said, "Well? Are you going to tell me how our project is going?"

"Probably the less you know the better," I said truthfully.

She looked at me curiously. "Then why did you call?"

Wally came back, dropped off her drink. He leaned against the back bar for a minute, looked uncomfortable, then left.

I swirled my beer in the glass. "I wanted to thank you for what you did the other night. You took a chance and you did great."

"You already told me that, Mike. Remember? In the car?"

I only remembered one thing in the car. "Yeah, well . . . I guess I wanted to tell you again."

Down at the other end of the bar a couple of guys were going back and forth arguing sports. Julie turned to look at them. I looked at the back of her head and the dirty blonde hair that brushed the top of her coat.

When she turned back toward me, she looked serious. She spoke seriously, too. "I don't appreciate being treated like a kid, Mike. I helped in this. I want to know how it's going."

She was pissed; she had a right.

"I'm only trying to keep you from getting hurt."

She stared at me. I drank my beer. She wouldn't take her eyes off my face.

I set the beer down, just as another one materialized. Wally was there and gone faster than the Roadrunner. Finally, I shrugged. Started to tell her what she wanted to know.

"I had a meeting with Brogna. He's agreed to a swap—the cook for Susan Worthman."

"When?"

"I'm not sure. Soon. A day or two, hopefully."

She reached over touched my arm; I jumped. "I don't trust him, Mike. Who's going to bring Elliot to Brogna? You? That'll be dangerous."

I looked at her hand on my arm, then at her face and that damn crooked nose. "I have to do it. It's my job. Besides, I'll pick the place and the time. And maybe I'll have someone come with me. It'll be all right."

Her voice grew louder, her blue eyes sparked. "And what if it's not all right? What if he does something?"

"Shhh," I said.

"He's a killer, for God's sake. He could kill you!"

I tried to calm her down. "Nothing's going to happen. I'll make sure we're in a public place with lots of people around. Even *he* wouldn't try anything in a situation like that."

She wasn't buying it. "What about later? He knows who you are. He could come after you then. Whenever he wanted. Can't you get the police to handle it from here? Mike, please." She was talking louder still, and she was halfway to hysterical.

I didn't want to tell her that the police were already involved and that if things went according to my plan, Myles Brogna wouldn't get a chance to go after me, or anyone else for that matter. The less she knew, the safer she'd be. "I can't do that, Julie."

She started to tear up and sniffled. And for some reason my mind glommed onto the thought of that night, the night in this exact same spot, both of us seated right where we were now, the night she stuck the knife in my shoulder and I deformed that one-of-a-kind-face of hers for life. All of a sudden, my throat tightened and my head felt light.

"I have to go to the men's room. I'll be right back."

I was off the stool so fast she didn't have time to respond. When I got inside, I stood at the urinal. My heart was thumping. I thought of leaving without her knowing. I could have probably gotten out the back door undetected. I almost decided to do it, then changed my mind.

What the hell was the matter with me? Was it just that night long ago that was driving me sideways? Sure, I'd hurt her and I'd always feel guilty about that. But the woman had stabbed me, for the love of God. And after all, it was only a broken nose. I hadn't slashed her face with a broken beer bottle. I shuddered when that thought entered my mind. It could've happened.

There was no one else in the bathroom, but someone could come at any time. I stepped into one of the stalls, locked it behind me. My hands shook, so I closed the toilet cover. I pulled out the coke, opened the folded paper, and dumped a small mound on the back of the toilet tank. Put the rest back and chopped at the pile like a madman with my driver's license. I wasn't fussy; the job was half-ass. I rolled a bill, snorted both lines quick as I could. I don't know how I felt when I was done. I didn't have time to take stock. I just got out of there, checked my nose in the mirror, went back, and took my seat beside Julie.

I think she looked at me funny, but I couldn't be sure. She seemed to have calmed down somewhat. As for me, the anxiety symptoms I'd felt had left me, but now I was jacked-up, my mind on something else. I signaled Wally for a refill for both of us.

Julie touched my arm again, this time squeezing it. "Promise me you'll be careful, Mike. If anything . . ."

I interrupted her. "I will be. Very careful. It'll be fine." I pretended I was looking over her head to see where Wally was. She was looking straight ahead now. I could see the side of her face, just that little dusting of makeup, the smooth neck. From this angle her nose looked perfect, like the rest of her. I caught her scent. I was getting hard. As I turned back, I saw her staring at me in the back bar mirror. She smiled.

She slid from her stool, her thigh brushed mine. She was close to me now. If we hadn't been in a public place I would've . . . "I'll be right back," she said, turning and walking towards the ladies' room. I watched her go. I wanted her so bad. But I couldn't risk going back to my place with her, even if she would. That could be dangerous for her. And she was staying at her friends. So we couldn't go there.

Wally dropped off the drinks. "You said Jake won't be in tonight?" I asked.

He nodded.

I felt ridiculous asking, but not so ridiculous that I didn't. "I wonder if I could use his office?"

Wally smiled. "I don't blame you," he said, then caught himself. "No insult meant. Ahhh. Yeah, I guess so." Then quickly added, "Don't tell Jake though."

"You don't have to worry about that." Then I asked, "Is it locked?"

"No. He keeps it unlocked so I can get in if I need anything."

Wally walked away when Julie returned. She'd only been seated for a moment when she said, hesitatingly, "Would you like to go to your apartment?"

She was leaning so close to me I could smell her minty breath. "*That* would be dangerous," I said. I felt stupid, but I screwed up my courage and added, "We could watch TV in Jake's office."

"Is it all right?"

"Yes." I waited for a moment, then said, "Why don't you go first. People'll think you're going out the back door. I'll come in a couple of minutes."

She smiled. "All right, Mike." She got off the stool and headed in the direction of the corridor that led to Jake's office.

I reached for my beer, drained the glass. I waved the empty in Wally's direction. He came right along with another beer. I was plenty nervous. Whether it was the coke, Julie, or everything else that was going on, I didn't know or care. I'd told myself I was going to stay away from her, but how could I? When I was thinking like this, I always remembered the way it was once, back then, when she meant everything to me. Maybe she still did. I killed the beer in three gulps, squared my bar bill, and headed for the office.

When I reached it, I opened the door, stepped inside, closed it behind me. There were no lights on; I didn't try to change that. I just stood there, waiting for my eyes to adjust to the darkness.

I saw her shadow move toward me. She said huskily, "Lock the door, Mike."

I didn't have to be told twice. I could see her now. She stood right in front of me. The thin gold necklace stood out in the semi-darkness. It was all she had on. My heart was beating heavily, my palms were sweating. I reached to unbutton my shirt.

She took a step forward, pushed my hand gently out of the way. "No," she breathed. "Let me do it . . . all."

She slowly unbuttoned my shirt, slid it off my shoulders, and let it fall to the floor. My chin rested on the top of her head. I felt her tongue touching my chest, then her lips planting little kisses, teasing me. I reached for my belt.

Again, she gently pushed my hand away. "No, let me."

She leaned her breasts against me and eased me across the floor until I was backed up to a leather couch. I dropped onto it. She came down to the floor on her knees. She slipped my shoes and socks off and pulled my belt free.

I could see clearly now, and I just stared at that beautiful face. Every so often she would look up at me and smile. When my pants were off, she used her tongue first on my stomach and then on the inside of my thighs. She slid my underwear off and stood.

She just looked down at me, said, "Don't you move."

I didn't.

She lowered herself, her knees resting on the couch, either side of my thighs. She took one of her hands, and with that soft palm, slowly stroked the side of my face and ran it through my hair. With her other hand she ever so gently, like a warm feather, stroked my cock. I don't think it had ever been so hard. My head went back against the couch, moving from side to side. I was in ecstasy; it felt so goddamn good.

I tried to reach for her shoulders. She moved away. "Don't. I want to do this for you."

Even with the coke in me, I couldn't have held off much longer. No man could have. She must have sensed that. She stopped, held my face with her hands, and kissed me. Her tongue tasted so good. I was afraid if she bumped me it would be over.

Somehow she must have been able to tell when I was ready, when it was safe. She circled her small, soft warm hand around me again as she rose up and directed me into her. She lowered herself and I was home. Just where I was meant to be.

CHAPTER 38

TANK DIDN'T WASTE any time. He called early the next morning, and we agreed to meet at a coffee shop on Route 28 in Stoneham. He gave me the rundown. Told me all about where I was going. I didn't ask but I assumed he'd talked with someone who'd done business with this dealer. He passed me what he said was a long-barreled .22 in a large paper bag just before we parted ways. He assured me it couldn't be traced. I was hoping I wouldn't need it for anything more than show.

My destination was just a few miles up the road in North Reading. An apartment complex with lots of buildings, all two-story brick garden-style jobs. Each building had below ground units, too. That's where my target lived—in a basement apartment—number 102, in Building 1.

Tank had said that mid to late morning was perfect for this type of operation because meth dealers weren't usually early risers, so I was likely to catch him at home. He also said that Creighton Larson—that was his name—was definitely holding and that it was Demons' crank. Their crank was Brogna's crank, so it was fitting.

When I arrived at the complex, I drove the Karmann Ghia in and circled around the area until I found the building marked -1-. I parked further down, near Building 4, behind a dumpster that kept the car out of sight. I put a few other items into the bag with the gun. I'd decided coke wouldn't have helped me with this job. My heart was thumping as it was. So I took half a blue Valium, placed it under my tongue, let it dissolve. I sat there for a few minutes, got my courage up. When I felt it was now or never, I got out of the car with the bag and walked casually to the front of my target building. I saw no one and there weren't many cars around. Most of the residents were probably at work.

I went up a few stairs and through the first set of doors. There were mailboxes with buzzers to the left. All were numbered, most with the tenant's name. Number 102 was blank. I started with the top buzzer, pressed it. Nothing. I repeated this process, skipping 102, until on my sixth try, an elderly sounding woman's voice came through the intercom.

"Yes," she said shakily.

"UPS delivery, ma'am," I said authoritatively.

There was a click and I quickly opened the inner door and stepped inside the hallway. I took the five or six stairs down to the basement level. Pushed quietly through swinging doors. The apartment was where it was supposed to be—on my right, a door with the gold numbers 102 on it. Also where it was supposed to be—on my left, kitty-corner from 102, was the laundry room. I slipped inside, closing the door all but a crack. The room was empty—of people that is. There was a large mustard-colored pay washing machine with a matching clothes dryer beside it. A long wooden table for placing and folding clothes stood in the middle of the room. A bare bulb was above the table, giving off a harsh light. I found the switch for that, turned it off. When my eyes were accustomed to the semi-darkness, I turned back to the door I'd left ajar. I had a perfect view of apartment number 102 across the hall.

I took a pair of thin black leather gloves from the bag and put them on. I also removed a roll of duct tape and put it in my jacket pocket. Next, I pulled a blue ski mask over my head. When I was done, I held the bag with the gun at my side, stared at the apartment door, and waited.

I wish I could say I didn't have long to wait, but I did. Before the first hour was over my neck had a very uncomfortable kink in it from peering through the crack. My face was itchy and sweaty from the ski mask. The only good thing was that no tenants had showed up during that time to wash their dirty underwear. If that had happened I would have had to rip the mask and gloves off quick. I had some half-baked speech ready about being there to look for some socks. Hopefully, the place was large enough that the tenants didn't know all their neighbors. Even still, if a tenant had shown up, I would have had to make tracks out of there before someone called the cops. Fortunately, it didn't come to that.

I'd been acting like a peeping Tom for almost two hours when the knob on 102 turned and the door opened. I had to blink a couple of times, make sure I wasn't hallucinating. I already had thought I'd seen that doorknob turn a couple of times before. They'd been false alarms, probably because of my nerves; this wasn't. A tall, lanky man stepped out into the hallway. He had medium-length black hair, a black leather car coat, and jeans. In his hand, he held a briefcase. As he closed the door and fumbled with the lock, I fumbled getting the pistol out of the paper bag. I dropped the empty bag to the floor and came out of the laundry room while he still had his back to me. I took the few steps up to him and pushed the muzzle against his back.

"Don't bother locking it," I said. I sounded calm, which surprised me. "Open the door and step inside."

He did what he was told. He didn't even turn to look at me. I stepped in behind him, nudged him forward with the gun. I reached my free hand behind me, quietly closed the door. I took my eyes off him just long enough to snap the deadbolt into place.

The apartment was your standard suburban garden-style set-up. A living room with two easy chairs, couch, TV, coffee table and a dark brown wall-to-wall rug. There was a small open kitchen with the usual appliances. On the far side of the living room were two doors I assumed led to the bathroom and the bedroom. From what I could see, it was pretty clean and neat. Not like my apartment. Or what you'd think a meth dealer's would look like. Resembled more that of a tidy middle-aged bachelor's. A legitimate one that is.

"Walk toward the red chair." He did; I followed. "Take your coat off and drop it on the floor. Slowly, carefully." He did, switching the briefcase from hand to hand.

"You got a gun?" He shook his head. "Don't even breathe," I said as I used my free hand to thoroughly pat him down. Clean.

"Put the briefcase on the coffee table, then sit." He set the case down where I'd told him, then moved the few steps to the red chair, his back still towards me.

Just before he turned to sit, I said, "Hold it." I moved closer, pushed him aside, and kept the gun on him. I tried to lift the chair's pillow seat. It was attached; it didn't lift. "All right. Go ahead. Sit." I stepped back.

When he turned and sat, I got a good look at him. He was a homely man but not particularly threatening looking. And even though he appeared like he might use his own product occasionally, he didn't resemble your average speed freak. Matter of fact, he didn't look much like you'd think a meth dealer would either. He more closely resembled a small businessman on his way to open his store for the day. Except for the smirk, there was no sign of aggression. Still, I had to be very careful.

"Anyone else here?"

He spoke for the first time. "No," he said. His voice had a touch of disdain in it, like I was an irritation.

I kept the gun on him as I walked around his chair and backed across the room to the closest door. I put my hand behind me, turned the knob and swung it open. I glanced at the interior. It was an unoccupied bathroom. I repeated the process, checking out the other room, more carefully this time. It was the bedroom, as I'd expected. I stepped into it, keeping an eye on Creighton Larson all the time. He hadn't lied. There was no one there. I returned to him, noticed his eyes dancing around. I wondered if he'd done speed today.

I stood over him, said, "Open it." I pointed the gun at the briefcase. "So I can see the inside when you do."

He spun the case toward me, released the two clasps, and lifted the lid. Inside were various papers, a small spiral notebook, and a clear plastic Ziplock bag with a gray powder in it. I picked the bag up, let it roll open so it was hanging loose. Even zippered tight, I noticed a chemical smell. I wasn't familiar with large weights of illegal powder but I knew it wasn't anywhere near what I was looking for.

"How much is here?" I asked.

"Half-ounce."

"What's it worth?"

"Why? You want to buy it?" He let out a sarcastic little chuckle.

I moved the gun a half-foot closer to his head.

"Six hundred."

I was right. It wasn't enough. I'd need much more weight for my plan to work. A small amount like this might not do it. In fact, it might be worse than nothing. An enraged—free— Myles Brogna would be very dangerous and not just to me.

"Where's the rest of it?" I asked Larson. Tank had assured me that there would be closer to a pound of methamphetamine here.

Larson sneered. "You got it all, Jack. Now why don't you just take it and get the hell out of here."

That was something I couldn't do. I'd come this far and I wasn't going to turn back now. People's lives, friends' lives, were depending on a positive outcome here, whether they knew it or not. Besides, I had no Plan B.

I considered giving the place a good toss but shelved that idea. I couldn't search the apartment adequately without giving Larson an opportunity to make a play. For all I knew there could be a gun hidden somewhere within his reach. That wouldn't be good.

"I want the rest of it, Larson." I was pissed now and he must have sensed it. He wasn't sarcastic anymore but he was defiant.

"I told you—that's all there is." He nodded toward the Ziploc bag I'd dropped on the coffee table. "I wouldn't be stupid enough to leave more here." He sat up higher.

Tank said he *was* stupid enough to leave more here. A lot more. And I believed Tank. I had too.

"That's not what I heard."

"You heard wrong, asshole."

I took two quick steps and swung the gun backhanded faster than Larson could get his hands up. It caught him flush on the cheekbone. I heard bone crack. His head snapped back and his hands shot up to his ugly face, covering it.

"You motherfucker!" he screamed. "I'll fuckin' kill you!"

I backed up as he lowered his hands and looked at the blood covering them. There was a nasty, deep gash on his cheek. As he stared at his blood-stained hands, more blood ran down from the wound on his face onto his shirt.

"Where is it?" I tried again.

He looked at me, his face bloody and angry. "Fuck you."

There was only one thing to do. I couldn't hesitate or debate the pros and cons. I held the pistol out straight. Larson reared back and I fired. It was only a .22, so the noise wasn't bad, and it didn't do the damage a magnum or even my .38 would have done, but you wouldn't have known it by the way he howled when the slug slammed into his kneecap.

He grabbed his knee with both bloody hands and pulled it to his chest like he was doing an exercise in the gym. His upper body rocked back and forth, his teeth bared and clenched. He let go of the knee and moved his hands to the sides of his thigh so he could stretch his leg out.

There was only a small hole in the material of his jeans near the knee, but there was a lot of blood. I couldn't tell how much blood was from the gunshot or from his blood-soaked hands.

"Jesus Christ," he said, not sounding quite so defiant now. "You shot me!"

I aimed the gun from his knee to the center of his face. "And I'm going to shoot you one last time if you don't talk," I said as calmly as if I shot people every day.

If he didn't fold, I don't know what I would've done next. Fortunately, it didn't come to that. "All right. All right. It's in the bedroom," he said, pointing his chin in that direction.

"Get it," I said.

"I can't walk."

I shifted the gun to his other knee. "Would you rather crawl?"

He was up and off the couch like a spring had popped under his ass. I followed him as he limped toward the bedroom. He left a thin trail of blood on the carpet as he went. Inside the room he headed for the bed, which was nicely made, and reached for one of the pillows.

"Hold it," I said. "I'll do that. Move over."

I motioned for him to back against a wall, where he stopped, leaned over, and held his knee with one hand. The blood from his face wound dripped constantly onto the carpet. I kept one eye on him as I grabbed the pillow and managed to shake it free of the pillowcase while keeping the gun trained on Larson. I placed the pillow on the bed, unzipped the inner case, jammed my hand inside with the pillow. I came out with a large Ziplock bag containing the same grayish powder that the smaller bag held. Actually the stuff was encased in two Ziplock bags. Definitely the amount was a lot more than what was out on the coffee table. The powder in these bags was as thick as a wrist. And even with the double bags, I could smell a sickeningly sweet chemical aroma.

"How much?" I asked.

He was still bent, holding his knee and bleeding on the rug. "A little over a pound," he said glumly.

That, I knew, would do it. Tank had come through again. I set the meth down on a small table beside the bed. "Lie face down on it, Creighton," I said, motioning with the gun at the bed.

He hobbled over, collapsed face down. The fight was all out of him now. Maybe he felt he had nothing left to protect. Until he spoke and I realized he still had one thing he was worried about.

"You aren't going to kill me are you?" He was serious and that didn't make me feel good.

"Would I be doing this if I were going to kill you?" I got on the bed, straddled his legs with my knees. "Put your arms behind your back." I stuck the gun in the back of my pants waistband, where I knew he'd have no chance of reaching it before I could. I took the gray duct tape from my jacket pocket, secured his wrists firmly together. I got off the bed and used the duct tape on his ankles.

"You can't leave me like this." He was almost whimpering. "I'll bleed to death."

I doubted that from the looks of the wounds, but on the other hand I wasn't a doctor. "I'll send an ambulance after I leave."

"Thanks."

"No, thank you, Creighton. You don't know what this means to me." To him this was probably just a run of the mill drug rip-off that he'd tell his associates all about. He'd probably never know the real reason his powder was taken until it was too late. If even then.

"Don't make any noise, or I'll be back." I knew he'd be quiet. He didn't even say anything as I grabbed the meth and left. He wasn't stupid, just happy that he was alive.

I closed the bedroom door behind me. In the kitchen, I pulled out a brown grocery bag from under the kitchen sink and tossed the meth into it. I peeled off my mask and gloves, and tossed them, along with my gun, into the bag. I didn't bother with the small baggie of meth on the coffee table. I wouldn't need it. When I opened the apartment's door with the brown bag to shield my fingerprints and leaned out, I saw the corridor was empty. I walked up the stairs to the building's outside glass door and saw there were no people in the parking lot either. I made it to my car, jammed the bag with the meth and the other items under the front passenger seat, and drove slowly out of the complex.

I drove for a short while until I was in Stoneham again. I stopped at an outside pay phone. I kept my promise to Creighton Larson and made an anonymous call to the North Reading police. By the time they got to Larson and had a chance to talk to him, I'd be safely back in Cambridge. Well, at least back in Cambridge. I wasn't sure how safe I'd be.

All in all, things had gone pretty smoothly. Except for Larson's new facial scar and a lifetime limp, there'd been no other serious injuries and I'd gotten what I'd hoped to. The next step might not be so easy. I wouldn't be dealing with a lightweight. Anything but. I was moving up the ladder. Right to the top.

CHAPTER 39

WHEN I GOT back to my apartment, I took out the bag of meth, felt its heft in my hand. Looked like Creigton Larson had been telling the truth when he'd said it was over a pound. Anyway, it was enough to put my plan into action. I put the meth on an overhead shelf in my bedroom closet, threw a couple of sweaters over it. It wasn't much of a hiding place, but I didn't need a great one—the stuff wasn't going to be there long.

I had a series of calls to make and headed out to use a pay phone. I stopped at the liquor store first, got a few dollars' worth of change. Once inside the booth, I made my first call. It was the number Brogna had given me to use when I was ready to reach him.

I called the number and repeated what Brogna had told me to say. It didn't take long for him to call me back.

"You ready, Malloy?"

"I'm ready."

"You took long enough. That better not mean anything."

"It doesn't."

"For your sake, I hope you're right," he said. "You wanted to call it, sport. So where?"

"Harvard Square. On Cambridge Common. Near the Arlington end."

There was silence for a minute. Finally Brogna said, "I guess I can live with that." Then added, "Just remember."

"What?" I asked without thinking.

He didn't say anything; he didn't have to. I remembered his threats.

"Noon," I said. "Tomorrow."

"Twelve on the button. Don't be late. I don't like people who are late." He slammed the phone down.

My hand shook as I placed the receiver back on the hook.

Now I had to make my second call—to Cousin Billy. He wasn't at the station. I tried his house. I was lucky; he was home.

"Tomorrow noon? Jesus, Mike, you're not giving me much time."

I wondered if I'd made a mistake in not running the time by Billy first before arranging it with Brogna. That doubt only lasted seconds. Billy would have had to get in touch with his fed friend and I knew how cops—local, state and federal—operated. There was too much red tape. Especially with two law enforcement agencies involved. They would have gone back and forth over it, trying to agree on a time and a place for so long that Brogna would have known something was up. No, I was right to take the chance. There'd been no other way.

"Can you get your friend to do what he promised?" I asked. If he couldn't, a big part of what I had planned would be dead in the water.

He was only silent for a moment. "Well, he did say he could move quick. And seeing who the target is, I think my friend would leave his dying mother's bedside to make this happen."

"Good." I mentioned a couple of the details, then added, "Can you keep your friend and whoever he brings with him out of the Common, Bill? At least until the last second. If our target gets even a whiff that anything's not right, it could endanger the girl."

"I'll do my best. These guys don't like taking suggestions from locals, even big city locals. But seeing they got a chance for a career-making bust, I think I can get them to play it that way."

"Okay. I'll see you when I see you."

"Yeah, sure." Then, he added, "He's a shrewd bastard, Mike. Be careful."

"I will. Thanks."

So I had those two pieces in place. Two of the major players—Brogna and the feds—hopefully would be where I wanted them, when I wanted them. If you could trust either party to play by my rules, that is. There was nothing more I could do about that, except keep my fingers crossed and wait to see what happened.

The next and final call was one I knew I could control the outcome of—I called Stoney at Hampton Beach.

"How's it going?" I asked when he answered.

"Good. Our big friend just left," he said, referring to Tank. "He spotted me a few hours' sleep."

"Where's our other friend?"

"In the kitchen."

I was wound tight and had a vision of Elliot taking off and blowing everything at the last minute. "Get out there and don't leave him again," I said into the phone.

"All right, all right, Mike. I had to answer the phone, didn't I?"

"Sorry, Stoney."

"That's okay." We were silent for a bit, then Stoney continued. "We're playing chess. And I'm going to win one game if it kills me."

"You better beat him quick. I'll be up early in the morning."

"It's going down?" he asked excitedly.

"Yeah. Noon. So watch him close. I don't want anything to screw it up now. We're almost home."

"Don't worry, Mikey. He won't be out of my sight. I'm going to make him play until you get here or until I win one."

I chuckled. "Good luck. See you tomorrow."

"We'll be waiting for you. So long."

"So long." I hung up and smiled, but only for a moment. Before I left the phone booth, I ran through my mind all the things that could go wrong at Cambridge Common tomorrow. And it was quite a procession too; a whole marching band. And the tunes they played were very disturbing.

CHAPTER 40

WHEN I WOKE the next morning, it was just after dawn. I felt fairly good considering how I'd been abusing myself lately and what I was going to be involved in soon. I wondered for a moment exactly what that would be. I knew how I hoped my plan would go, but I had enough common sense to realize that any part of the scheme, or maybe even all of it, could end up being the exact opposite of what I was shooting for.

I got myself ready, took the .38, the bag of meth, and pointed the Karmann Ghia in the direction of Hampton Beach. I'd been going to Hampton since I was a kid. Spent a lot of my teenage years there, too, chasing girls through the Casino, the entertainment center of the beach. T-shirt shops, arcades, ice cream stands. And later, when my friends and I were old enough to have cars, driving the loop up Ocean Boulevard and around on Ashworth Avenue. Again, looking for girls. We were rarely, if ever, lucky. I guess the chase was some type of rite of passage. I could remember my father saying someone, he or his father, I don't remember which, made the same endless circles during summer nights in a

Model-T. So the tradition went way back. I had some great memories of Hampton Beach.

Those memories didn't make me feel any better about the trip I was making now though. I was worried. Within a few hours, it would all be over one way or the other. I couldn't be sure which way it would go. I could even be dead. That was a possibility. You might be surprised, or think I'm lying, but that didn't bother me much. My life hadn't really amounted to more than a hill of beans for a long time now. I knew I'd been kidding myself all along with this PI thing. I didn't love the work. It was more that I couldn't do anything else. With my lifestyle, I wouldn't have lasted at a nine-to-five job. I didn't know if I'd even last at this. Right now, the investigation business was no more than a way to make a few bucks—a very few—and more importantly a way to keep my mind off things I didn't want to think about.

There was one person I couldn't help but think about though—Julie. I hated to admit it to myself, but I knew deep down inside there was still something real between us. Something that said Julie was the answer. She knew it too. And she wanted to help me—with my doubts, my night-mares, and my demons. A dope could see that. And maybe she was the only one who *could* help me. Even so, I couldn't let her get too close. I didn't know what the hell I might do to her if I went crazy again. And that was always a pos-sibility with me. And then there was the guilt too. The only time I didn't feel guilty about what I'd done to her—and what I might do next—was when I was high on one thing or another. And the irony was that those were the times I *really* couldn't trust myself, the times I might easily lose it, and, God forbid, hurt her. All I had to do was stop the beer, and…yeah, the other stuff too. But even more ironic was that without the beer and the coke, I'd have to face what I'd done to Julie. And even worse, much worse, what I'd done to that young girl in Vietnam. The one I'd killed. Learn to live with all that knowledge. I wasn't sure I was capable of that. I was afraid I might end my own life. Besides, Julie deserved better than me. Almost anyone did.

By the time I crossed the Hampton Bridge, my thoughts were dangerously dark. Strangely my attitude felt right for what I had to do. I hadn't intended it that way, but I realized it could be helpful.

I pulled into the driveway. The cottage was only a couple of buildings from the beach itself and built right on the sand. It was raised up, to protect it from the tides I imagined, even though the area looked like the ocean hadn't risen this high in a century. The cottage had no ocean view because of the buildings in front of it. I walked up the steps and into the cottage. I shouted for Stoney.

"We're out here."

I wasn't surprised what I saw when I got to the kitchen— Elliot and Stoney seated at the table, both hunched over the chessboard. Neither looked up; they both mumbled something. Except for a few dirty dishes in the sink and a greasy frying pan on top of the gas stove, the tight little kitchen wasn't in bad shape.

"You haven't beaten him yet?" I asked.

Stoney shook his head. "No, but I will this time."

"Well you better make it quick, because we're all leaving soon."

I didn't have long to wait. Within two or three moves, Elliot declared, "Checkmate."

Stoney just sat there, staring at the board. Finally, he said, "I always hated this game anyhow."

"All right," I said. "Come on. We've got a noon appointment with Brogna."

Elliot looked up at me, his eyes big behind the glasses. "I'm not so sure I want to go."

I didn't blame him. No one could be sure what Brogna's reaction to any of this would be. Still, I honestly didn't think Brogna would hurt his moneymaker or that he'd even get a chance to.

"You're the last one he'd cause any harm to, Elliot," I said. "The man needs you."

I'd barely gotten those words out of my mouth when someone spoke up behind me. "You bet your ass he does."

I turned. It was the Devil's Demons' sergeant at arms and another biker. The second man was taller and heavier than the sergeant. Also unlike the sergeant, who had short hair and a scruffy beard, the second man was clean shaven with long greasy black hair that hung to his shoulders. They both looked like they lifted iron. Their hard faces told me that hobby was probably picked up in prison. They each wore denim jackets and jeans.

Apparently I'd forgotten to lock the door when I'd come in and apparently they were quiet men. The sergeant stood in the kitchen pointing a pistol at me; the other man was beside, and a step behind, him. I backed into the stove, my right hand behind my back looking for the gun I had in my waistband. Elliot and Stoney just sat there, bug-eyed.

"Let me see your hand," the sergeant said to me. I pulled my hand from behind me. Held my .38 barrel down. The sergeant stepped closer, took my gun. I kept my hands down at my sides, palms against the stove. "Keep your hands on the table," he said to Stoney and Elliot. They did as they were told.

The other biker stepped up beside the sergeant. His long hair fell in front of his face. Every time it did, he'd pull it back like he was going to rip it from its roots. He was sniffling and breathing through his mouth. Either he had a colossal head cold or he was overusing some type of powder. Maybe both. He looked from us to the sergeant and back again. I couldn't tell if he was jacked-up, nervous or just anxious to do whatever it was they'd come to do. Maybe all three. The sergeant handed him my gun and told him to check out the other rooms. When he turned, I could see the bottom rocker on the back of his denim jacket announced him as a Demons' prospect, someone who was working to become a full-fledged member. That wasn't good for Stoney, Elliot, and I. It meant he'd do *anything* the sergeant told him to do.

"So you thought you were gonna actually fuck over the Demons, shithead?"

The sergeant was addressing me. I didn't answer.

He continued. "You weren't careful comin' here this time, Malloy. You was easy to follow. What, was you daydreaming?"

I wondered that myself, then realized I had been. I'd been careless. Maybe it was because I knew it would be the last time I'd be here anyway. Or maybe I'd been lazy. Or maybe just tired. Whatever the cause of my being so lax, it didn't matter now. I'd fucked up. Now I had to see if there was a way out of it.

"No smart answers?" The sergeant looked around the kitchen. "Chess? Cozy. You must like it here, huh, Malloy?"

The prospect returned, stood beside the sergeant, and shook his head.

"I hope you like it, Malloy," the sergeant said. "Because this is going to be your home now. Your permanent home."

The prospect snickered in between sniffles.

Elliot spoke up in a whimper. "You're not going to kill us, are you? Mr. Brogna needs me."

The sergeant let out a little snort. "Don't worry, college boy. You're gonna live to cook again."

You could almost see the relief on Elliot's face. He didn't say anything about me and Stoney though—so much for chess friendships.

Through this whole thing, Stoney had just been watching the proceedings. Now he finally spoke up. "Can't we work this out somehow?"

"Shut up, dipshit," the sergeant said. Then he turned to Elliot. "Get up. Go in the other room and wait for me."

Elliot headed into the small main room. I couldn't see him from where I was standing.

Before the sergeant followed, he turned to the prospect. "Do it on the couch. But give us five minutes to get out of here. We'll pick you up where we talked about."

The prospect nodded. His gun hand actually shook a bit. I heard the sergeant and Elliot go out the front door and close it behind them. None of us moved. The prospect kept glancing at the clock on the wall above the sink. The only sounds were his sniffles. After five minutes had passed, the prospect motioned with the gun, *my gun*, for Stoney to get up.

"Both of ya in the other room. On the couch."

As we walked toward the kitchen doorway, the prospect stepped out of the way.

Stoney whispered, "What's that . . .?"

"Shut up, Stoney," I whispered back. I'd wondered when someone was going to notice the odor. I hoped the prospect's schnoz was as jammed up as it sounded. I glanced at Stoney's smokes and matches on the table before I left the kitchen.

In the main room, Stoney sat on the tattered couch. Just before I joined him, I said to the prospect who'd walked in behind us, "How about letting us have a smoke first?"

"I don't have any."

"Mine are on the kitchen table," I said. Stoney was good; he said nothing.

The prospect stared at me for a bit, then finally nodded. I don't think it was a humanitarian gesture; I think he was trying to delay doing something he was very uncomfortable doing.

"You go first." He motioned with my gun toward the kitchen doorway. I headed that way. He walked behind me, probably keeping one eye on Stoney. When I got in the kitchen, the prospect stood in the doorway where he could see both of us. I picked up the smokes and matches.

He quickly stepped into the kitchen. He probably couldn't see Stoney, but he could see the front door. Again he said, "You go first." He motioned with his head toward the living room.

Just as I reached the doorway, I stopped. Took a smoke from the pack and put it to my lips. I glanced over my shoulder. The prospect was a couple of arm lengths behind me. He held the gun straight out, pointed at my back, said, "Come on, come on. Get in there. I wanna see the other shithead."

There was a refrigerator on my right, between me and the stove. I lit the match, but instead of bringing it to the tip of the cigarette, I turned the flame on the entire pack of matches. The matchbook ignited.

"What the fuck?" the prospect said.

I heaved the flaming matches up and over the refrigerator, so the pack would fall onto the stove—if it made it that far. It just about did. There wasn't actually an explosion, noise-wise that is. The sound of gas igniting was more like a giant whoosh. An orange-blue fireball shot though the kitchen like a burning meteor. I was protected by the refrigerator. The prospect wasn't so lucky. The fireball engulfed him. The screams coming from him were horrible.

He'd dropped my gun and was rolling around the kitchen floor, trying to put out the flames dancing through his clothes. I pulled the table cloth off the kitchen table, sending chess pieces flying in all directions. I used it to smother the flames on the prospect. His hair was crinkled from the heat and his eyebrows were completely burned off. He was still rolling around the floor, wailing in pain. Even though I wasn't an expert, I'd seen men with burns in Nam. I didn't think these looked too serious. Sure, the smell of singed flesh was sickening and it must have hurt plenty and he was probably in shock. But he'd live.

Stoney was in the doorway now, jabbering away. I didn't pay any attention to him. I was on automatic pilot. Fortunately the fireball hadn't ignited anything but the prospect. It had scorched the walls heavily though. I didn't have time to survey for further damage.

There was only one thing to do with the prospect. I found my .38. Except for being a little warm, it hadn't been damaged in the explosion. The prospect was in pain and I needed him out of the way quick. I raised the .38 over my head and tried to hold him still while I bashed him in the head with the gun. He groaned but didn't go out. I glanced at Stoney; he looked horrified. I whacked the prospect again. This time he went out cold.

Stoney shouted, "What the hell's that?" He raced to the kitchen window. I followed him, turning off the stove's gas jets as I passed. The ones I'd discreetly turned on earlier. Outside, below, on the sand that surrounded the cottage, I saw Elliot dash by the window and out of sight. Apparently he'd escaped from the sergeant somehow. Seconds later, the sergeant came by running after him. Except for the pistol raised skyward in his hand, he was a comical sight. He was making slow progress in the sand with his heavy motorcycle boots. He'd probably never catch Elliot. We watched as he disappeared around the corner of the cottage.

"Come on, over this way." I waved at Stoney and we hurried across the kitchen to the other side of the cottage, stepping over the unconscious prospect as we went.

Inside the bedroom, we headed to the far window. There was a large window air conditioner in it that the owner had either failed to remove after the last summer season or had put in recently in anticipation of the coming warm weather. We both leaned over it to look out. The cottage was raised high on the sand, so the window was about ten feet above the ground. We were just in time to see the sergeant stumble past, sinking in the sand in his motorcycle boots.

We stood there for a bit until Elliot came barreling by on another pass. Apparently the sergeant was chasing Elliot around and around the cottage in some *Three Stooges* routine.

"What are we going to do?" Stoney said.

I didn't know. I had my gun, but the sergeant was armed, too, and any gunshots could bring the law before we could get the hell out of there. We'd already been lucky that the gas igniting hadn't been loud enough to attract any notice. I certainly couldn't afford any attention. I had a date at Cambridge

Common. But if this footrace went on any longer, I figured the cops would get a call from someone and show up anyway.

I wasn't any closer to a decision on what to do when Elliot whipped by the window again. Behind him, still losing ground, came the sergeant. This time he stopped, put his hands on his knees, looked like he was trying to catch his breath. Only for a few seconds though, because he turned and pointed the pistol at the corner he'd just rounded. He must've been hoping Elliot would run around the building right into him.

The sergeant was standing directly below us. I took one quick survey of the air conditioner. It was unplugged and nothing was holding it in place but the bottom of the window, which was resting on the top of the unit. I brushed Stoney out of my way. With one hand, I pushed the window higher and with the other gave the A/C a shove. It broke free and fell.

The air conditioner caught the sergeant on his shoulder with a glancing blow to his skull. The impact caused a nasty sound. His scream I mean, although the sound of the A/C hitting the sergeant was unpleasant too. I hung out the open window and looked down at him lying on the sand. How bad he was hurt, I couldn't tell. He wouldn't feel like lunch today, that was for sure.

Just then Elliot came flying around the corner and almost collided with the air conditioner. He made an awkward but successful jump over it. He turned, took a look at the sprawled-out sergeant, then up at me.

I kept my eye on Elliot. "Put Elliot's stuff in a paper bag," I told Stoney without looking at him. "We're leaving in a minute."

"Are we still going to meet Brogna?" Stoney asked.

"Yes. If Brogna had the Demons follow me here to get Elliot, he'll realize they failed. So he'll be there."

I carefully lowered myself out the window, hung on the windowsill, and dropped to the sand. I didn't take my eyes off of Elliot; I still didn't trust him as far as taking off was concerned.

"Is he dead?" Elliot asked.

I could see the sergeant breathing. "No. Help me get him inside."

When we'd finally lugged the sergeant inside, we spread him out on the kitchen floor on his back beside the prospect. The sergeant had an ugly gash on his head and one arm looked out of whack. I couldn't decide who looked worse— the prospect who'd been badly singed and love-tapped twice on the head with a hunk of iron or the sergeant who'd had an air conditioner fall on him.

"You got his clothes?" I asked Stoney, nodding toward Elliot.

Stoney held up a large brown shopping bag full almost to the top with shirts, underwear, and whatever else Stoney considered Elliot's clothes.

I walked over to the sink, opened a couple of cabinets underneath it until I found what I was looking for. I pulled out a couple of sandwich-size plastic baggies from a box inside. "Wait here," I said.

"Mikey, we got to get out of here," Stoney said. "The cops could be on their way."

"One minute."

Out in the car, I used my driver's license to transfer what I estimated was around an ounce of the speed from the big Ziploc bag into both of the small baggies. I put the large bag of meth back into the brown bag and placed it under the seat.

Back in the cottage, Elliott and Stoney watched as I jammed one of the baggies of speed into the jeans pockets of both the prospect and the sergeant. Neither said anything— Elliot and Stoney that is. The other two wouldn't wake from their naps for a while.

When we pulled out of the cottage driveway and headed for Ocean Boulevard, I was driving, Stoney was jammed in the tiny back and Elliot was sitting like a statue in the shotgun seat. His head touched the car ceiling. He hadn't spoken since his question about the mortality of the sergeant. I figured he was in borderline shock.

Stoney was moaning about how his friend was going to react to his scorched kitchen and the two bikers found unconscious in it, their pockets loaded with meth. I assured him we'd get his friend out of any trouble he found himself in once this was all over.

Then he asked me about his car that was parked one street over from the cottage.

"We'll get it later," I said.

On the far side of the Hampton Bridge I found a pay phone, called the Hampton cops. "Some guys were making meth and the place just blew up," I told whoever answered. I gave them the address, hung up.

We made a beeline for Cambridge and our rendezvous with Myles Brogna. I glanced at my watch. I could make it, even without speeding. Speeding wouldn't have been too smart. Not with what we were carrying.

CHAPTER 41

WHEN WE WERE almost halfway to Cambridge, I decided to stop. We had time. Close to an hour before noon. It didn't really matter if we hadn't had time, though. I would've stopped anyway and risked being a few minutes late. And it wasn't because of my jittery stomach either. I turned off the highway where I knew there was a combination gas station/ convenience store. I pulled up to the pumps, rolled down the window, and told the zit-faced kid who approached to fill it up.

I nodded at Elliot. "Take him for a piss," I said to Stoney who was crunched up in the rear.

"I don't have to go," Elliot said.

I didn't care whether he had to or not. I wanted him out of the car for a bit. "We're all going," I said. "I have no idea when we'll get the next chance." I felt like a father talking to kids on a cross country trip. "I'll go after you two."

When they were gone, I paid the zit-faced kid. As soon as he walked away from the car, I took the brown bag with the speed from beneath the seat and placed it in Elliot's bag under his clothes. When Stoney and Elliot came back, I hurried to the men's room. I was glad I didn't have to use it. The place stunk of urine and crap and looked like they'd given up on cleaning it long ago. I stayed there with the foul smell for as long as I could, then hurried back to the car.

When we reached Cambridge, I parked about two blocks from the Common. Elliot and Stoney got out. I grabbed Elliot's bag of clothes and followed.

We were a strange group, on our way to I wasn't sure what. The straight-looking PI, the hippie, and the goofy MIT nerd. Then I remembered where we were and what year it was and realized we were probably the least weird-looking group of people in the area. If anything, we stood out only because we looked so unusual together.

We walked to the side of the Common where I'd agreed to meet Brogna. There was a bench and the three of us jammed onto it. Elliot was squashed in the middle. I kept Elliot's bag on my lap. I felt, and we probably looked, ridiculous.

On the other side of the Common, I could see a large throng of people. Some of them were swaying to the sound of a rock group pumping out the Doors "Light My Fire." I could smell the pot smoke from here, although after studying some of the people heading past us in the direction of the music, I couldn't be sure the odor wasn't coming from them. As I said earlier, pot was as common a smell around Cambridge as morning coffee. Probably more so.

I let my eyes survey the area. No sign of Brogna and nothing I could spot that looked out of place.

"Where is he?" Elliot said.

"He'll come." I wasn't as sure as I tried to sound. I could feel the .38 at the small of my back, covered by my jacket.

I continued to scan the Common. I didn't notice anyone who looked like an Irish gangster or a cop. But that didn't mean that one or both groups weren't already here. Even some undercover cops and trying-to-be-cool gangsters wore hip garb and their hair long nowadays. So that meant anyone could be a threat. Except the three of us sitting here on the bench—the MIT nerd, the hippie, and the PI.

A girl in a peasant dress and tie-dye blouse walked past us. She had a jar of bubble-blowing liquid and a wand. She was blowing huge bubbles like she didn't have a care in the world. I turned away for a moment and when I looked back, a bubble burst on my nose. Elliot laughed. I was irritated.

Stoney said, "Oh, oh."

I looked in the direction he was facing. Three men were walking across the common in our direction and I had no doubt, even at this distance, who it was—Myles Brogna and two of his associates. Brogna was walking just like he had when I'd met him at the steakhouse—like he owned Cambridge Common. There were small groups of people between us, and when Brogna came up to a group, people just seemed to part and he and his companions walked right through.

As they approached us, I stiffened and felt my heart rate pick up. Elliot let out a heavy sigh. I didn't think Stoney was breathing. And there was one more thing—I didn't see Susan Worthman.

Brogna marched right up to our bench. His two associates, one on either side of him, could have come out of central casting for Irish thugs. Both had middle aged, ruddy faces. One had a scally cap on like Brogna, the other was hatless with slicked back jet-black hair and blue eyes—black Irish. They were a tough-looking threesome.

The black Irishman leaned over and looked in the bag on my lap. Moved around a few of the clothes on top. I held my breath. Apparently satisfied, he straightened back up.

"Where's Susan Worthman?" I said. "You were supposed to bring her."

"Hold your horses, sport," Brogna said. "I'm asking a few questions first."

Brogna doubled his right hand into a fist, then massaged his Claddagh ring with his other hand. "You tell them anything, kid?" he asked, looking down at Elliot.

Elliot shook his head. "Nothing, Mr. Brogna," he said, his voice shaking more than his head. "I haven't told them anything."

"What have they asked you?"

"Nothing, really. Nothing."

Brogna looked at Elliot doubtfully. "They haven't asked you anything about me or anything related to me?"

"Honest, Mr. Brogna. Not a thing."

"What the hell did you do the whole time you were with them then?"

"Played chess," Elliot answered.

Brogna's eyes narrowed, probably wondering if Elliot was being a smart ass. Then apparently satisfied that he wasn't, he dropped his hands and said, "What about this?" He waved his arm around. "Have they planned any surprises?"

I jumped in. "We just want the girl. No surprises."

Brogna gave me a look that probably would have intimidated the mayor of Boston. "I'm talkin' to him." He looked back at Elliot.

Elliot was wringing his hands in his lap. "I don't think they're planning anything, Mr. Brogna."

"That better be right. You know what I mean?"

Elliot's face went gray.

I looked across Elliot to see if Stoney was still alive—he hadn't spoken the whole time. He was alive but stiff as the barrel of a gun. He probably could have used something to ease the tension right about now; I know I could have.

Brogna turned and nodded to the thug with the scally cap. The man took out some type of walkie-talkie and mumbled a few words into it. I tensed up; Brogna noticed.

"Don't worry, sport. You kept up your end of the bargain. The chick's coming."

We only had to wait a couple of minutes before both Brogna and his men looked over my head toward the other end of the Common. I turned and saw a large gray Cadillac on the street at the edge of the Common. The back door opened and a woman got out. She started walking towards us, weaving around the various clusters of people as she came. I couldn't see who else was in the car.

"Look back at me, sport."

I did, along with Stoney who'd looked in the direction of the Cadillac too. Elliot hadn't budged.

When she reached us, I saw it was a girl. She stood at the end of the bench near Stoney where I could see her clearly. There was no doubt it was Susan Worthman. She looked just like her photos. Except she was worse for wear. She was still pretty, but she'd lost a lot of weight, her face was drawn and her eyes darted around as if there was more than this situation bothering her. She'd aged and not in a normal way. And it looked like she'd been slapped around a bit. There were red welts on both sides of her face. She had all her fingers—that part had been a bluff. I wondered for a moment whose finger had been in the box.

Brogna spoke to me. "All right, sport. It's been nice doing business with you. Now you and your buddy," he tipped his chin toward Stoney, "are just going to watch us leave, and after we're out of sight, you're going to sit here another five minutes before you leave. You got that?"

I nodded.

"Good." Brogna looked at Elliot. "Come on, kid. I got a few more questions I want to ask you."

Elliot got up reluctantly from the bench, turned to look at both Stoney and me. I thought he was going to say something, but he must've thought better of it.

Brogna had one last comment. "And remember what I said, don't get up 'til we're out of sight for five minutes."

Brogna, his associates, and Elliot began walking in the direction Brogna had come from. They'd only gone a short distance when I hollered, "Elliot." They all stopped, turned. I jogged over to them and slowly started to hand the bag to Elliot. "You forgot your clothes," I said.

What I hoped would happen, did. Brogna reached over, grabbed the bag, started to move some of the clothes. The black Irish thug said, "I already checked it. It's his clothes, Myles."

Brogna took his hand out of the bag. "I'll check it again when we get to the car," he said.

They resumed their walk. I returned to the bench, sat the Worthman girl down between me and Stoney.

"You okay?" I was looking at Stoney.

"Yeah, man." He stared at me like he was naturally high. "Wow, was that heavy."

"How about you, Susan? Are you all right?"

"I'm . . . okay," she said, though she sounded anything but. I couldn't imagine what she'd been through all that time with a sicko like Myles Brogna. Or maybe I could. Anyway, I knew it would be a long time before she got over it, if she ever did.

"Are we going to stay here the five minutes, Mikey?" Stoney asked.

"No." And it wasn't because Brogna and the rest of them were out of sight now, which they were. It was because I didn't trust Brogna and I didn't see the cavalry. For all I knew, Cousin Billy's federal connection hadn't come through. Maybe there was no backup here. If that was so, I wanted us to get out of there fast in case Brogna had something else cooking besides meth.

When I got up and started to help Susan from the bench, I saw that I'd been right—Brogna hadn't been playing square. Coming in our direction, from the Caddy Susan had been in, were two men in black leather car coats and they were moving fast.

"Quick," I shouted.

Stoney was up and off the bench like a shot. The three of us, with me supporting Susan, made a mad dash for a granite memorial near the center of the common, dodging knots of people as we ran. The structure might give us cover. There was a statue of Lincoln in the middle of the tall monument and some other guy I didn't recognize on top. I glanced over my shoulder. The two thugs'd seen us bolt and had broken into a run after us. They pulled guns out as they ran.

When we reached the memorial, we were lucky. It was surrounded by a wrought iron fence but the gate was open. We pushed through it. I pulled the .38 from the back of my waistband. A workman saw us and the gun. He dropped his rake and sprinted out through the gate. We ran behind the monument, where I shoved Susan to the ground. Stoney hunched over her. I leaned around the granite structure, held the gun with two hands, and let a slug fly high in the air well over the two thugs and everyone else that was there. The thugs stopped and went to their knees. Hippies scattered in every direction faster than if the Cambridge police had lobbed a few tear gas canisters. I'd hoped the shot would scare the thugs off. It didn't. A few moments later they separated and headed for opposite sides of the monument. They were trying to encircle us.

Just then I heard a volley of shots coming from the other end of the common, behind us, in the direction Brogna had gone. The shots were rapid, continuous, and from a variety of weapons. One sounded like an automatic rifle.

I hopped up on the ledge near Lincoln's statue, shimmied along the side. One of the gunmen had come in through the gate and was rounding the corner of the monument, but I couldn't get a shot off. I needed both hands, including the one with the gun, to hold onto the edge of the granite. The gunman stopped and raised his gun in Stoney's direction. I let go of the statue and fired off a shot in the thug's direction just as I started to fall backwards to the ground. I landed hard on my shoulder. When I rolled over, I saw that the gunmen had stumbled forward and fallen next to me. I was looking into his eyes. He was inches away from me and he had a bullet wound where his nose used to be. My stomach did a flip-flop.

Susan was screaming. The other gunman ran out from behind the monument, stopped dead in his tracks when he saw his partner. My gun had flown from my hands during the fall; it was ten feet away. I got to my hands and knees and made a mad scramble for it. I didn't make it. A bullet slammed into the ground between my hands and dirt sprayed my face. I moved onto my side, faced the shooter. He must've been a bad shot. He couldn't have been much more than twenty feet away. I didn't think he'd miss again. His hard face was red and his eyes wild as he aimed the gun at my face. I tensed as I waited for the bullet.

That's when a human blur slammed into the thug's side and he went flying like he was a tackle dummy. The person who'd bowled the gunman over landed on top of him, and was pounding the thug's body with both fists. As Brogna's man struggled to get up, I remembered my gun and crawled after it. As I was doing that, the thug managed to get loose somehow. He got up, still holding the pistol, and pointed it at his attacker. At that instant, still on my hands and knees, I reached my gun. I grabbed it and was ready to get a shot off when a phalanx of men came racing around the statue. The one in the lead had his right fist drawn back; I couldn't believe anyone that size could move so fast. He was a huge gorilla, built like Paul Bunyan.

When Brogna's hood saw the gorilla and the group with him, it was too late. He turned his pistol in their direction, but never made it. The running blow the gorilla hit him with landed bingo on his jaw. The sound of breaking bone was sickening. I've seen a lot of fights in my life, some with sucker punches, but never a blow like that. The thug flew backwards and slammed flat on his back on the ground. It looked like something you'd see in the movies. I wondered if he was dead. I looked again at the thug I'd shot; I didn't have to wonder about him.

I struggled to my feet. Stoney came around the corner of the monument, supporting Susan Worthman. She was shaking in his arms.

"Are you all right?" I said to both of them. Stoney was pale but he nodded. Susan didn't answer.

"Susan, are you okay?"

Tears streamed down her face, and she seemed more like the young girl her father had hired me to find than the girl I'd seen just a few minutes before stepping out of the Caddy.

"Who . . . are . . . you?" she said, barely getting the words out.

"We're friends of your father, honey. We're taking you to him. It's all over. Everything's all right now." I wasn't sure about that last part. Brogna was out of the picture. I was pretty sure of that, judging by the gun-battle sounds we'd heard earlier. As far as damage from the drugs and what that animal had done to her, and how long it would take her to get over it all—if she ever did—I didn't know that part. But at least she was safe for now.

The gorilla who'd clocked the gunman suddenly put a huge hand on my shoulder. In a voice like a foghorn, he said, "You guys all right?"

I looked up and nodded. "Yeah, we're fine. Thanks. Thanks a lot."

I noticed some of his companions were standing behind him and others were over near the man he'd decked, trying to revive him. I didn't know if they'd have any luck. All of the gorilla's friends were large guys and most looked young. I realized the gorilla was just a huge kid too, twenty maybe, and he had on a purple-red unbuttoned sweater with the letter H embroidered on it. Some of his friends had the same sweater on.

"Who are you guys?" I asked even though I already had a good idea.

The gorilla smiled and said, "We play football, mister."

He didn't have to tell me anymore. My guess had been right—our rescuers were none other than members of the

Harvard varsity football team. It hadn't been a hard guess. You could see Harvard University from where we stood.

"We were heading over to the Square," the gorilla continued. "Coming through the Common and saw what was going on. So we did what we could. You sure you're okay?"

I sighed, nodded. "We're fine. Thanks again."

"No problem, mister," the gorilla said. "Anyone would've done the same."

I said to myself, *Yeah, but not anyone could have.*

There were sirens coming from everywhere and I noticed Cambridge police running towards us, some with guns drawn. All of us—Stoney, the football players, myself, everyone except Susan Worthman—put their hands over their heads. No one wanted a good ending going haywire at this point in the game.

CHAPTER 42

TWO WEEKS HAD passed since the big shootout at Cambridge Common. The incident had received more media coverage than the recent burning of a bank in Harvard Square and the Vietnam War put together and the hubbub still hadn't died out. After all, it was a great story—drugs, the arrest of a long-time Irish crime kingpin, police corruption, outlaw bikers, Mafia involvement, the Combat Zone, sexual abuse of young girls…even MIT had been dragged into the press frenzy along with the Harvard football team.

In the past couple of weeks, I'd seen a few of the people involved, like Stoney and Jake, but mostly my time had been taken up giving police and prosecutors interviews and fending off a swarm of reporters looking for any loose morsel of information that hadn't already been chewed to death by the Boston media outlets. So except for maybe a quick phone call to touch base, I hadn't really talked to or seen most of the players.

Things had finally quieted down a bit with the press coverage, so I'd thrown out a trial balloon to see if anyone wanted to get together. To my amazement, they all did. Even Cousin Billy—after a little hesitation and after he made me swear to keep a couple of bits of information just between me and him. Jake asked the same. Tank too. I agreed with all of them.

That's why we were all at O'Toole's now. We'd arrived earlier, late in the afternoon on a weekday—a slow time. Jake had taken the day off so he could relax during our little get-together. He had wisely put us in a back booth and pulled a table up beside it, giving us enough room for the whole gang. I took a sip of my Schlitz and looked around. To my right was Stoney. He was talking a mile a minute. For some reason, that made me anxious. I quickly looked at Tank seated beside him. The beer bottle in his huge hand looked like some type of miniature. Across from Tank sat Cousin Billy. He gulped his beer and looked uncomfortable. I figured he must be wondering why he'd agreed to come in the first place. Beside him, and across from Stoney, was Jake. He was more gregarious than usual. Probably because this was one of the rare times he actually got to enjoy his bar as if he was a real customer. He was drinking from a sixteen-ounce bottle of Knickerbocker. My eyes shifted to Jake's right. Julie sat directly across from me. She had her soda water and lime and played with the swizzle stick.

This was the first time I'd seen Julie since our romp in Jake's office. She'd called me a few times, but I didn't feel good about seeing her. I don't know why. Maybe it was just that I knew she was doing so well. I wasn't and I didn't want to derail her. Except for that damn nose she looked good—real good. And to think, I almost hadn't invited her to this little shindig. But I had. Stoney or Jake would have anyway.

We'd made idle chit-chat for quite a while before Jake finally started the ball rolling.

"How's the Worthman girl doing, Mike?"

All eyes at the table turned toward me. I shrugged. "I talked to her father. She's in rehab. Probably will be for a couple more months. They're keeping their fingers crossed."

"That's all you can do," Tank bellowed. "Works for some people . . . don't do nothin' for others."

Cousin Billy spoke next. "Doesn't work for anybody." He sounded bitter. I was the only one there who knew why. Dottie, his daughter. "Once a junkie, always a junkie."

"That's harsh, man," Stoney said before excusing himself to go to the men's room. I watched him go.

"It's more than harsh, Bill," Julie said, sounding angry. "It's wrong." Her cheeks were red. "Anybody can quit anything. It can take a lot of tries, though. Like cigarettes."

Cousin Billy said, "I haven't seen anybody get off the hard stuff."

Julie's brows were furrowed. "That's because you only see the people who fail. The police don't see the ones who beat it."

Billy raised his voice. "That's because there aren't any."

Julie lowered her voice. "Yes, there are." She turned her gaze on me. "And believe me, there's something out there with everyone's name on it. Most people have just been lucky to have never bumped into theirs . . . yet. I bumped into mine. And I beat it. Anyone can. I have to believe that."

Billy shrugged and sighed. "I pray to God you're right," was all he said.

There was an embarrassed silence at the table. Jake broke it. "Wally," he called to the bartender. "Another round."

Tank jumped in before another stretch of silence descended. "That was quite the cavalry that came to your rescue, Mike."

He let out a laugh that only a man his size could. "The god-damn Harvard football team. You couldn't have done much better, unless it was me and a few brothers." He let out another laugh.

The whole table laughed with him. Mine was forced. I could still see the face of the dead thug lying beside me on Cambridge Common with that ugly bullet hole in his face. The hole I'd put there. He'd deserved it, but I still didn't like thinking about it.

"Christ," Cousin Billy said, "the hood the kid clocked is lucky he's alive. He was in a coma for three days. He'll probably never be the fucking same." He short a quick glance toward Julie. "Pardon my French."

She flipped her hand up. "I've heard it before."

That brought a laugh of relief from the table. At least Billy and Julie were talking.

Just then the bartender showed up with a tray of fresh drinks and began distributing them. Then he gathered up the empties and was on his way.

Stoney returned. I watched him closely as he made his way to the seat beside me.

"It was even worse over the other side of the Common, eh Bill?" Jake said, looking at the detective.

Cousin Billy brightened. "Jesus, you should've seen the look on that pervert's face when he saw us all coming at him." Then his face turned sour. "He's a smart son of bitch though. Threw his hands straight up, still holding the bag of dope in one. His two boys weren't as bright. They were going for their pieces." He cleared his throat. "At least the feds said they were. I couldn't really see it too good. I was behind someone. They blew both of them right out of their shoes, though. Tough guy Brogna was screaming, 'Please, don't shoot me.' Just like a little girl. I wish they had drilled him. Would've saved us all a lot of tax money."

Jake and Tank nodded solemnly.

Stoney finally spoke up. "What was Elliot doing while this was happening?" I heard him sniffle softly.

"Elliot?" Billy said, looking suspiciously at Stoney. "Elliot was hugging the ground before the first shot."

"I'm glad he didn't get hurt," Stoney said emphatically. "What's going to happen to him, do you think?" He was looking at Billy.

"Well . . ." Billy began. Everyone at the table turned to look at him. "He's flipped on Brogna. No surprise there. I don't know if they'll cut him completely loose though. He was the cook after all. There wouldn't have been any meth without him."

I jumped in. "If it wasn't him, they would've found someone else."

Billy shrugged. "Probably. Anyway, after he testifies, he won't be able to stay around here."

Jake held the Knick bottle in one hand and studied it thoughtfully. "Why? Brogna's going away for a long time. They got him holding the pound of speed. He won't be around to hurt the kid."

"He might get out on bail, Jake," Billy said. "His lawyers are working on that now. And there's always a chance he'll beat the charges."

"There's no chance!" Tank thundered.

"Keep it down, will ya," Jake said.

"Ahh, sorry," Tank said, flustered. Then regaining his composure, he continued. "I know something you probably don't even know." He jerked a thick thumb toward Cousin Billy.

"What's that?" Billy asked. He didn't look happy.

Tank's beard-covered face spread wide in a huge smile. "They picked up the Devil's Dinks president and a few other club members last week."

"I didn't hear anything about that," Billy said. He sounded doubtful.

"It was some kind of secret federal drug indictment. They're trying to keep it quiet. Anyway, I heard they're rolling over like ten pins. Fuckin' punks." He looked over at Julie. "Sorry, hon." He turned back, said to everyone at the table, "You know what that means."

"Sure," Stoney piped in. "The president's going to rat on Brogna, too."

"You said it, Jack," Tank said. "And he knows plenty. That slimeball's been working directly for Brogna for years. He'll crucify him."

"Couldn't happen to a nicer guy," I said. "So between the speed they caught Brogna with, and the cook's testimony, and the Demons' president turning against him, do you think there's any way he can get out of it, Bill?"

Billy shook his head. "Probably not with all that. I hope. He doesn't have anyone he can roll over on. He's the one they want."

"What about your two friends?" Jake said.

Billy's face flushed. "Cummings and Dalton? They aren't any friends of mine."

Jake held up his hand. "Sorry, just a figure of speech."

Billy frowned. "There's nothing Brogna can do there. They . . ." He hesitated a moment, then said. "Well, what the hell.

It'll be in the papers soon anyhow. But keep it quiet, please. They've rolled over on Brogna, too. Before he had a chance to roll over on them. They're out the door. No pensions. But they aren't going to jail. Too bad on that part."

"Holy shit," Stoney said. "He's got everybody testifying against him except the pope." He pushed his chair away from the table, said, "Bathroom," and hurried in that direction. I watched him go again.

"Twenty years easy, I figure," Tank said.

Billy grinned. "That's if he pleads guilty. Life if he fights it. He'll be a very old man or dead when he comes out."

"Let's drink to that," Jake said, raising his Knick bottle. "Maybe Southie will return to a half-decent place again—minus Brogna's drugs."

"Harvard Square too," I added, then realized, even before I saw the other faces at the table, how doubtful a statement we'd both made. There'd be someone else to fill Brogna's shoes. There always had been and probably always would be.

We all clinked our glasses and bottles. Julie held hers toward me. She was trying to say something with her eyes; it went over my head. We touched glasses.

There was silence at the table for a minute or two. Everyone was lost in their own thoughts. Then, naturally, Billy ended the party.

"Well, I got to work tomorrow." He stood.

"But it's early," Jake said. I figured he was reluctant to end his first day off in who knew how long.

"Yeah, but I'm a lightweight, drinking-wise," Billy answered, placing a finger on his half-empty beer bottle. He reached for his wallet.

Jake shook his head. "It's all on me."

"Thanks," Billy said. "And nice talking with everyone." He waved over his shoulder as he hurried for the door.

"I got some things I got to take care of, too," Tank said. He heaved his bulky frame up from the chair. "I'll see ya all down the road." He was looking at me when he said that. He nodded to Julie, shook hands with Jake. "Thanks for the hospitality, Jake."

"Anytime," Jake responded.

Just as the big man was lumbering away, Stoney returned from the bathroom. Before he could sit, I said quickly, "Don't bother. Everybody's leaving."

"So soon? I was just getting into it."

"I'm sure you were," I said irritably.

We all stood up. Julie, Stoney, and I said our goodbyes to Jake.

Out on the sidewalk, it was dusk.

The three of us chatted for a minute.

Then Julie said, "Why don't you guys come over for a drink? It's early."

She spoke to both of us but meant me. Of course Stoney knew that too.

"Naw, I got to get back to my place," he said. "Thanks anyway, Julie."

"Mike?" She looked at me hopefully.

I wanted to go with her; I should have gone with her. Instead, I said, "I've got to talk to Stoney about something important."

She looked at me doubtfully, then at Stoney, then back to me. Stoney threw me a disapproving glance.

I cleared my throat, spoke to Julie. "It won't take long. I'll stop over a little later."

Just then the door to O'Toole's opened and a group of boisterous customers spilled out onto the sidewalk. We had to move to get out of their way. I moved toward Stoney.

I touched Stoney's arm, directed him gently away from Julie whose apartment was in the opposite direction. "I'll be by in a while."

She stood there looking at us; she looked more worried than angry. Why she should be worried, I didn't know. I'd told her I'd stop by soon. I waved; she didn't. Stoney and I turned and headed down the street in the direction of his apartment.

It didn't take us long to get there. I hurried Stoney along. Inside, I'd barely plopped myself down on the red bean bag chair before Stoney said, "Jesus, Mike, I hope you don't take any offense but how the hell can you say no to Julie? She is one smokin' hot chick." Then he quickly added, "And a real nice person, too."

I threw up my hands. "I'm going over there a little later. I just wanted to talk to you alone for a minute."

"Yeah?" Stoney said. There was sadness in his voice. Or maybe it was resignation.

I leaned forward in the bean bag chair. "I just wanted to tell you how grateful I am for all the help you've given me on this. And as soon as I collect my fee from George Worthman, I'll show you, too."

Stoney looked at me doubtfully. "Thanks, but you had to come all the way here to tell me that?" I didn't answer, so he continued. "And you don't have to give me anything. I was glad to help get Susie Sparkle out of that mess."

I shook my head. "No, no, no. I want to. I couldn't have done it without you."

Stoney just looked at me. He was sitting across from me in a chair that was a twin of mine, although his was mustard-colored. We didn't say anything. I looked around the room, studied everything and nothing. I was very uncomfortable and it wasn't because of the chair.

Finally, after what seemed like hours, but was probably only a few minutes, Stoney said, "I'm going to do some blow. You want some?"

Jesus, did I want some! But to Stoney, I said, "Ahh, a little taste, I guess." I tried to hide the excitement or nervousness or whatever the hell it was from my voice. Who knows if it worked?

Stoney pushed himself awkwardly from the bean bag chair, went to his bedroom, and returned with a glass vial filled with cocaine and something else in his other hand. He sat back down and I watched, trying to act nonchalant, as he removed the top from the contraption and dumped a generous pile of coke from the vial into it. He twisted the cover back on what I now realized was a grinder. He held the grinder over the polished stone lying on the table between us and rotated a small handle on the grinder's top. A fine white powder floated from the bottom of the grinder and accumulated on the stone. He didn't stop until the grinder was empty. I had to catch myself from licking my lips. By now my heart was racing and my bowels felt loose.

Stoney brought out his driver's license and used it to draw out four long lines of coke. He handed a cutoff straw to me. I could feel his eyes watching me as I leaned over the stone. I tried to act cool; I felt the opposite. When I had inhaled two of the lines, my world changed. The unpleasant anxiety left me, replaced by a different anxiety—an anxiety I liked. A lot.

I watched Stoney do his lines. "Beer?" he asked when he was done. His eyes were sparkling.

"Sure."

When he'd gone to the kitchen to get the beer, I hurried to the bathroom. I did my business on the toilet; it took less than a minute. Washing my hands I looked into the mirror. I was ready; I felt good. I knew where I wanted to go.

I stayed in front of the mirror for another minute, then went back into the main room. Stoney was sitting in his bean bag chair, looking at me oddly. He'd brought back two imported beers. They were on the table. I sat and drained half of mine in one long swig.

I looked at Stoney. He looked at me. I looked at the walls. I was afraid if I spoke my voice would shake like an earthquake. I had to get out of there. But I couldn't go yet. There was one more thing I needed. And Stoney gave me a way to ask for it when he said, "Shouldn't you be going to see Julie? You told her you were coming." He sounded very calm. I didn't know how he did that. Why couldn't I?

I nodded rapidly. "Yeah, yeah. You're right, I better get going." I didn't get up though. I had to say it first. And even though I tried, there was no way I could stop my voice from shaking, no way in hell. "Can I buy some of that to take with me?" I pointed my chin toward the cocaine.

Stoney hesitated, then shrugged. "Yeah, sure. What do you want? Half gram, gram?"

Again, I tried, but there was no way I could hide the quiver in my voice. "An eight-ball, I guess." Then stupidly added, "It's such good stuff. I better get a little extra to put away." Even before I said it, I knew Stoney knew better. We'd done this dance before. Still, I had to play the game.

He looked at me with genuine concern. "Are you sure you want that much, Mikey?" he asked.

I held my hand up, let it shimmy. "Oh, yeah. I'll do a little, save the rest."

"I get stuff this good all the time. You don't have to stockpile."

I was flustered. "I don't like bothering you. Might as well get some extra while I'm here." *Jesus, let me get it and get the hell out of here.*

Stoney was torn; I could tell. But he didn't say anything else. Just got up, went back to his bedroom. I went to the kitchen, grabbed and opened two bottles of beer. Placed one on Stoney's side of the table, one on mine. That's when he returned and sat back down. He reached across the table and handed me a cutoff plastic baggie with a yellow tie securing it. I could feel how fat the baggie was.

I asked him how much. He answered like he was asking for a million dollars. And he could have, I wouldn't have cared. I stood, handed him the money from my wallet. I was up, so I took advantage of it. I said, "I guess I better get going." I grabbed my beer, took two steps toward the door and stopped. "Got to take a piss before I go." Stoney didn't say anything, just stared at me as I walked past.

In the bathroom my hands shook as I opened the baggie. I didn't have the patience to chop and snort. I put my thumb and forefinger in the bag, found a rock that was probably close to a gram. Stoney treated me special; I knew that. I dropped the rock into the beer, watched it fizzle. Shook it gently and when the liquid began to rise out of the bottle, I drank the overflow. It had a strong medicinal taste, but I loved it. I secured the baggie, put it in my pocket. When I returned to the main room, I held the bottle in my fist at its base so Stoney wouldn't be able to see any coke that hadn't dissolved yet.

"Okay, I'll talk to you later," I said as I passed Stoney. No worry about my voice shaking now. I had more important things on my mind.

Stoney was up like a spring was under his ass and followed me to the door. "You're going to Julie's, right, Mike?"

"I'm on my way," I said, reaching for the door knob.

"Mike, are you going to be all right?"

I held the door open and turned just enough to see Stoney's face. He looked at me like I was falling down drunk and about to drive away on a motorcycle. I guess in that case he would've taken my keys. What could he do in this case? Not much.

The words tumbled out of my mouth. "Sure, sure, I'm fine. I'll call you tomorrow."

As I hurried down the stairs to the first floor, I didn't hear his door close. He must've been watching me go.

I barreled through the two doors out into the Cambridge night. The streetlights were sparkling; I felt good. I hustled down the stoop's stairs to the sidewalk and began a fast walk toward Harvard Square. I took a couple of small sips of the cocaine beer as I walked. I waved to the first cab I saw. The cab pulled to the curb a few yards in front of me. I held the beer bottle under my coat, my thumb over the opening, and jogged up to the cab. I hopped in back.

The driver didn't even look at me. All I could see was the back of his head. White hair and a scally cap. "Where to, sport?" he mumbled in a South Boston accent.

I thought of Julie—for all of one second. "The Combat Zone."

"Okay," the driver said. When he threw the meter up, I noticed the Claddagh ring he wore. The cab pulled from the curb out into light traffic.

I took another pull of the cocaine beer; what a wonderful taste it had. As we drove through Harvard Square, I barely noticed it. All I could see and think of were the lights and delights of the Combat Zone.